REBEL

A Breathless Novel

SAVANNAH KADE

GRIFFYN INK

❦ 1 ❦

Abelle never shares an address with a man she isn't married to. Engaged doesn't count.

EM TOOK A DEEP BREATH IN AND SLOWLY LET IT OUT. HER head hurt. Vegas had managed to be both less and more than she expected. Her left hand felt weird, lying on something like a tutu. She was likely still in a weird dream.

Emma Kate had rolled in under the bright lights around five p.m., her U-Haul too big for the things she'd had in her dorm and they'd all been rattling around the whole drive. The rental shop had not had the small trailer she reserved and they acted as though they had been very nice giving her the larger one. The problem was, she didn't want the larger one. The excess space made it nearly impossible for her to keep her things safe. She'd packed her stuff in a two-foot layer on the floor of the trailer and hoped nothing broke. So, when she'd hit Vegas, she decided to call it a night, rented a cheap room, and grabbed a cab to the nearest luxury casino.

Now she lay on the bed, looking up as the ceiling came into focus. This ceiling was beautiful. If she could sit up, she could check it out. Emma Kate prodded at her brain and tried to figure out what she'd done last night.

She remembered playing the nickel slots and the guy next to her pointing out that drinks were free as long as you were feeding money into a game. Then she... well, she didn't really remember much after that.

Em took another deep breath in and out and only just then noticed the crown molding and the gold flecked wallpaper border. It was nice. Again she asked herself, how was a ceiling *nice*? But it certainly didn't look like what she expected from the cheap motel room she'd rented.

Wait, her brain stopped her. Frowning, she rolled her head to the left. The wall was very far away, the room much bigger than she remembered. She squinted. The wallpaper missing, the paint a peachy tan, beautiful and perfect. Not a peeling strip of tacky floral print in sight. She looked right.

Shit.

The curtains were barely open, revealing a slice of sky, but through that slit she could see daylight. She could also see that she was somewhere in the neighborhood of fifteen to twenty stories up in the sky. No, this was not the one-story motel room with one window and one door.

Where in hell was she?

Em knew that any normal person would have bolted upright just then, but Em also knew that she'd had too many free drinks the night before. Her head was pounding and spinning at the same time. She felt like a typical college student—though that might be a thing of the past. She cringed to herself and regretted that she remembered dropping out of school so clearly.

She wasn't generally one for doing really dumb stuff—she wasn't internet stupid—but she'd made more than her share of bad decisions. Emma Kate also wasn't one for freaking out. She'd had her freakouts earlier in the year when first her mother had died of cancer, and then her father had followed a few months later, apparently unable to go on without the love of his life.

Em was finished with freakouts. Now was not the time anyway. On the plus side, she was warm, comfortable, and clearly in a nice hotel room. She smiled to herself, pleased when that didn't make her brain protest. Maybe she'd won a lot of money and gotten herself a suite comped right here in the... *No.* She didn't remember which hotel she was in. It didn't matter anyway. The lamps were beautiful. The painting on the wall was much, much classier than the one in the room she'd rented.

She frowned. She was clearly in a different section of town from where she'd parked. She wouldn't have driven when she was drinking. She'd never done anything like that. So, her paid motel room, car, and trailer were probably still down the street. She'd gotten a ride to the casino because parking her trailer in the high-end parking lot would have made her look like she was coming to Vegas for the sole purpose of losing her shirt. She would look like Poor-down-on-her-luck-Emma-Kate, and that was not who she was. She'd made a decision to leave school. That was all.

After another deep breath, she slowly sat up, and that was when the troubles really began.

Though Em reminded herself that she wasn't one for freaking out, as she sat up, Emerson Kate Mayfair realized she had a serious problem on her hands.

For a moment, she thought the pounding in her head was also lying to her eyes. Surely, she was not seeing what she was seeing...

Being a smart cookie, she checked things out before flipping her lid. So she moved her hands around, feeling along the fabric, and realizing she had another sense confirming what she saw. *Well, shit.*

She did not remember how she'd gotten here, but the king size bed was softer than any she'd slept on in the past several years. Underneath her hands were yards and yards of white tulle. It looked like she'd slept on the puffy cloud.

Far too scared now to just look down at her clothing, she

touched the front of her chest. *Yup. That was lacework. And beading.*

When she did eventually look down, she saw a beautiful sweetheart neckline with cap sleeves, one of which had slid off her shoulder at some point in the night. The dress itself was gorgeous, but she had no idea why she was wearing it.

Damn. She looked amazing. Although, she reconsidered, there was every possibility her makeup had run down her face or smeared off onto the pillow. The dress might be amazing, but she might look like Frankenstein's monster was wearing it.

Reaching up to touch her hair, she instead felt the crisp reply of hairspray and curls. Clearly, it had been expertly coiffed and then slept on. Reaching around to touch the back, Em realized the hairspray wasn't as crunchy as she'd originally thought. That was more tulle... on her head. This did not bode well...

She found the tulle was trailing down her back from the tiara pinned into her hair. *A tiara. Of course, she was wearing a tiara.*

As she rolled her head to the side and looked down, she saw *him*. Dark hair, high cut cheekbones, long, inky lashes unmoving because he was out cold. Broad shoulders splayed across the bed on the other side.

She wouldn't have believed him being there was a problem, but he was wearing a tux, and Emma Kate was pretty sure she'd just gotten herself in a world of trouble.

✺ 2 ✺

Keith hadn't closed the bathroom door, and why would he? He hadn't come in here to do anything except stare at the mirror and deal with his existential dread.

The mirror told him he had a bow tie hanging open around his neck. Though he had questioned everything when he leapt out of the fluffy king-sized bed, the large mirror over the dual sinks made it clear, he was *dressed up*. He was wearing a very fine tux and a now-crushed red rose pinned to the lapel. He didn't even recognize his socks. The cuff links at his wrist told him what they were—gorgeous and expensive.

Shit, he could afford neither gorgeous nor expensive.

He was also pretty sure that "gorgeous-and-expensive" was pacing around the room behind him, muttering to herself. It wasn't enough that he'd rented a tux apparently—or had he bought it? He didn't know. It didn't matter because it still wasn't the most expensive thing on his list of "things he'd apparently done but couldn't afford."

She was pacing around in the open space of the room, her hands waving and her mouth moving. Her deep ruby lipstick had stayed perfectly in place and he could see every word that passed those lips. If only he could read them. She, too, was clearly trying to figure out what they had done.

If the dress she wore was also *gorgeous and expensive*, the woman inside it looked even more so. Keith wondered for as many times in as many seconds what the hell he'd gotten himself into.

If appearances were correct, *he'd married her.*

"Check your phone!" she called out to him, the voice sweet and lilting, with a southern accent. He might have liked her—certainly would have been attracted to her—had he not been appalled by what he'd most likely done. He would have even liked the sweetness of her voice and the contradictory crisp drawl that was not quite appropriate to the situation.

Still, he stared into the mirror for another moment, ignoring her voice.

This was also not the hotel room he'd intended to stay in. He'd been driving all day, starting early from Berkeley. Just two days ago, he graduated from the veterinary school there. He'd been so pleased with his life, since he'd managed to line up a job and do it in a town where he wasn't completely on his own.

So he couldn't have fucked it all up like this. He just couldn't have.

He had a job to get to! But, apparently, he'd managed to snag himself a wife along the way. With a deep sigh, he did as she'd suggested and pulled out his phone.

"What am I looking for?" he called back, still not quite prepared to head out into the main room and face what may have been the most colossal mistake of what had been up until now a very orderly life.

"Check your bank account. I'm checking my purchases," she called back. He would have worried about her calm tone, but the glimpse he caught in the mirror told me her appearance might be perfectly put together, but she was freaking out, too.

Hers was a good idea, and he logged into his banking info and began to scroll through his listings, hoping like hell that she had paid for the hotel room because he could not afford... *Shit.* He had paid for it.

In fact, the numbers in his bank account were far fewer digits than they'd been when he'd left Berkeley yesterday morning. His heart sank.

Keith had this trip planned out perfectly. He had an apartment waiting. For a moment his heart tripped and then he sighed in relief. He'd already paid the deposit. Thank God. But his relief was short-lived. He'd not paid his first month's rent. That was due when he arrived...and no longer in his account.

He also had a job waiting. He had three more days to arrive on the other side of the country, get settled, and report for his first day of work.

He was screwed. *So screwed.*

Rapidly calculating the numbers in the checking account, he realized there was hardly enough money left for gas. Well, he could cover gas, but not also food unless he ate Cheetos the entire way there. Doing that would mean he arrived sick to his stomach. *Way to start your first job after graduation.*

He sighed. He did not want to call his grandparents and ask for money. He did not want to live with them because he couldn't afford the rent on his own apartment. He wanted to return as many of the items littering his spending from last night as he could and get his money back. But it appeared that he'd bought the tux outright and had it tailored...a rush order. And that was the most returnable item on the list. His stomach turned.

The overwhelming urge to throw the phone, as though *it* had done this to him, was something he tamped back down. Keith was not one for throwing things or having temper tantrums but it sure looked like he'd well and truly fucked himself this time.

"Check your pictures," came the voice from the other room. Somehow, even more dread filled him.

What could be worse than the missing digits from his bank account? But he looked anyway. He didn't shy away from things.

Keith Lee worked hard; he was dedicated, a good student. And he didn't deny the truth. So he pushed the button on his phone and opened the pictures.

Holy hell. How many were there? It looked like she had taken several of him with his phone, or maybe someone else had, because there he was, smiling in his tux, doing up the expensive bow tie.

There were pictures of her walking down the aisle and him standing there watching her with that awed look on his face. It appeared as though—at some point during the evening—he'd been sober enough to download a batch of pictures.... He checked. The Little White Wedding Chapel. *Oh, yes.*

There was also a copy of their marriage certificate. Just in case he'd been in doubt, that was cleared up. He didn't open it to read the fine print but kept scrolling through the pictures and downloads.

There were the two of them standing at the altar, with Elvis seemingly officiating from one red velvet step up. There was another of the two of them, her with a richly hued bouquet in her grasp, the two of them holding hands as they came down the aisle. Another with the requisite kiss under the floral arch. And damn but that picture was hot. He wished he remembered it. He'd certainly paid for it.

Keith's heart thudded in his chest. God, she was beautiful, stunning in her dress and curls and wide smile. He'd wondered in the past if he'd ever have that moment when he saw the woman he loved walking toward him, dressed in white. He'd seen more than one of his friends married off, but he'd never had the urge to leap in himself. But here he was, already married, and to some beautiful, southern blonde. And he was torn up inside.

Because while this one was beautiful, he had no idea who she was.

He hadn't read the marriage certificate, and so he hollered out now, "Hey, I'm sorry, but what's your name?"

☀ 3 ☀

K eith watched as she dipped her French fry in the pool of ketchup she'd made. It had been interesting watching his new wife open her burger wrapper, carefully lining up the waxed paper square to the edge of the table. She moved the burger to one side and anchored one corner with her coke...all while not paying attention to the fact that he was watching her rather than eating his own food.

It amused him that she tipped her fries onto the place setting she'd handily created. It petrified him that he now had a wife.

They were eating at McDonald's, not her favorite place or his, but the only one where he could get enough food to keep his brain going. God knew his brain was fried.

"Emerson," he started, but she shook her head.

"Emma Kate. Everyone calls me Emma Kate, or Em."

Emma Kate, he thought, the syllables rang perfectly for the off-beat southern belle sitting across from him. While at first he worried that maybe she'd roped him into some kind of scam, the idea had passed very quickly.

One, if it was a scam, she was doing a really crappy job. She'd picked entirely the wrong mark. Emma Kate should have been running a pick-up on a much richer man than him. Though he

9

didn't remember all that much from last night, he knew he would have told anybody who would listen that he had just graduated from veterinary school and had exactly enough pennies to get to his new apartment.

Hell, he wasn't even driving a car cross country, he'd been using a bike because the gas was cheaper. He'd mailed his clothing, his vet supplies, and everything else he'd needed to his grandparents' house a few weeks ago. He'd had enough money and clothing in his backpack to arrive and that was it. He'd budgeted everything out and was barely going to be able to eat until his first paycheck showed up. Though now, apparently, he'd ruined that. So if Miss Emma Kate was looking for a rich husband, she had dicked it up royally.

The second thing, though, was that her actions didn't read like any kind of scam. If she was acting, she deserved an award, but she seemed just as upset by the whole thing as he was. She also didn't remember his name that morning, which strangely made him feel better rather than worse. Though she was eating her fries one at a time, and mostly ignoring the small, flat burger that sat listlessly in front of her, she was tapping away on her phone.

Having given up on finding anything helpful online, he still hoped she would come up with a different answer than he had. She looked up, her eyes wide, tears starting to form.

"So apparently," she started with a quiver in her voice that made the dread squeeze in his chest. *This was not going to be good news.* "You can get married in about fifteen seconds for equally few dollars here in Vegas, but," *here it came*, "an annulment takes a lot more effort."

Sadly, that's what he'd found, too.

"It's a lot more money and it's going to take several days just to get the papers filed, and then we have to wait. If we leave the state, it will take even more money and more time." She was shaking her head at him, her frustration showing through. "I don't have enough money to stay here for four more days and file the paperwork."

She was looking at him as though she hoped he did.

Great. He thought. There went his hopes that maybe *he* had been the gold digger and *she* was independently wealthy.

Then she took a deep breath and looked off to the side. It was her thinking face. He already recognized it, she'd made it so many times in the short shit-show of time that he'd known her. "I mean, I might have the money. My parents died. My sister's handling all of the finances, but ... right now, all of my inheritance is caught up in properties and stocks. Honestly, my parents had some money, but my sister is still trying to find it, because my dad turned out to be a crappy financial manager."

She shouldn't be telling him this, Keith thought. What if he was gold digging? Though her dress from last night had been extravagant, so had his tux. But everything else about her said that she was broke, from her dented silver hatchback, to the U-haul trailer, to the scared expression she'd worn all morning.

"If you have it, I can pay you back. When the condo sells, and once the assets are liquidated." She was stumbling over her words, but Keith was shaking his head. It didn't matter how long it took her to pay him back; he simply didn't have it.

"In fact," he said, "I don't have enough money to stay here for four more days either." And that was *if* the paperwork went right through. If there were any snags at all, it would take even longer. "I was supposed to have left early this morning. I just thought I was spending the night in Vegas and playing the slots for a couple of hours."

He remembered sitting down beside her, both of them on nickel machines. The servers kept coming by and keeping their glasses full. Maybe they'd done too good of a job of that. He had glimpses of memories, many of them jogged by the pictures that had popped up on his phone, but most of the night before was just gone.

What wasn't gone was the tux he had folded as neatly as he could and put into a backpack, which felt wrong. She had treated the beautiful tulle dress better than him. Though she'd started to shove it down into her suitcase, Emma Kate had stopped and called for a garment bag. He hadn't even known that was a possibility.

Feeling like a fool, but not wanting to be a dick, or ruin the only expensive piece of clothing he had, he asked her to get him one too. They arrived, cheap dry cleaner style bags, but they were free. After he pulled the tux back out, she brushed out the wrinkles for him and then went to the job of tucking her very poofy dress into her own bag.

They'd walked all the way from the hotel to the cheap motel she was staying at. He would have bitched, but she was carrying what looked like twenty pounds of dress and walking in heels. He offered to help, but Emma Kate shrugged him off. It would've been embarrassing, but ironically they weren't the only couple on the streets having a clear "morning after." Many of the others he saw were still in their wedding wear making their way down the strip.

They'd even wound up waving to the others, though the others held hands, or bouquets, and looked happy. They showed off rings. That was when he had looked at her hand and first seen the stunning rock that now perched on her third finger. *Holy shit.* He suffered a small heart attack as he wondered if he'd bought it for her. He hadn't worked up the nerve to ask yet.

Instead, Keith told her about his job, about what was waiting for him. She told him about her family, and it jogged his memory then—why they had hit it off in the first place.

The town of Breathless, Georgia, where his grandparents and his aunt and uncle lived was her hometown. That was what had started them really talking. But that wasn't what he talked about now. Clearly, they were obviously a bride and groom with their see-through garment bags slung over their shoulders. He waved to another couple as he threw out the worst thing he could think of to say.

"I don't have enough money for gas for my bike. Whatever we spent last night barely leaves me enough to eat for the next few days."

She didn't take it as an attack or even a request for money. Emma Kate simply nodded and tried for a solution. "Well, I have extra space in my trailer, and we're going to the same place."

Emma Kate sat in the driver's seat, her hands at ten and two on the wheel. She was rolling down the interstate, just as she had planned, except now she was sitting next to her new *husband*.

Even thinking the word "husband" gave her the wiggins. She wasn't supposed to be married. Not now. Not this young. Not to someone she *barely knew*.

Unlike both her older sisters—who'd taken to their mama's prescribed life plan like fish to water—Em had had no idea what she wanted to do with the rest of her life. She hadn't wanted to get her degree, get married, raise a couple kids, and join the Junior League. None of that had been on her radar even in the future, let alone now. Yet, here she was, driving her new *husband* across the country. There was a legal document and everything making it all way too official. She told herself they'd get it annulled when they reached Georgia.

It would take longer than staying in Vegas and doing everything quickly, but he wouldn't lose his job, either.

They'd loaded his bike into the trailer. It had taken some repacking, but a closer inspection of their finances revealed that they couldn't afford gas for her car *and* gas for his bike *and* food.

They had two out of the three at best and they both had to eat. So gas for his bike had been the thing to go, since they couldn't very well pull the trailer with it. There had been a terse discussion of selling it for the money, and while it wasn't off the table yet, Em was glad they hadn't had to sell it.

They would stay in the cheapest motel rooms they could find. This was only one step down from her original plan so, sadly, it didn't free up a lot of money.

They hadn't yet discussed getting one bed or two. They hadn't discussed whether or not they'd slept together the night before either. Emma Kate suspected they had not. All of her bridal wear was in the exact right place when she woke up. It really seemed they'd just been a couple of crazy, punch drunk kids.

Luckily, Keith Lee seemed like a really great guy. He wasn't angry at her about the crazy shit they'd done, about the fact that all of his money was gone, and that she seemed to be wearing a large chunk of it on her left ring finger.

He'd been planning on leaving early that morning to stay on his schedule to arrive in time to claim the apartment he'd put his money on and find his new life after school. Their attempts to find out how to get the marriage annulled, return the wedding dress and the tux, or even find out where her ring had come from so they could at least get that money back, had all come up short.

None of it was returnable. Still, he was sitting in the passenger seat, scrolling through his bank records on his phone while she drove. Em had a good idea what he'd find though: nothing. The name that the bank posted for the charge didn't match to any of the jewelry stores they'd found listed in town. It appeared to be a shop owned by some parent conglomeration. Unless they spent another day and went door-to-door and got lucky with a return, nothing would change. Keith sighed and looked up, his eyes rolling with frustration.

Em understood. He'd been riding a nice bike and now he was

in a car with the lining on the roof starting to pull loose. There was no wind in his hair, because the passenger window didn't work anymore. The little car was just loud enough to probably remind him of being on the bike. Lordy, she thought, she was too old to be this much of a mess. Lennon was getting her masters degree and probably going to marry Gabe Zemp. Em was still in this little car and could barely afford the oil changes. And she didn't have a degree—or any accomplishments, really—to show for it.

"I can't find anything," Keith eventually told her, though she wasn't surprised by that. "And I don't know what to do about it."

"Could you stop the payment?" she asked.

"I guess I could, but the fact of the matter is, I walked out with the merchandise. Since it's a jewelry store, they'll have cameras, won't they?" He looked at her, his black-coffee eyes looking bleak. "They'll have video of me there, purchasing that ring. Probably video of you, too. And since we're still together—still legally married—it will be even harder to get out of it." Another sigh, and she could almost hear the gears working in his mind. "I handle schedule three drugs. I can't have a felony on my record."

She almost asked what a "schedule three drug" was but figured he was talking about dog morphine and cat heroin and didn't ask. She hadn't thought of it as a legal issue, but he was right. It seemed they'd gone into the store and legitimately bought her the ring. Well, they couldn't prove otherwise.

She shrugged her shoulders and shook her head and tried to explain. "I mean, I was hoping if you stopped the payment, they might demand the ring back. Then at least we'd know where to send it, and you wouldn't be out the money."

She felt bad. The dress and the tux were both packed up and put away. That part seemed equal. They were both broke—so that part also seemed equal. They'd at least both seemed to realize that getting mad at each other didn't do either of them any good.

But the ring...it weighed a little on her hand and heavily on her heart. She'd asked him if she should take it off, but he'd said no. If he was going to pay that much for it, the least they could do is both enjoy looking at it.

Em didn't really enjoy seeing it. Though the ring itself was beautiful and would have turned her heart in any other circumstance, she felt as though she'd stolen it from him and he was decent enough to let her. Under the ring sat a perfectly sized gold wedding band, too. Keith wore a matching one.

Damn. Their drunk selves had their shit together, she thought, *better than her sober self did.* Keith Lee seemed like he had his life figured out. Then again, *everyone* had it more together than Emma Kate Mayfair. Hell, Keith had not only graduated from college, he'd gone on to Veterinary school. It wasn't easy to get into vet school, and he'd graduated from that and found himself a job.

Emma Kate was running home on her *third* break from college. She hadn't told her sisters she was coming. She hadn't even graduated *once*. Not since high school anyway.

Looking over, she saw Keith had put his phone away, and she guessed he'd given up on getting the money back for the jewelry. There was just enough money left on their credit cards, and in their bank accounts, that they thought they could eat relatively cheaply and make it all the way across the country.

"I don't know what we'll do when we get there," he said. "I need a chunk of change to cover my first month's rent. I already paid the deposit, so that part's okay." He seemed to be thinking while he talked.

She wondered if he did that all the time, but rather than think about it, she volunteered, "I can get the rest."

He shrugged off her offer. "You don't owe me the rest."

"I feel like I do." The road curved to the right, and she turned the wheel as she watched the shiny sparkle of the diamond on her left-hand wink. Yes, she felt like she owed him.

"We'll figure out how to get the ring returned," he said.

"We'll figure all of this out. At least we're going to the same place."

She nodded because there was nothing to say. They were both headed to the tiny town of Breathless, Georgia. Her hometown, where she'd once been a princess. Daughter of Con Mayfair. Her aunt GiGi was the daughter of a former mayor. Her older sister, Bailey Ann, had been captain of her cheer squad and homecoming queen, just like their mama before them. Though Em had been wild and crazy, she'd been treated like a princess nonetheless.

Keith said he'd been in Breathless as a kid several times visiting his grandparents during the summers. His cousins Grace and Jimmy had grown up there, though they were a little bit older than him, and they hadn't been close. But from his stories, he knew Bobby's Pizza and the park by Chandler Elementary and Libby's Ice Creamery downtown.

Em wondered if the two of them had ever run into each other as kids. If he'd been there during the summers, they might have... She and her sisters had run free. They'd played with all the neighborhood kids, but Emma Kate couldn't remember a beautiful-eyed dark-haired boy with that cut to his cheeks. Wouldn't she have remembered Keith Lee if she'd seen him before? Then again, he didn't remember her either. But she was pretty sure she'd grown out of an awkward phase and maybe it was better if he didn't connect her now with the kid she'd been.

"My rent isn't your problem," he said into the space of the car.

She couldn't help her feelings though, and this felt like her fault. Of the two of them, it seemed far more likely that she would be the one to suggest they up and get married one night in Vegas. She was grateful he didn't remember, but then he asked the question. "Where are you staying when you get to town?"

❦ 5 ❦

"**Y**ou don't know where you're going to stay?" Keith's thoughts stumbled, but they stumbled because Emma Kate's voice did when he'd asked her where she was going to live.

She shook her head as though that wasn't it at all, and Keith jumped right back in. "You're driving all the way across the country. You seem to be going home. Is there..." He didn't want to ask but felt he should know. "Is there no home waiting?"

"Oh, there's a home," she replied easily enough, and his heart untwisted. "My sister even just re-did the entire house. She pulled mama's nasty wallpaper out of the dining room and repainted the living room—brought the house into the new century. It's just not waiting for *me*."

"Why?" he asked, still not quite comprehending how Emma Kate was answering so cheerfully about the fact that she was heading back to somewhere that wasn't ready for her.

"Oh, they'll take me in, that's not the problem. They just don't know I'm coming." In the last sentence the tone of her voice turned down, and he wondered what that was about.

Deciding that they were married and every good marriage was based on communication—even though he was pretty sure they didn't have a *real* marriage so how could they have a *good* one?—he pushed. "Am I allowed to ask why that is?"

Emma Kate took a moment. Her eyes darting left and right as her brain churned, still scanning the road. She'd proven to be quite a capable driver, and it only took him a little while to relax in the passenger seat. He hadn't had to grab the "oh shit" handle up on the roof, but the car was a little rattle-y, and he was almost afraid if he grabbed it, it might come off in his hand.

He waited her out and eventually she answered. "Well, I was at UCLA."

That was good, he thought. He realized he didn't even know how old she was. That would be his next question, depending on how this one went.

"Anyway, I'm an honor student."

Also impressive, he thought.

"...and I'm supposed to be doing my thesis, but..."

Uh oh.

"...but, I need a break. I'm not ready for the thesis. I'm not ready to graduate. Really, the problem is, I did this twice before, so I've actually been there for the right number of semesters, but I'm two years older than your average graduate because I... I can't get my shit together," she said, huffing her way through the last words. "Ask my family. They'll tell you."

She was looking out the window. He wondered if she thought he'd think less of her, because she "couldn't get her shit together." She seemed relatively together to him. She had a U-haul. Her car wasn't even stuffed with her crap, like a normal college student's would be. The back seat was clean and empty, except for the small suitcase she seemed to be traveling with.

Her car, though it rattled, seemed to run just fine. He'd surreptitiously checked the oil change sticker. She was well under her three thousand miles to her next change, though they'd be pushing it by the end of this trip. Keith noted it was the beginning of January, so likely she hadn't skipped out mid-term.

"Why didn't you tell them you were coming? I mean, if they're going to welcome you with open arms, make up the guest room and all."

She laughed, "Oh, there's no guest room anymore. I'll be on the pullout couch downstairs in the den, which will annoy my nieces that they can't just run around down there if I'm asleep."

She sounded like it would annoy her, too, but instead he asked, "Nieces?"

"So, my oldest sister Bailey Ann moved back... Do you really want to hear this whole thing?" She turned and looked at him then, blue eyes searching his face for a moment.

"Yeah," he said. He didn't add, *After all, I am your husband.* The words still didn't come naturally. For a moment, he hoped they never would. He'd not intended to get married in Vegas. Instead of dwelling on it, he blurted out, "Tell me your life story. I'll tell you mine next."

She grinned as though he had no idea what he was asking, then proceeded to tell him about her oldest sister, Bailey Ann, who was apparently the belle of every ball. His new wife—who he now realized looked the part despite her occasional swears and dropping out of school—was literally a southern belle.

She moved on to talk about her middle sister, Harper Rose, but then he interrupted her. "Do you all use both your first and middle names? All the time?"

Emma Kate laughed at him like he was silly. "Oh no. My middle name is Charlotte. I'm Emerson Kate—first name—Charlotte Mayfair."

"Not Emma Katherine?" He'd known the "Emerson" part from having finally read the marriage certificate. He'd been more concerned with finding an error so he could claim it wasn't real, but now he was hung up on her name. "How do you get a name like Emerson?"

"Family name. My sister is Harper. Bailey Ann just got lucky, I guess." She'd gone on to tell him about her middle sister, who'd done everything right and gotten shafted anyway. If he had his pieces put together right, Bailey Ann had lived in the house but now she'd moved out and Harper Rose was there with her three young daughters.

"I'm not sure how they have it arranged." Emma Kate told him, "but I'm pretty sure they're in all the upstairs bedrooms, which means I'll be downstairs on the pullout couch. And I didn't call ahead, because I'm not looking forward to the lecture. Bailey Ann doesn't even live in the house anymore, but she'll find a way to let me know I screwed up. And Harper Rose... Well, they're ten and seven years older than me. I'm pretty sure I was a mistake."

"*What?*" he blurted it out, flummoxed that any parent would let their child think that. "Did your parents *say* that?"

"Oh God, no. My parents don't talk about sex or anything. Well, they *didn't*. They certainly never mentioned that I was a mistake. But it's pretty obvious. All their friends have two kids. And those two kids are my sister's ages, not mine. They had their whole family—they even had the professional family portrait made before I came along—and then seven plus years later, *boom!* there I am. So I think it's pretty obvious that I wasn't an intentional pregnancy." She was looking out over the long stretch of interstate in front of them, and Keith couldn't help but think how long the real road was in front of her. "My sisters are enough older than me that they've mothered me all my life. I've had damn near enough, and I don't want to hear about dropping out of school again."

He understood the heavy sigh in her voice. He understood about being overly parented, though his had been different. He nodded. "I spent the summers with my grandparents in Breathless. I think a lot of it was because I was an only child, and my folks needed time to not be parents. Maybe a few months out of each year. I love my mom and dad and I know they love me, but I don't think they were really cut out to have kids, so they quit after me. I'm pretty sure they had an arrangement with my grandparents, to give them some alone time each summer. I was fourteen before I figured it out."

Em smiled at him. "My parents never got rid of me."

"My new apartment has two bedrooms," he said, the words tumbling out, before he could stop them. That was unlike him. He was the kind of man who always thought before he spoke. As the only child of two adults who didn't really understand or seem to want kids, he'd never run wild and crazy. But here he was, less than twenty-four hours around this impulsive woman, and he was making offers he hadn't thought about at all. He might as well finish it off. "You could live with me."

❧ 6 ❧

If you must break a rule, don't do anything small or tacky. Go all out and take no prisoners.

EM BLINKED AND PROBABLY ALMOST SWERVED OFF THE ROAD. She wasn't paying enough attention to know if she'd even done it or not. Well, if she'd swerved like an idiot, at least she'd saved them, because she was still on the road and no one was honking at her.

Had Keith Lee really just offered her a room in his apartment? He surely couldn't have meant it, as even he looked surprised by the offer.

So she did the right thing and politely turned him down. "I don't even have a job or money for rent. I was fully intending to mooch off my sisters for a while."

That would be the end of it, she thought, but Keith only laughed at her.

Her head swiveled sharply to the right, and she must have looked at him as though he suddenly appeared in her car, instead of having been there for all of today's drive. His wide grin lit up his face and those black-coffee eyes sparkled with mirth. *Holy crap*. Emma Kate was suddenly hit with the realization that Keith Lee was *hot*.

No, actually, she'd known that already. She'd known he was attractive from the moment she'd woken up beside him and seen him sleeping on the other side of the bed. His shoulders were broad, his waist narrow, and his face looked like he could be modeling. He probably wasn't tall enough, she thought. That was probably why he'd gone into veterinarian school, but that just meant he was smart, too.

She tried not to think about the way her heart pitter-pattered in her chest at the way he smiled at her. She could see why she'd married him, and she also understood why it was prob-ably best that she not be attracted to her own husband.

"I can't pay half the rent," she admitted. Once again, she figured that would be the end of it. But, once again, he only laughed in response.

When she asked him what was so funny, he told her, "I can't pay half the rent either. At least, not until I get my first check. Once I get my paycheck, I can pay all the rent."

"Well, then you don't need me for anything," she said, although the thought of having her own room in an apartment was so tempting. What would it be like not having Harper Rose, with her three beautiful daughters and her should-have-been-a-perfect life hovering over her? What would it be like, knowing every day that at least Harper Rose hadn't been the one to screw up her own life, while Emma Kate was always her own worst enemy?

Being on her own sounded like heaven.

"What could I possibly do that would make it worth your while to have me living with..." She cut that question off right there and watched as his eyes sparked again for a moment.

"Nothing like that," he said with a grin that let her know he wasn't thinking *that*. "I would never."

See? She told herself. *Keith Lee was a great guy.* She'd picked well, even if she'd done a damn fine job of messing everything up.

"What I was thinking..." he explained, "is that the new job is supposed to have really long hours. This sounds stupid because it sounds really wifely, but my God, if you just did the grocery shopping, I'd be thrilled. You could pay whatever rent you could afford, when you could afford it. If you made dinner once in a while, I would be so grateful."

"Like a wife for hire?" But she didn't let him answer that. It sounded too easy anyway. She tried again. "Wouldn't you want the second bedroom for your office?" Emma Kate was still trying to think of a way to get out of this proposition. But she knew herself, too: She was also actively trying to find a legit way to get into it.

She didn't want to be seduced by the idea of a room of her own, of not having to fold up her bed in the morning, of having a place of her own and at least appearing more adult to her sisters, even if she really wasn't. But if she did it for the wrong reasons, she would just mess up her life even more than she already had. She might be a screw up, but she wasn't stupid.

Keith shook his head. "I don't need a home office. All my work is at the clinic. And I fully intend to leave it behind for the few hours I do get to come home. The apartment came with the job. Well, at least the vet who offered me the job offered me the apartment."

"Is he your boss *and* your landlord?" Emma Kate asked, thinking that could get sticky. What if the job didn't work out? She knew that could happen from her own personal experience.

"No, he's not the landlord. The apartment is on a farm, and the farm is one of the ones where he works for the owners a lot. I'm going to be his assistant for just a little while, until I get the hang of the routine and the area and what needs his clients have. But I'm a full-fledged vet, and he intends to make me his partner, soon. I'm hoping he'll like me and he'll sell the business to me when he decides to retire."

"Will that be soon?" Emma Kate asked, frowning, wondering if she was sitting next to some kind of wunderkind. He'd not only graduated with a doctorate but would likely even own his own business in a couple of years. She couldn't even pick out her thesis topic.

"I think so. I got the impression that he's ready to retire, but his clients aren't ready to let him go yet. So he's looking for someone he can get them to trust."

"That sounds wonderful," Em said, a jealous knot forming in her little heart, even though she understood Keith had earned every bit of his good fortune and she'd caused all her bad.

"Exactly. So take the room, help me out. Find a job when you can, or will you head back to UCLA?" he asked.

She shrugged and shook her head. Honestly, going back had not occurred to her. She was one semester away from graduating. She had no more required classes—at least not if she did the thesis. But that thesis was like a Navy SEAL obstacle course and she didn't see a way over it. She had no idea what topic to cover for the thesis, no idea who should be on her committee, and if she didn't do it, she wouldn't graduate with honors. To make matters worse, if she didn't graduate with honors, then she was subject to a different set of requirements and she would have two more classes to take.

She was between an academic rock and a hard place, so she sucked in a breath and said, "If you're sure."

He held out his hand, reaching across the middle, offering to shake on the deal. That was funny, she thought. He'd married her but would offer a handshake to give her a place to stay.

Then he said it. "Of course, wife."

Emma Kate grinned back, but she felt her heart turn over at the word "Wife." What had she done?

❄ 7 ❄

Emma Kate woke to a smushed feeling along the side of her face and a hand shaking her shoulder.

It took a moment to remember what was going on. When she'd gotten sleepy and suggested calling it a night in Tucson, Keith had asked to aim for the Texas border. He'd even volunteered to drive while she slept. So instead of getting a cheap room, she'd pulled out her pillow, wedged it against the car door and fallen asleep to the rumble of the old car on a long cold road.

This was a drive she'd expected to make alone, so it was odd to wake up in a different state sitting in her own passenger seat.

"We're in Amarillo," Keith told her in his relatively quiet voice.

When she looked up blinking and focused out the front window, she saw yellow incandescent light that did nothing to improve the view. She saw that it didn't matter if they were in Amarillo or Omaha. Where they could afford to stay would look roughly the same. A glance up and to her right revealed they were in front of the Starlight Motel.

She sighed and wondered if they were going to get asked if they wanted the room by the hour. Would that make Keith the hooker, or her? Flipping the visor down, she checked her reflection. She would definitely be considered the sex worker. At least neither of them looked like they'd been doing meth.

"What time is it?" she asked, the words rolling like gummy candy in her mouth.

"Almost one a.m."

It had been close to nine or ten when she'd been ready to stop back in Tucson. But he'd offered to drive if she'd let him. How could she say no? She'd *married* him, for Pete's sake. At least he'd be covered on her car insurance-not that Bailey Ann would be happy to cover another driver.

It suddenly occurred to her that the idea that she could keep this marriage secret only worked if she didn't have any accidents. A car accident? Even a fender bender, and Bailey Ann would be notified, because she was still paying out the insurance. Her parents had covered it, but when they'd both died this past year, her older sister had taken over all the family paperwork and finances. It hadn't made Em feel any better about any of it.

She'd like to keep this whole "Married in Vegas" thing under wraps until it was annulled. If she had her way, she'd play this as a card in a rousing game of "Two truths and a lie" in about a decade. She'd win, that was certain.

But right now, if anything happened, she'd have to tell her sisters what she'd done. Part of the beauty of having her own room in Keith's apartment was not having to confess what a mess she was in.

Right then, she pledged to herself that she was going to get a part time job, as soon as she could. And she was going to pay Keith back for the ring. She'd have to pawn it, probably, which would probably only also get her about half the value. She'd have to earn the other half.

Carefully, Em twisted her hand around and tried to look at it without looking like an adoring bride gazing at her lovely new rock. She didn't want Keith to think she was getting attached to it. The ring had cost way too much money for either of them to be attached.

"I'm going to go inside," he said into the silence she'd allowed in her slow waking, but there was a catch in his voice.

Em understood. They'd mapped out everything earlier. It was part of the reason that they were so late getting here. They'd spent the morning figuring out that they couldn't return anything or get an annulment. Once they'd decided to travel together—as there were no other real options—they'd laid out what money was left and decided who would pay for what.

They'd planned how much they thought they could get away with paying for each part of the trip—lunch, dinner, motel rooms, gas, snacks, everything they would need to get home. Luckily, her car was old and it was from an era when gas mileage had been a priority.

She pushed her eyes wide and hopefully her brain awake. "I've got this," she told him. Pulling the pillow down from where she'd wedged it and opening the side door, Em tumbled out into a night a good bit colder than she'd expected.

This one was hers. Their plan was to spend credit card money on motel rooms, because there wouldn't be enough cash to eat when they arrived if they didn't do it this way. It would put them in more debt for later, and they were both already in way deeper than either of them planned, all because of a wedding neither of them remembered. At least they had beautiful photos of the fun time they must have had, she thought wryly.

Heading inside, Em asked for a room for the night and was pleased when the clerk cited her a lower-than-budgeted cost. She fished her card out of her wallet, thinking that if anyone came looking for her, they'd easily be able to trace her movement across the country. Either of her sisters would probably shudder if they figured out where she'd been and what she'd been eating.

She and Keith had left a trail of debit and credit card purchases. Taco Bell, McDonalds, and now, the Starlight Motel.

"One room." she told the man, then quickly tacked on, "Does it have two beds?"

Only, as she asked that—with a quiver forming in her voice at the thought the answer might be "no"—did she realize Keith had come in behind her. For a moment, she pushed her thoughts to the practical, and hoped he'd locked the car. But her concern about the mundane didn't last long. He pushed the car keys into her palm, wrapping her fingers around them and smiling. Keith was clearly not offended by the two beds question.

On the one hand, he shouldn't be. They really didn't know each other. Well, she thought, they knew each other pretty damn well after almost twelve hours in her small car together today. If he asked for one bed, she'd still say no, but it was a lot harder to justify saying "I don't" after legally saying "I do."

"Two queens," the motel clerk told her and slid a key across the desk. No plastic card, this was an old, diamond shaped tab with a gold key dangling from it. Em didn't like the lack of security and figured there was probably a chain lock on the back of the door. At least she had Keith.

Taking her credit card back, she asked for a receipt and then turned and headed out. She had to examine the key for a moment before she found the number. "Looks like we're in seven."

"Lucky seven," he said, with a smile on his face, though Em was struggling to agree. She unlocked the car, grabbed her pillow, pulled out her little suitcase, and the cloth grocery bag that she'd pushed on top of it. "Do you have what you need?"

Her voice still felt gummy. She'd already slept for several hours. Keith had not. "I'll take the first shift driving in the morning," she volunteered.

He nodded. "That would be nice." But then he sidestepped in front of her on the sidewalk and for a moment, she frowned. Was he one of those guys who always had to go first? He held his hand out for the key, making her wonder a little more. As she handed the key over, she heard her brain go "Oh, hell, no." But instead of saying it, she watched, wondering how he was going to handle this.

But Keith Lee seemed to lack all asshole-y intentions. He

simply unlocked the door, checked out the room, and motioned for her to enter first. Crap, here she'd been thinking poorly of him and he was a perfect gentleman.

Her turn. She needed to make up for her bad assumptions, even if he hadn't caught them. "Why don't you use the bathroom first? Brush your teeth, whatever. Then you can go right to sleep. You're probably tired."

He hadn't napped all day and she figured it was the least she could do. So she stayed back as he headed into the restroom, a small travel bag clutched in his hand.

She had her pajamas and her quilt laid out, and her phone turned to her newest book by the time he came back out. But he didn't really look at her. Keith Lee almost fell across the bed.

Taking that as her sign, she took over the restroom. Changing in the tiny space was another thing she'd not expected to do. She'd thought she would have her motel rooms to herself. But she brushed her teeth and thought again that she'd probably sleep better with him beside her than she would have alone.

She trusted Keith Lee. It felt good to know that she might be an idiot who'd spent all her money on a drunken Vegas wedding, but she'd done it with a good guy.

When she came out from the bathroom, she saw he'd managed to crawl under the polyester covers and was out cold. His eyelashes lay like soot on cheekbones that begged for a photograph. His head tipped, his lush mouth quieter than her thoughts.

Emma Kate Mayfair wasn't tired anymore. So she turned out the light, crawled under her quilt and tried to read her book. Instead, she found herself watching her husband.

❧ 8 ❧

"Wait," Keith said, trying to keep his hands on the wheel and working hard not to laugh. "You dated Chad Bass? Didn't your sister marry Chad Bass? Your sister who is seven years older than you? She married your ex?" He was frowning but laughing.

As Em had told the story, he understood the most important thing: Chad was a Class A asshole, quarterback on the football team, who thought he was all that. Em did not agree with Chad's self-assessment of total awesomeness.

"No," she told him. "I dated *Chad* Bass, little brother of *Thad* Bass, whom my sister married."

"And he died right?"

"Right. And it turns out, he was also a lying asshole."

Keith cringed. It was one thing for Emma Kate to have dated a loser in high school—funny even—but for her sister to end up married and left destitute for it was another. He was not a fan of the Bass brothers. Keith tried to remember if his new boss/partner Ed had mentioned any Basses on the rounds. He shook off the thought and said, "I thought all your parents' friends had kids your older sister's age."

"Yeah, the Basses didn't seem to do such a good job with

having the kids. They had Thad, and then there was a big break between him and Chad and then the youngest brother."

"Wait. There's another Bass? He's not named—wait—he's not Brad! Right? Is he *Brad Bass*?"

"Of course he is." Em was laughing as she said it, and it was all Keith could do to keep the car on the road.

The landscape had changed in the past day, it had gone from brown, straight and flat and long to curvy, green, wet and almost icy in places. They were getting closer, he thought. It was starting to look more like what he remembered, though there was still another full day on the road.

They'd stay over tonight in Little Rock and make it in tomorrow to Breathless, hopefully before two p.m. That would give them three hours of wiggle room. At least, that was his plan so that he could meet the owners of the farm with the apartment and get started getting settled in hopefully before five.

Showing up any time later would be rude, he thought. He'd spent enough summers in Breathless to know Southerners judged harshly on "rude." If everything went well, he would officially start work the next morning. On his original plan, he'd included almost a full day's wiggle room but that didn't exist anymore. He'd wiggled most of it away on his quickie Vegas wedding.

Luckily, with two drivers they'd been able to get a little further each day than he would have been able to alone. It helped make up for having left so late. He should thank her for the car. He'd not planned for the chill in the air, and he would have been freezing on his bike. He'd thought Tucson was warm, but all the elevations around it were not. They'd seen ice warnings galore.

"Why would they do that?" he asked her. "Chad, Thad and Brad. I mean you and your sister have these elegant family names."

"I don't know that *Emerson* is elegant" she almost snorted, making him wonder if she was commenting on the name or herself as a person.

"Oh, come on. It's unique. And Emma Kate is pretty awesome."

She grinned. "Emma Kate is pretty awesome," she offered, once again making him wonder exactly what she was referencing.

God help him, he liked her. It didn't hurt that she was pretty. She was short but had some curves on her. If you'd asked him two weeks ago, he would have told you he didn't really have a type. But now, it seemed he did. He couldn't say he hadn't noticed the morning he'd woken up next to her, but it hadn't made him feel anything other than fear.

He'd assumed for the first petrifying moments that she was the wrong woman. He didn't care that she was pretty, only that she had a bad game, and he was going to have to shake her loose without letting her get any of the small amount of money he had. But it had become clear pretty quickly that she was not a gold digger, and they'd *both* screwed up. When he might have liked her, he'd been dealing with the fact that he was stuck with her.

He hadn't said anything yet and he wondered if she'd noticed that their budget did not account for an annulment. They simply didn't have the money to file the paperwork. Though they'd agreed that ending their little farce of a marriage was the best thing to do. Food, gas and shelter all had to come first. So they were stuck being married for the time being, at least legally.

Then he'd gone and invited her to be his roommate. He wanted to say he was doing a kind deed—that she looked like she needed a place away from her family and he could enjoy a few home cooked dinners. But that had not been all of it. He actually really liked her.

The worst part was he was married to her. If he'd simply met her, he might have asked if she *wanted* to drive cross country with him. She might have shared a bed with him, rather than wondering just how creepy her new *husband* was. He might have at least asked her out in some semblance of a normal way. Now? It wasn't even an option.

Each night, his wife pulled an old quilt out of the bag she carried and wrapped it around her as though she needed armor to shield herself from him, despite the fact that he was on a different bed. The second night, he'd worked up the nerve to ask about it, but she laughed at him. Despite his very polite question about her quilt, she'd caught on to what he was really asking.

"I'm not afraid of you. And if I was, a quilt wouldn't save me. It's my grandma's quilt; she hand-stitched it and then handed it down to *me*."

He heard that in her voice, the tone in the "me" that implied "not my older sisters." He wondered how much Em had had that hadn't been hand me down. What of her sisters' things had been passed directly to her? Clothing, parental love, even expectations?

He'd been wondering that all morning, and when she'd voted to stop the car for lunch, it stopped his thoughts. Even though it was just another fast food place—this one attached to a gas station—she wanted to go inside and sit down. Closing the car door, she shuddered at the cold. Then she turned and leaned against the hood of the small car, working the kinks out of her legs.

He'd watched as she stretched... putting one leg forward, the other straight back, lengthening her calves, first one then the other. She insisted she needed to get out a little bit. Maybe she'd just needed to stand upright, get all her muscles to their full extension.

While he understood she wanted to stop, he didn't. Still, he compromised. Their timing was okay. While he had a real need to get to the other side of the country, she didn't. He forced himself to stretch alongside her. If he had to stop, he'd make it useful.

His nerves were kicking in. About the apartment he hadn't yet seen, about the job that might blow up in his face. What if he didn't fit? What if all his rounds in vet school didn't fully prepare him? But he couldn't fix those things now and an anxiety attack wouldn't do any of them any good. So he took a few deep breaths and told himself he was just copying her.

He saw a few other people around the gas station looking as well. They couldn't quite help it, there was something magnetic about her. When she was afraid, it made her eyes wide. When he asked something she didn't want to answer, her face went carefully blank. Her smile lit up her eyes when it was genuine. Her frustration was always clear. It was a good thing they hadn't been playing poker in Vegas or they would have lost even more money that night.

So he knew she was grateful and relieved as she stretched. But then she stood and held out her hand to him, as though to pull him into the restaurant behind her.

God help him, but he started to wonder, how do you ask your own wife out on a date?

❧ 9 ❧

Emma Kate felt her eyes go wide as Keith turned the steering wheel and they pulled up to the Barker farm. As her eyes looked from one side of the broad property to another, she tried to find where their apartment building might be located.

There was a main house relatively square in the center of the cleared land. A huge barn stood off to her right, the wood old enough that light might shine through the slats. On her left, there were new stables, with black painted horse fencing marking a corral beyond the main house. Several other little outbuildings looked squarish and made her think about western ranches, kitchens and living quarters for the help, and she began to wonder if she was going to be living in a bunkhouse.

Well, she thought, *she could always tell Keith that it wasn't working out.* If she did that, she was going to have to tuck her tail between her legs and go beg a room—or at least a pullout couch —from Harper Rose.

For a moment Em set her mouth, thinking she should be welcomed with open arms, then she remembered they all thought she was still in L.A. finishing up her thesis. Finding out she was home, and *married*—of all things—was going to be a shock. Finding out that she'd quit school once again probably wouldn't.

Hoping Keith had a better handle on things than she did, she turned to him and asked, "Which one's ours?"

They'd done that over the past forty-eight hours, begun talking about the apartment on the farm as "ours" instead of "his."

But he shrugged. "I have no clue. I've never been here before in my life."

"They didn't send you pictures?"

"No, just some basic dimensions. It's not that big," he warned her again. But it wasn't the size that worried her. It was the fact that it might be as drafty as the barn to her right, or as square and dorm-looking as the building straight ahead. Or it might be full of ranch hands.

"Let's go up the driveway," he said. "We'll knock on the door and figure out where we fit. They're expecting me. I texted earlier today."

Of course he did, Emma Kate thought. Keith Lee had his shit together.

"Mr. Barker is expecting us." Sure enough, Keith turned the wheel to the left, taking the section of gravel drive that headed for the main house. Before they even made it halfway to the parking area in front of the home, an older man came out the front door.

He had shocks of white hair sticking out from under his cowboy hat. His dark skin was hidden, mostly by the shadow of a ten-gallon hat that wasn't out of place in this range of the South, Emma Kate thought. But what she liked best about Jay Barker was the wide smile. She climbed out of the car, already feeling better. If it was the bunkhouse, she'd say "no, thank you" and go home. So she'd wait and see. Decision made, she headed up the drive, her footsteps crunching along right behind Keith's as they approached their new landlord.

"Hey," he said by way of greeting. "You must be Keith Lee.

I'm Jay Barker." He didn't even let Keith nod in confirmation. Who else would be driving up the driveway exactly when Keith had said they would arrive? Emma Kate was pretty sure he'd given an exact ETA. "My wife, Julani, will be out in just a moment."

Jay Barker's eyes darted to her face and Em nodded then suddenly, she froze. What was Keith going to say about her presence here? Had he texted that, too?

Jay Barker, for all his wide smile, seemed a little old fashioned. As he looked at Emma Kate, who'd not yet been introduced, his smile faltered. Apparently, that answer was No, Keith had not mentioned that he was bringing a roommate. *Roommate, girlfriend, wife?* She had no idea what to call herself in this situation. They hadn't defined it yet, but they were going to have to now. Right now.

"Hello," she said, figuring a good offense was the best defense, and put her hand out. "I'm Emma Kate Mayfair."

She hoped her last name would mean something to the man. They were all of ten miles outside of the Breathless city limits, and the town had once been called Mayfair. Mostly, she didn't like that her family was so well known around town, but right now, she would use it to her advantage.

"It's very nice to meet you. Are you helping Keith move in?" The old man shook her hand with a warm grip that was welcoming again.

She opened her mouth, though all she was prepared to say was, "Well, uh..."

But she didn't get any sound out, as Keith jumped in to fill the awkward gap that was opening. "Actually, Emma Kate and I met up in Vegas, and one thing led to another."

He grinned, shrugged one shoulder, and held up his left hand. It was brilliant, Emma Kate thought. He didn't have to say anything. He hadn't defined her in any way, shape, or form, but Jay Barker saw that ring on his finger and immediately looked to Emma.

As it was all she could do without boldly lying to a nice old man, Em held her hand up too, her rock winking in the sun as the light was sinking behind the hills.

The grin that had faltered momentarily now became very, very wide. "Well, congratulations, you two." Then Barker tipped his head. "The place is tiny, but I tell you what, as a wedding present, I'll make your lease month to month. If it's too small, and you find somewhere bigger, I won't hold you to it."

"Oh, that's not necessary," Keith told him.

"Well, wait until you see it," Barker spoke in a cautioning tone and made a motion for them to follow him.

Julani had stepped out on the porch, a towel in her hands. "Are you showing them the house?"

"I am."

Emma Kate wondered why they were getting a tour of the home. Mostly, she'd been in the car for almost four days, and she desperately wanted to unpack, or just fall face forward onto a floor somewhere and splay out like a starfish. If she could, she would sleep for three days.

Jay, however, was not walking them into the main house, but around the corner.

He looked back over his shoulder at them, a red and black cowboy handkerchief having appeared in his hand. "I turned the heat on for you," he said, and Emma Kate thought she might never have heard more wonderful words. At least they weren't heading toward what looked like a bunkhouse.

As they rounded the corner, she saw it—a tiny, perfect cottage, built up on a small foundation, with wooden steps leading up to a front door. It was small, she thought, but it had a huge front porch. Her breath sucked in. The porch was wood plank, made from old rough-hewn beams, and it already had two rocking chairs. A small table stood between the two chairs waiting for a warmer day.

The building itself was small, but it had been painted a sunny yellow, probably twenty or so years ago. The shutters were a glossy black that had also sun-faded over time. The raised foundation was skirted with lattice and it wasn't the Taj Mahal, or anything like what she'd been raised in, but it was cute and looked to be well built.

She could see herself bringing her laptop out on the porch on a sunny day. The chairs begged for cushions and a tea glass for the table. She could see herself hanging Christmas lights in pine boughs along the railing—not that she'd still be here next year.

Jay Barker turned and pointed out the section of gravel drive that came up to the side of the cute little house. "You can park here." Then he led them up the stairs. "It's not much," he warned them again, but he turned the knob and stepped aside so she could see.

Emma Kate got one glimpse, and she gasped.

❦ 10 ❦

K eith pulled another box from the trailer. There was more in there than it had initially appeared. More than he had remembered moving to make room for his bike. But as he hauled it inside the house and stacked it against the wall, it seemed to grow. Maybe too much for the tiny house. Definitely too big for what he could only call "the dining area."

He thought again how he had heard Emma Kate gasp when the front door swung open. She had covered it beautifully, telling Jay Barker how quaint and adorable the place was. She was a true Southern belle, Keith thought. She hadn't hidden the gasp, but by the time Mr. Barker left, he thought Emma Kate was in love with the place.

Keith was not in love with it. But the good news was, he didn't have to be. It was just a place to live while he got his job under his feet. He might not even decide to stay in Breathless, though he'd wanted to be closer to his grandparents. And—as Mr. Barker had just let them know—he didn't even have to stay in this small house.

Keith let the box settle down onto the top of the one below it. It said "Dishes" across the side in bold black marker. He felt he'd known Emma Kate just long enough to wonder if she'd borrowed the box from someone else who'd put *their* dishes in it or if the weight really was due to her dishes. He asked.

"No, the labels are mine." She smiled up at him from where she bent over another box. Despite her horrified gasp upon seeing the inside, she seemed happy enough to be unpacking here. Or maybe he was misreading her and she was simply grateful to be out of the car and making the best of it. He'd offered to haul the boxes in from the cold if she would arrange everything. After all, most everything was hers.

He checked the swishy-looking labels on the boxes again, rethinking things now that he knew they were correct. *Interesting.* Each word was written in beautiful cursive with a fat marker, almost as though they'd been designed onto the box.

"Do be careful with it, please," she called out. "It's my china. I'll carry it if you want."

"You have china?" he asked.

Emma Kate put her hands on her hips and very clearly gave him a look that asked, *you don't?* Then she seemed to re-think his question and make sense of it. So she replied, "Look, I know I'm not married, or I am—I mean *we are*—but no one gave us china. The thing is, there's a Mikasa outlet between L.A. and Vegas, and I've been more than once." She said it as though she was confessing she'd run off to Vegas and married a man she'd barely met. But no, this was about dinnerware.

He blinked.

He'd thought he had a pretty good grasp on her after riding in the car with her for three straight days. The car had not been big enough for them to get away from each other, and he had been pleased that he liked her. However, now, moving in with her, he was starting to see a different story. He had a backpack. She had neatly labeled boxes that said things like *dresses*, *dishes*, and *shoes*. He was curious if she also had one that said *guns and ammo* or *pearls to clutch*.

Keith couldn't help himself, and he asked, "Is your silver in there?"

She gave him a dirty look. "I don't have silver."

He was raising his eyebrows, getting ready to ask why she was so irritated by that question, when she told him, "That Mikasa outlet? It's at an outlet mall. I got myself a fine set of sterling ware, but I don't have real silver."

She was a college-honors-student-drop-out and she seemed bitter that she didn't have real silver. There was a story there, and he didn't think he had said it out loud until she turned around and almost glared.

"Remember I told you I have two older sisters and I was this mistake third child? Well, Bailey Ann got Grandma Mayfair's silver and Harper Rose got Grandma Brown's. Everything worked out!" Her voice rose a pitch. "Harper Rose married Thad Bass, so the B monogram was exactly what she needed. And Bailey Ann Mayfair just married Finn Malloy—another perfect monogram match. It was written in the stars!"

It sounded more like it was written on the ends of the forks, he thought.

But Emma Kate wasn't done. "Sadly, there are only two grandmothers. No more grandmas left to give Emma Kate their silver. So Emma Kate took herself to the outlet mall and bought her own."

And that was the end of that, Keith Lee thought. Emma Kate was not getting her silver handed down from her grandmother, and she'd apparently had enough of their shit. He almost laughed but managed to stifle it.

Turning away from him, Emma headed toward the back of the little unit, taking the door on the right. A stubby hallway led directly into the one small bathroom that was shared for the whole house. He hadn't thought about it before, but he wasn't surprised. He had been told the square footage and that it was only two bedrooms.

The two bedrooms were equal in size, though Emma Kate had made it clear over the previous days she would gladly take the smaller one. He laughed now. There was no *smaller* bedroom.

They were both small enough that anything smaller would have to be called a closet.

Out where he stood was a kitchen area off to the right. Appliances and cabinets snugged up against the wall. A desperately old oven from another era featured a pull front that didn't have a window and a warming center up above. He'd never seen one of those except in catalogs and old paintings. A tall pantry was built into the corner, the door stretching floor to ceiling. Next to it, a row of cabinets ran both bottom and top, creating the only real counter in the "kitchen." The woodwork was solid, not cheap, but he wasn't sure about the curlicues carved into the bottom cabinet doors, or the fact that the top row was all open with only chicken wire across it to keep the dishes from falling out if an earthquake hit.

A refrigerator butted the end and almost made the hallway seem longer. It too came from another era but not the same one as the stove. It had the kind of door handles that pulled out like car handles, unlocking and letting either the freezer on top or the refrigerator down below open. There would be no ice maker.

He told himself it was okay. He was prepared to live without the conveniences, after all, he'd been a poor student, then grad student, for nearly a decade. But he wasn't so sure about his new wife who had brought her own Mikasa. No ice maker, no TV, just a couch and a mantle over a small woodstove heater. The bedrooms didn't even have closets, just a dresser and a hanger rack.

With a deep breath, Keith hollered out to her, though the sound didn't have far to go. Once again, he offered her a chance to leave, but she came back wide-eyed. Emma Kate surprised him once again.

"No, really. I *love* it."

❧ 11 ❧

Keith rode his bike toward his new, tiny home. He was feeling every bump in the gravel drive and every gust of cold air that blew past him. Every bone in his body ached.

It wasn't that he'd done so much work today, it was that he'd had to be "on" from the moment he met his boss/mentor/partner Ed Housley in person for the first time. The old man believed in getting right to business. So within moments of saying hello, Keith was on a tour of the veterinary clinic, memorizing all of the assistant's names, and soon after heading out on three separate runs to three separate farms in three separate directions. In one case, he and Ed had to inoculate a herd, which was not easy work and he wasn't sure why the owner wanted it done in January.

He was sweaty and he smelled bad and all he could think was that maybe he shouldn't have let Emma Kate live here. He wanted to stand in the shower for an hour and sleep for ten.

Charging up the steps to fight the cold and officially end his day, Keith wondered if she'd be in the bathroom. There hadn't been much counter space around the tiny sink, and he thought perhaps she'd have curling irons and makeup and hair brushes all over the place.

He'd never had a female roommate before, and he didn't know what to expect. Though he suspected even if he had known, he wouldn't have been prepared for Emma Kate. He pushed the front door open, wondering if he should be surprised that it was unlocked. Perhaps the people in Breathless didn't regularly lock their doors. It had a small town feel to it and maybe they just wanted the doors to be open in case people got cold. Or maybe it was because she wasn't even quite in Breathless, but just out of town on a private farm with a house relatively nearby. He didn't have the energy to ask.

Whatever he'd thought it would be like in Breathless, he hadn't been prepared. He'd only been in town for the summers, but the cold was sharp and gusty, and felt like it was biting at him. And there wasn't any snow! Keith Lee was a firm believer that if it was cold there should be snow to compensate for the frostbite.

At least the land around town was beautiful and even the little house had great views. At the top of a small knoll, it looked out in all directions across the farm. He was grateful that the Barkers were no longer running a big operation. They had only a gentleman's herd of cows and a handful of horses.

So at least it didn't smell like a cow farm, at least not that he noticed yet. Then again, maybe it did because right now he sure smelled cow farm. The problem was that he was ninety-nine percent certain it was coming from him.

Worn out and wishing to be alone, he'd had no idea what would happen when he walked into the tiny house.

When they'd moved in the night before, it had been cleaned, but it had been a while since that had happened. Julani had intended to scrub it down but was just getting over a virus. He didn't fault her for that. He couldn't fault any of it—the rent was cheap and they'd been willing to offer it to a recent graduate from across the country that no one had met in person. So he was grateful that Julani had come in and apparently scrubbed it at one point, but last night it had needed a good dusting in more than one place.

The lone twin bed in each of the bedrooms looked like they had come from an orphanage for bad children. They were entirely metal, with rail headboards and footboards. They sat only a foot off the ground and had a spring layer directly under the mattress. Again, he couldn't complain. It was "furnished" and they'd warned him it was nothing to write home about. But the bed had creaked during the night each time he rolled over. At three a.m. Keith had mentally added "box springs" to his growing list of things to buy with money he didn't have and hadn't yet earned.

He hadn't thought ahead far enough, though he had mailed his things to his grandparents. He hadn't thought that he would need to go and get them immediately upon arrival in town. It hadn't occurred to him there would be no sheets. But Emma Kate had opened one of her magic boxes. It said "Linens," of course, in that beautiful script and she produced clean sets of twin sheets.

She smiled, "Luckily, most dorms have only twin beds."

"You were in a dorm with china?" he'd asked.

"I was in an apartment style dorm. So yes. I guess if you stay long enough there are some perks."

Tonight, when he walked in, he'd expected... little. She'd said she would make dinner. So he'd hoped there would be leftover food. Something he could re-heat after she'd gotten tired and eaten without him at six or seven.

He stood there with the door held wide, his eyes taking everything in, stunned.

Emma Kate stood in the kitchen section of the tiny house and she looked up at him, blue eyes bright and a smile on her face, "Are you going to let the cold in?"

Finally thinking, he turned around and closed the door behind him wondering if he should lock it. Though it was just a little flimsy knob lock, he did it anyway. He inhaled the warm air in the house and thought it smelled good. But again he smelled himself, too.

She looked at him, her head tilting, "There's some time before dinner's ready, do you want to take a shower?"

There wasn't much he wanted on earth more than to take a shower and she was fixing dinner now. It was almost eight p.m. and she was fixing dinner to be ready for when he got home. He almost wondered if it was a mirage.

But Emma Kate just smiled and said, "You told me you'd be late and I promised I'd make dinner." She said it as though that explained everything he was seeing. If she had an apron, she'd look like a fifties housewife—though that was partly due to the fact that she was standing in front of a fridge that he was pretty sure was still hanging on since the fifties.

He couldn't even figure out what she cooked with. Had she brought pans? But even if she had, there was no food. Last night she'd put a large glass of water in the fridge so it would get cold. She'd poured it from the tap after running the water for long enough to get the yellow out. Two partially opened bags of chips had sat on the counter. They'd had cute little clips on them—because Emma Kate had brought them along for the car trip.

But there was food in the oven. He could smell it. Blinking, he took all ten steps it required to get to the fridge. Yanking on the old-style handle, he jerked his head back when he saw the food inside. "You went shopping?"

She nodded.

"With what money?" He was stunned. They'd portioned out enough funds to feed them—barely—until he got his first check. But it was not enough to stock the fridge. "Did you spend all the money?"

She must have. He must not have been clear about the time-frame before he would get his first check. About what had to be set aside for gas if she was going to drive her car to a job. They'd laid it all out, had she misunderstood?

Emma Kate just shook her head. "I was paying the motels,

remember? Well, we managed to stay cheaper than what we budgeted for, so I added it to the grocery money. Then I couponed the hell out of it."

He must have been looking at her like she'd grown another head, because she was talking again. "I made a huge tray of lasagna, because the beef was on a last-day sale. I had to cook it today. That tilapia? We'll be eating that tomorrow night, or it will re-animate and kill us in our sleep."

He was laughing, but he heard his stomach grumble. Standing next to the stove, the scent of newly baked lasagna was invading his senses and making his insides twist. "I need a shower."

"Go, then." She waved the tongs at him and he thought he saw a salad sitting on the counter.

He'd thought he wanted a long hot shower and sleep, but now, he knew he was wrong. He wanted Emma Kate and everything she brought with her. Smiling, he leaned over and kissed her.

It was just a short thank-you kind of a kiss. Not deep and soul searching. But damn she tasted good.

The surprise on her face compelled him to head to the shower and not examine what he had done. But all he'd done was kiss his wife, right?

Trying to act normally, he turned away from her, which was when he finally saw the rest of the house.

A belle might never serve a meal that requires a shrimp fork, but she has a full set of them and she knows where they go on a table setting

EM SAT DOWN AT THE TABLE, FAR MORE NERVOUS THAN SHE expected to be.

She hadn't thought about the size of the house as being a problem. After all, they'd been staying in motel rooms, trading out of the bathroom and living in one open room. She'd thought this would be easier, after all, now she had a bedroom with a door that closed. But something about walking into the house, and maybe because they knew it was their house—even in just the twenty-four hours they'd been here—they'd dropped just a little of the polite formality.

Just a moment before, she watched as Keith walked from the bathroom into his bedroom—all two feet—with just a towel around his waist. She told herself she hadn't noticed, that she wasn't really *watching*, and went about setting the table. She lied to herself that the rest of him wasn't as much of a kick to her heart as his smile was, and she went back to setting the table for two.

He came out, fully dressed, and stood in the short hallway with a frown on his face. She wondered, pausing in her work for a moment, if he was going to kick her out. He seemed to think she'd overspent the grocery budget, and probably would have fed himself Taco Bell if left to his own devices. Maybe this wasn't going to work out...

Not one to wait around for things to happen—probably why she'd dropped out of school twice—she looked up at him from where she stood with a fork and knife in her hand. "What's wrong?"

"I'm running out of clothes."

It wasn't the big life conundrum she'd been expecting. In fact, she was pretty sure they could deal with it.

He continued, the frown still stuck over his features. "I have to get to my grandparents and get my things, but I don't have time to go. I'm due at work at seven a.m. tomorrow. And I can't even wash what I have. The time issue again and we don't have a washer and dryer."

"I'll take a load to a laundromat tomorrow."

But he shook his head, "We didn't budget for laundry."

"I did."

"What?" The frown finally disappeared, replaced by confusion.

"I put a buffer budget in," she said. "We couldn't possibly have thought of everything we needed, so I tried to find as much buffer budget as I could. I have room on one of my other cards." She didn't like using the buffer budget. The buffer was there to be exactly that, and once it was gone, they would be shit-out-of-luck. But she didn't believe in suffering when the light was just over the horizon. Em was simply grateful that the buffer problem was a trip to the laundromat, and not a muffler.

"Oh. So that's okay? We have it?"

Em nodded and thought again what a good sport he was

being. If their quickie was the fault of either of them in particular, neither remembered it, so they weren't wasting time being angry about it. So far, the situation had sucked, but the company had not.

Keith finally stepped into the main room and looked around. "Holy crap."

She looked up from the table once again, wondering if that was a good *holy crap* or a *holy crap, what the fuck did you do?* From the look on his face, she couldn't quite tell. He looked at her and frowned, making her decisions from the day feel even worse. But she'd had to make them herself. She couldn't just call or text every five minutes and ask if he was okay with spending the food budget through the end of the week even though she could get enough if she spent it all at once on some bargains. She couldn't ask how he wanted the house done. But—aside from the food— she could undo any of it.

"You know," he said, "when you saw the house and you gasped, I thought you were horrified."

Emma Kate felt her head jerk back. "No. Before I saw it, I expected to be living in some square little cracker jack box of a cheap apartment. This place is *adorable*. It's a real house, even if it's small. And it's well-built and it has *character*," she said, almost hating the words once they'd come out of her mouth. Who would even believe her?

"I didn't see it when we walked in last night, but I can see it now," he said. "This is amazing."

"What's amazing?" she asked. Em had spent her time cleaning the place up certainly, but he had to have expected that. When they'd walked in the night before, it had been obvious the place had been sitting untouched for a while. So, she'd dusted and mopped and made dinner, feeling ever so much like the wife, far more than she'd expected to.

While both her older sisters had intended to get married and become household moms—and Harper Rose had even succeeded —Em had never had that desire for herself. But here she was. All she needed was her hair up in curlers and an apron around her waist, and she would have reached the pinnacle of wifeliness. Well, except for... She let the thought trail off.

Keith smiled then frowned at her again, though this time it didn't make her panic. "Paper napkins? Really?"

She frowned back. "I'm not getting out my cloth napkins for a lasagna that I made with beef the butcher sold me on sale."

He laughed. "I was teasing you, but you just revealed something very important."

What was he talking about?

"You actually own cloth napkins."

"Of course I do."

"How many?" he pushed.

"Only eight."

"*Only* eight?"

"It's because I'm in college," she defended. "If I owned my own home or was married..." She paused. Actually, she *was* married, but she decided to keep plowing ahead. "I would need at least sixteen of each color."

"*Holy shit*," he replied. "Who raised you?"

"My mama, and apparently my older sisters, too. And, as I look around right now, I can see that it rubbed off a damn lot more than I thought I was going to let it."

He laughed then, the wide grin showing off his teeth, his head thrown back, and he looked happier than he had when he walked in. "Well I like it," he said. "The place looks great. I thought we were going to be living in a square box, too."

That smile hit her, and she felt her stomach twist with the memory of that kiss.

❧ 13 ❧

Emma Kate woke up the second day ready for an all-day shift just as crazy as the first had been. Keith may have thought she stayed home all day, but her day had been blazingly nuts.

Sure, she'd done all the *wifely* things. She'd cleaned the whole house, top to bottom. Its small size was the only blessing. Scrubbing had eaten up more of the day than she'd thought. And she'd only made a small dent in the work before she realized that water and the cleaning rag she'd found were not going to cut it. It hadn't made her feel safe enough to eat an apple that had rolled away onto her counter.

Each thing had snowballed into the next. If she needed to go out and get cleaning supplies, then she should do the grocery shopping. After all, she'd had the last of the bag of Doritos and water from the fridge for breakfast. That meant she had to make a list and the size of the list meant she couldn't afford it all without some coupons. So she'd done the cleaning but it had taken about three hours just to get to the point where she *could* clean.

When she'd finally finished with a satisfactory scrub, Em next unpacked all the boxes and of course they were all hers.

Only the backpack had been Keith's. Unpacking had also taken longer than she expected. She'd pulled everything out and set it on the counter—dishes, hand towels and hotpads, spices she couldn't handle throwing away so she'd packed them up and brought them.

On top of all that, she'd applied for three jobs the day before. Well, it took an hour just to get to that point because she had to hook up her computer and she set up Keith's while she was at it. That meant getting wireless passwords and information from the Barkers. Thank God they'd offered it and the utilities as part of the rent.

The first job she'd applied for was as a grocery checker, another was to work the front desk at a beauty salon, and a third was to become a file clerk at a law office. The law office one was the one she wanted, but to be fair, she had no real experience as a file clerk. However, it paid the best and seemed the least depressing. What would people think of Emma Kate Mayfair checking their groceries? She needed a job, but nothing she could find was anything she would count as "good." Apparently, no one cared if you *almost* had an honors degree from UCLA.

Her sisters had nagged her about it. Her mother had pushed. Her father had gently nudged, but they'd all said mostly the same thing: "It doesn't mean anything until you finish." Here she was, so close but she sure hadn't finished. She hated that they were all right. She hated that she needed the kind of jobs that she was applying for. That wasn't even the fault of her silly hit-and-run marriage. That would be the same no matter where she lived. So she sucked it up and did what she had to.

Emma Kate promised herself she would apply for several jobs each day and take the first one she got. She could keep looking for something better but at least she'd be generating income.

Keith's job was salaried. Luckily, it would pay out biweekly. So—as long as everything went okay and nothing messed up with his direct deposit or anything like that—they would have an influx of money in another two weeks. It would just figure that they had just happened to come in on the exact day that the employees had previously been paid. Anything else would've cut that turnaround time shorter, but they had no such luck.

Emma sat on the couch with her laptop and trolled the web for other jobs. It wasn't as though she could go on any social media or anything. What if her sisters saw her? She'd made a video of making the lasagna the other night. It was her special dorm room recipe. She had a handful of followers on her channel and they would be wanting something new soon. But she didn't want to lie to her sisters or Lennon if any of them saw it and called her asking where that strange little kitchen was.

She looked up into the kitchen where the chicken wire grating across the top cabinets showed off her Mikasa dishes stacked neatly in the plate racks. It was probably good they didn't have a house that was any bigger. There would have been too many empty spaces, not enough furniture. For the second day, she sucked up her pride and hit the buttons necessary to apply for three more sub-par jobs and closed up the computer, setting it into a cloth bin she'd put beside the couch for exactly that reason.

Today, she also needed to go by Keith's grandparent's house and pick up the boxes he'd had shipped there. She hoped he'd managed to get in touch with them and let them know the strange blonde woman was coming to get his things. She also needed to go to the laundromat, and not waste a drop of gas. They couldn't afford it.

Both of those things happened within the city limits of Breathless and that was what finally forced her hand.

She wasn't ready, but she had no choice. After a moment's contemplation, she decided that Harper Rose was her better bet. Bailey Ann would give her an earful, tell her all the bad decisions she'd made all along and just why she'd wound up in a tiny house on a farm with no job prospects. The fun part was, Emma Kate wasn't even going to tell them that she'd gone and gotten herself married. So, even without that colossal fuck-up on her plate, this was still going to be relatively unpleasant but she couldn't do anything else until she brought both of her sisters up to date.

Bailey Ann now lived just a little way out of town, with her new husband Finn. They co-owned a small company that flipped houses. But Harper Rose was living in their old house, with her three daughters, smack in the middle of town across the street from the elementary school playground. If anyone saw Emma Kate, they would talk to her and before she could even pick up the phone and dial, her sisters would know she was back, that she'd dropped out of school, and that she hadn't contacted them. She had to be preemptive.

Harper Rose had been thrown a massive curveball lately, and just might be applying for some of the same jobs Em was. She might have a skosh more sympathy for a little sister who'd skipped out on her last semester and come home. Really, coming home had been the wise thing to do. L.A. was far too expensive to live there just because.

So Em sat at the table eating one egg and a piece of toast while she framed her argument. Why pay for a semester when she didn't even have an idea for her thesis? That would be a waste of money. Of course she would go back and finish it! But she needed a topic that fell somewhere between sociology and economics and she had exactly jack squat. It wasn't smart money to stay in such an expensive place or pay tuition for that.

By the time she'd formulated her argument, she'd finished her brunch. Slowly—honestly, procrastinating—she carefully washed each dish by hand, putting them one by one into the drying rack. There was an oven and a stove top and a fridge and for that she was grateful. They lacked a dishwasher and a microwave and even a television set, but she understood.

When there was nothing left to put in her own path, she sat down on the old couch—listening to it give underneath her weight. She cradled her phone in her hands as she stared at it for one more moment, but eventually she gave in. She couldn't leave the house until this was done so she pushed the buttons and dialed.

"Emma Kate!" Harper Rose answered, excitement in her voice. "How's the new semester going?"

And there it was. She couldn't just say *hello*. Nope, Harper Rose had to ask whether or not she was completing the task they had all set out for her.

"Actually, that's why I'm calling," Emma Kate tried to keep some cheer in her voice. "I'm in Breathless," she said and waited as her sister's voice paused on the other end of the line.

She could almost hear her sister sighing. "Why are you in Breathless when you should be finishing your thesis in Los Angeles?"

❦ 14 ❦

By the end of the first week, Keith found he was actually excited to come home at the end of each day. Who would have thought?

Emma Kate made the home warm, both literally and figuratively. She kept the heat running during the day and had dinner waiting when he got in. He found himself calling and letting her know when he expected to be home, just like a real husband with a real wife.

Except for one evening, when she'd gone out to have dinner with her sisters, she'd fed him home cooked food each night. She had a crock pot—of course his Southern Belle wife had her own crock pot—and she made chicken soup with rice and fresh spinach. The one night she wasn't home, she'd prepped him the leftover lasagna. Somehow, it was even better the second time around. She'd put it in a small baking dish for him with a note about how long to heat it. He'd needed that, since he hadn't progressed to non-microwave cooking skills. Still, it hadn't been the same sitting at the table, eating it by himself.

Left to his own devices, he'd explored the tiny house that night and had been shocked by what he discovered. He found a series of multi-colored spray bottles under the sink, but not what he expected. No name brand items, just four identical bottles in four different colors. Each bore a neatly cut piece of masking tape with her swirly handwriting on it in Sharpie—"Disinfectant," "Windows," and so on. Apparently, his wife had made her own cleaning solutions. In the back of the pantry, he discovered bleach, ammonia, lemon juice and vinegar. His pre-vet chem courses told him she knew what she was doing.

She'd also managed to make the crappy chicken wire cabinets look elegant, with her china stacked neatly behind it. Her china, it turned out, included two sets of eight full place settings. One was all white with a design carved around the edges that she called her "everyday" dinnerware. The other was clearly fine china that Emma Kate said she'd gotten for a song at the outlet. It had silver around the edges and swirls painted in royal blue on white. Keith didn't think his own family valued any of their dinnerware this much. She even had teacups, though he'd not seen her drink tea. Her silverware had teaspoons and sugar spoons and possibly shrimp forks. If they were really married, that would mean he now owned shrimp forks. It boggled his mind.

Emma Kate had placed both sets of dinnerware into the cabinets sideways, not stacked flat like he'd always seen. It almost looked like it was in the rack of a dishwasher, and he had not seen anyone do that before, but had to admit it classed up the farmhouse-looking cabinets.

Each day, he would have figured she was done. That she would have finally run out of things to fix or improve—apparently on zero budget, too—yet each day he was surprised. He was almost to the point now where he *expected* to walk in and find something different.

The night she'd spent out with her sisters, she must have either raided her sister's home or she'd been hiding some wild raw materials in those moving boxes. Because, the next evening, there had been fabric covering the chicken wire cabinets from the back. Silver and shiny, it didn't match the blue fridge or the old stove with the chipped cream-colored paint or the white tile countertops and whitewashed cabinets, but it looked as though it belonged there.

The night after that, he'd come home and found that a slip-cover had been put on the couch. The only reason he knew she hadn't bought it was because she'd sworn she wasn't spending money.

For a moment, he'd frozen. Should he ask if she had a money problem? Was that why she was leaving school and playing slots in Las Vegas in the first place? Maybe she was lying to him about what she was spending.

But he calmed himself down and didn't ask. He was a trained observer, and he put that to use. The slip-cover was made out of blankets, but it fit the strange little couch perfectly. Also, there was now a sewing machine sitting next to the basket he'd seen with his and hers laptops in it. There was a multi-port surge protector and both were plugged in. But the perfect fit and the sewing machine told him she'd invested time and talent and not dollars into making the place nicer.

When he looked a little closer, the couch even looked softer and squishier. When he sat on it, it didn't squeak quite as much as the day before. He'd looked up at her, still finishing dinner in the kitchen. "Why doesn't it make as much noise? Why does it feel better?"

"Is that a *bad* thing?" She looked at him over her shoulder and when he shook his head, she went back to chopping something. "Yes, it *is* softer and fluffier. It's nice that you noticed. I found the blankets and some old batting in my sewing stash at the house the other night. You were asleep when I got back but I hauled in a bunch of stuff."

"Where is it?"

"In my room. You don't deserve to sit among fabric scraps and bolts of batting." She'd smiled as she said it, as though she believed he didn't. He was impressed she thought that of him. That despite the ridiculous way they'd wound up married, she was making the best of it. She was certainly making things better for him.

There was a tablecloth over the antique table tonight and he'd found a six pack of beer in the fridge. For a moment, he wondered if there was a coupon for that. "So, tell me, magic wife woman, how do we afford beer? Good beer at that."

"I remembered you said you liked Sam Adams and some California microbrewery you were going to miss. So I found this in the downstairs closet at my house. I think it belonged to my dad, but Harper Rose doesn't want it in the house with the girls. I asked, and everyone agreed I could take it. I hope it's something you like."

She smiled at him, and—*holy shit*—he had himself a real wife. He'd been hoping for the occasional dinner. He hadn't even begun to expect folded laundry. But it had appeared, in neat stacks on his bed, sorted and smelling like a spring day in the dead of a Georgia winter.

She'd met his grandparents, having picked up his boxes the second day. She hadn't unpacked them for him, and he wondered why. And it wasn't until late in the meal that night, that she'd asked, "Do you want me to unpack your boxes for you? I didn't want to get into your things without your permission."

His immediate reaction had been *no, he'd like to do it himself*, but then he realized that was a stupid decision. She could clearly do a far better job than he could, and when would he do it? He tended to leave early and come home late. He'd thought he would do it the next day, his one day off, but maybe he should do something better... like take his wife out.

It was Monday night, and he had worked seven straight days. But this night, he tipped back one of the amazingly good beers from the brand he didn't recognize. "I'm off tomorrow," he told her. "My first day off."

"That's fantastic. I mean, that's planned, right?" Then she answered again, "Never mind, that was stupid. They can't work you twenty-four-seven."

"It'll slow down in a few weeks too," he told her. "I'll have much more regular hours. Right now, I'm the one pushing it. Housley isn't making me work this hard, but I'm trying to go out on every run that I can and meet every client."

"You don't have to do that."

"No, but it's easier to meet the clients this way. They trust me more when he's there to introduce me. And it's easier to watch him do the work and see how he interacts." He was thinking as he talked. What could he do to thank her? Could he afford a movie? Not yet, not the good date kind with popcorn and candy.

But maybe he could. Maybe his grandparents would have an old TV. His brain was still thinking about ways to make Emma Kate smile, when her voice cut right through his thoughts.

"I got a job."

❧ 15 ❧

Em had watched in awe as Keith spent his one day off working again. She'd expected him to sleep until noon and then ask her what was for dinner. But he'd done no such thing.

Though she was used to getting up at six with him, they'd both slept in until almost nine. It felt wild and decadent to be lying in bed, awake, but not getting up. As she stared at the ceiling, she thought about her weekends in the dorm, when she'd wanted to sleep in and she'd managed to stay in bed but hadn't been able to sleep because of someone running up and down the hallway. In the fall, she often heard the marching band practice —though they weren't right outside her window they were close enough and loud enough. She thought of the Tuesdays and Thursdays when she decided she was too tired and the information too useless and sometimes skipped her nine a.m. class and just stayed in bed.

Nothing like that had occurred since she'd headed back to Breathless. She'd expected to mooch off of Harper Rose, letting her sister feed her and mother her as both her older sisters were wont to do. But, instead, she'd gotten herself married, even more financially strapped than she'd been, and was now running her own tiny household.

Emma Kate Mayfair was up with the dawn most mornings, and she found she was pretty happy with it. So having Tuesday off felt odd. Knowing Keith would be home, she'd set oatmeal into the crock pot the night before in case she wasn't awake when he got up. She'd added raisins and brown sugar and set out a little bowl of blueberries beside the waiting pot with a note. She was more fond of strawberries, but her fondness didn't fit her finances. Blueberries had been on sale.

On the one hand, it all rang a little too wifely for her. On the other hand, cooking and cleaning seemed the very least she could do for a man supporting her. So she spent her morning lying in bed contemplating her feminist principles.

If anyone would have asked her just two weeks ago, she would have laughed and told them she'd not be willing to let a man pay her bills while she cleaned his house. And yet, here she was. But if she was being honest—and she was trying hard to be, at least with herself—she had to admit that she'd been more than willing to let her sister pay her bills. If her parents had still been alive, not only would she have lived in their house, eaten their food, and maybe not even have gotten a job for a while, she would have thought *nothing* of it. They were her parents, sure, but she realized her willingness to let others support her had to be examined a little more carefully.

She'd put in so much effort around the small house, she'd had to dramatically re-think what she was counting as *work*. Though she'd always liked playing house, and doing home-maker things, it had been a hobby, not a necessity. She guessed she could have left the place as it was, but she couldn't avoid cooking or cleaning. If she didn't cook, they'd eat fast food and blow their budget before the week was out. If she didn't clean... well, the place was so small it would be a pigsty in under ten minutes.

So she'd done those things willingly. Keith was at work sun-up to sun-down, yet he never made her feel as though she wasn't contributing her share. So she'd laid in bed for a little while, but found she got antsy pretty soon. More comfortable with the lack of distance between them now, she'd walked out in her flannel pajamas and found he was already sitting at the table eating the oatmeal, fishing out the raisins.

"I'm sorry." He didn't like raisins. *Uh-oh.* "You've eaten everything else I fixed." But as she said it, she realized maybe he was just being nice.

"No worries. I can pull out raisins. This has been fantastic." He pointed with his spoon, first to the bowl with its little raisin gathering on a tissue, and then to the rest of the house.

"I won't put them in next time," she said, turning toward the counter and scooping up her own bowl. She wanted pecans but they were too expensive, definitely out of the budget. And no more raisins, she thought. She couldn't afford to be cooking food someone wasn't going to eat, at least not for another week, and probably not for a while after that. Despite having his paycheck soon—and her hopefully having one to contribute as well, fingers crossed—they had plenty of debt to pay off from Vegas. She ignored the thought of her student loans not deferring because she wasn't in school. While they'd be better off next week, there was no cake walk coming, probably not for at least six months if not a year.

He'd asked if he could borrow her car, and she saw no good reason to tell him that he couldn't. So, Keith had disappeared for the morning, and she was stuck at home without any transportation. Inspired by his work ethic, she decided to tackle her next project. With the house to herself, it was the perfect time.

Glancing around, Emma Kate turned on all the lights, grabbed her flourescents and laid them on the table. Next, she set up her flexible tripod for her phone and set it to record. She pulled Keith's beer bottles out of the sink and set them out before heading into the bathroom to do her hair and makeup. When everything was ready, she turned on the camera and sat down at the table with a smile.

Em began speaking directly to the small screen. "Hi, everyone!" Okay. There were probably only five people who would watch this, but they were *hers*. "So, my guy only had two beers last night, so this means I can only show you two of these. But we're going to make this into a vase..." she tipped the bottle back and forth to the camera. "And it's going to look great. There are a few tips we need to do it right."

The kitchen was nothing to write home about but it was at least clean now. With her intro filmed, Em paused the camera, moved everything toward the sink and countertop, and showed the camera how she used her spray vinegar to release the labels off the bottle. She explained to the camera how important it was to clean them out thoroughly with hot soapy water.

She proceeded to use a trick with acetone, a string, and a lighter to snap the tops off the bottles. She turned to the camera and said, "I'm going to do the first one wrong, because it's good to see what mistakes can be made and how to avoid them. There's always a possibility with this trick of breaking the bottle. And, if you break the glass wrong, you can cut your finger pretty badly." Em lifted her hand toward the side of the sink to show off her set up.

"I recommend having a first aid kit pretty much on hand and *open*." She lifted the lid to demonstrate. "If you cut your finger with glass, it could be pretty bad, and the last thing you want to do is fumble for supplies, but if you do it right, this should be pretty easy."

Em started talking her way through the steps, explaining why straight acetone was better, and not to use a poly twine. "I didn't make the water cold enough either." So, she watched over the sink as the first one snapped incorrectly, leaving shards in her sink. "Now, let's clean up our process and do one correctly!"

As planned, she cut perfectly, using ice water to snap the bottle just below the neck. "Now, here's the real trick. I know there are other videos of this technique, but here's what I don't see on a lot of those videos." She talked her small audience through sanding the edge and sanding it again, and again. "It takes *at least* five times, or you or someone you love could cut your finger on this." She tapped her finger against the still sharp edge, demonstrating.

When at last she had it right, she demonstrated putting the leftover glass into a paper bag, "so it doesn't rip open your trash." Then she added one of her cloth napkins and a set of wire flowers which she referenced to a previous video into the vase. "Be sure to subscribe to my channel so you can see more tips and tricks on a budget." Emma Kate signed off with a smile.

She'd been doing these little videos for a year now. She'd started by showing off deals she found, then talking her fellow college students through decorating their dorms. A few of her friends had let her re-do theirs. Interestingly enough, the one she liked the least had been the one with the biggest budget. It hadn't forced her to get creative. But then she'd veered more into how-to, painting picture frames, sanding designs out of the wood, making wire flowers, cheap holiday decorations, and more.

Though her audience was crazy small, the house had been a gold mine of video ideas. The dorm had limited what she could do. She admitted there were several times she had changed up her dorm décor just because she wanted to add another video. But now, she was stockpiling pieces. She'd made one about the slip-cover for the couch, and another for making up her spray cleaners, just like her Mama had taught her. Another on setting a table with limited supplies.

Keith didn't know it, but one of the nights he'd come home to a nice dinner, she'd posted it online. At least now that her sisters knew she was in town, she was able to check her accounts, post her videos, and admit where she was. Several friends had reached out to her and were at least staying in touch.

But though she and Lennon had been chatting about everything, Emma Kate hadn't told her the one big thing. And she didn't want to do it in a text. It was time. No, she corrected, it was well past time. She reminded herself of how she would feel if it were Lennon who'd gotten married and didn't tell her. So, she picked up the phone to make yet another hard call.

It was a Tuesday morning. There was every chance Lennon wouldn't answer, but she picked up on the third ring. "Emma Kate!"

Em loved that her best friend sounded so excited to hear from her. But, before she could change her mind, she blurted out, "I have news! I went and got myself married."

"You're married!?!?"

"Yes, but it's not a big deal. Actually, it was an accident..."

❦ 16 ❦

E m turned as the door opened behind her and Keith came into the small house, the cold lighting his face up. She watched as his eyes glanced around the room and she wondered what he was looking for.

"You made a table arrangement while I was out."

She nodded, then had a second thought. "If you don't like it, I'll take it down." She'd had to get creative. There weren't any flowers available in the winter in Georgia, nothing she could just run outside and pick—nothing for free, that was.

"How did you make the flowers?" He asked.

"It's just wire, glue, and nail polish," she said and watched as his face became more and more confused.

He walked over and looked down at the arrangement on the table. Reaching out one finger but not actually touching the petal, he mused, "They look like enamel."

Em thought about it for a moment. "It's a lot like enamel. It's definitely a home job." He was shaking his head and she smiled at him. "Not only did I make the centerpiece, I also made a video."

"What?" She'd managed to truly confuse him.

"I make videos of all my little around-the-house crafts and

projects," she told him. Though it was no secret, she wouldn't want to find out later that it bothered him, having his home on the internet.

"What do you do with them?"

"I have a channel." She watched as he seemed to take the information in and it wasn't clear how he felt about it. "Don't worry, I asked Mrs. Parker before I posted anything with the house in it." *Shit.* She should have asked him, too. It was *his* house. Well, it was theirs, but he was the only one paying rent right now. "I mean, I'm using her internet to upload the videos and some of them would show some of the things in the house so I wanted to be sure I had her permission first, but she thought it was a great idea. She subscribed to my channel," Em said with a smile, hoping he wouldn't object.

"I had no idea you have a channel. What's it about?"

Em grinned, "Living on a budget."

And there went his smile. "Did you start this because of me?"

"No, I've been doing it for well over a year. I mean, I was in a dorm room. I was a college student."

He nodded, seeming to feel better that her budget domestic goddess tendencies had not been caused by him. The pained expression slid from his features and he changed the subject. "I have to go back out to the car, can you hold the door for me?"

Em nodded and moved over to the door, now wondering what it was he'd gone out to pick up. This was why he needed her car. As she stood behind the closed door and waited for his footsteps, she figured out that whatever it was wouldn't fit on his bike. And he hadn't been able to bring it in the first trip, so it must be big. As she pulled open the door and saw him hauling the large box, she realized it was definitely too big for his bike.

"What is that?" she asked.

"Hold on." His voice strained as he carefully maneuvered the wide, flat box through the door. She read the markings on the outside of the cardboard and almost slammed the door on him. "You bought a TV?"

"No," he shook his head as he struggled. The box didn't seem heavy, but it was clearly hard to maneuver.

Pausing for a moment, Em rethought her position and then she asked, "You *stole* a TV?"

Keith laughed at her, setting the TV down on the other side of the room. "No again. My grandparents will tell you they came over from a small house in China. They think they have so much space that they think they are wealthy now. They don't throw out any of the boxes for any of their major appliances in case they ever want to pack them back up or ship them. They also have a slight hording problem."

Em laughed, she'd noticed the same thing when she'd gone by to pick up his things. "So they just *gave* you a TV?" She asked.

"Well, they bought a new one about a year ago and they hadn't thrown this one out. It's not that big—" he said.

"Oh my God, it's a TV," Em replied. Then her heart sank, "... but we don't have cable."

"No we don't. But I do have a streaming account I paid at the beginning of the year and another account that apparently I forgot to turn off the auto-pay. So, we should decide if we want to keep that or not, but for at least the next three weeks, we've got it."

She was opening her mouth, but Keith turned around and headed back out to the car. He came back with another cardboard box, this one more rectangular and the top flaps splayed open because it was too full to close.

He held it out toward her, letting her inspect the contents. There were a handful of DVDs. A DVD player sat wedged into the bottom. On top of that sat an old-fashioned red popcorn maker and a bag of popcorn. A bottle of wine snugged into another corner.

"They gave you all of this?"

"They gave *us* the TV. This box," he told her, "... is on loan."

"They loaned us a bottle of wine?"

"Okay, they gave us the bottle of wine," he conceded with a laugh.

Em was laughing, too. "Good thing. I'd prefer not to return it." Then she paused, "It's not a wedding present is it?" They didn't need wedding presents—she didn't deserve wedding presents—since they weren't really married. Wedding presents would make her feel guilty.

"The wine is, the rest is just my grandparents being nice to me."

Em figured that was the best she could hope for. She wasn't going to drive into town and tell the nice couple that she hadn't really married their grandson. Not when she wasn't sure what he'd told them already.

It took almost an hour to get the tv set up, turned on, and the programs logged into. In the end, the TV was sitting on the floor, propped against the wall. There was no table to put it on.

Em mentally added a coffee table to her list of things she needed, along with a TV stand. Her list was getting longer and longer each time she thought about it. Though Keith was busy unpacking the other box in the kitchen, she stopped and looked around.

How long did she plan to stay here? She didn't know. This was a temporary stop-gap. She might move out if her job was steady and paid enough to get her own place. Did she really intend to nest here?

But when she thought about it, maybe she should. Keith would likely stay. He'd originally intended to lease the unit for a whole year. Now that it was not an apartment, but an adorable house with a porch he might want to sit on in the summer... or bring a date to... he might want it as nice as it could be.

Em decided she would nest. She would leave the little house as homey as she could. And she would ignore the twist in her heart at the thought of him bringing a date here. Or dating anyone else. Or kissing anyone else.

Trying to keep her hands busy, she picked up the popcorn

maker he'd set aside and popped popcorn while he set every-thing up. They ended up on a blanket on the floor, like a popcorn and wine picnic and watched one of the movies first.

"This is from the nineties," Em told him, holding one up.

"I think they may all be. My grandparents are generous but not trendy."

Two movies and a bottle of wine later, Keith leaned over and kissed her.

But it wasn't fair to say that. She'd been leaning into him, too. By fifteen minutes into the first movie, they'd been curled into each other. Like old friends, or more like lovers. His arm had easily slid around her waist and pulled her closer. Her head had drifted onto his shoulder and she'd been unsurprised at how well they fit.

So when he leaned toward her, Em discovered she was leaning toward him, too, and she didn't know who had initiated it. His mouth was warm and soft and searching. It felt like the kiss in her wedding pictures looked.

A building exploded in the background on the TV but it didn't faze either of them. They kept going, kept searching... and finding. Em's heart pounded harder with the lazy, drugging kiss. Her head tipped back as his hands first found her jaw then wound into her hair.

Her own fingers traced the seams on his long-sleeved t-shirt, the thermal weave creating texture over muscles that came from lifting big dogs and pushing cows out of the way. There was something about Keith—smart, steady, focused—that was so different from the wild guys she'd dated in the past. Em would never have thought she would fall for a guy like this, but she was tumbling, hard.

Then she was pulling his shirt off, and feeling his hands on her bare skin, though she had no idea when her own shirt had moved from being on her body to being on the floor beside them. But his mouth was moving over her skin and his hands were waking something long dormant up deep inside her.

Her jeans were next, his long fingers pulling them down her legs. God, it felt more decadent being here on this floor with this man, than it had even when she'd dated the Hollywood agent and he'd taken her to the nicest hotels in town. She reached for Keith, her naked body hot and wanting him, not even sure if this was the first time they'd been together.

Then he was over her, and inside her, and she was arching her back, and calling out his name.

E mma Kate woke up warm, sated, and unable to see. A few
blinks later, she realized the "unable to see" part was
because she was in the dark. It took another moment to realize
the "warm and sated" part was because she was lying on a
blanket on the floor of the living room of the little house with
Keith next to her.

It was pretty instantly clear that they were both naked, and
that her head was still fuzzy. For a moment, she wanted to ask
herself *what had she done?* but the answer was blazingly obvious.
She'd just had sex with her husband... and maybe not for the first
time.

As her eyes adjusted to processing what was actually dim
light, she realized it must be the middle of the night. Keith lay
on his side facing her, one arm tucked up under her head making
a pillow for her. His other arm was draped around her waist, the
heavy weight of it comforting. Their legs were intertwined. Her
own arm was snaked around his back, holding on to his shoulder
and holding on to him.

Even asleep, they were still as entangled as they were in the
daytime. Em was still as confused as she had been about what it

all meant, or what it all should be. Taking a deep breath, she tried to focus her thoughts on the situation at hand. Did she like it? Had it been a mistake? There were no clear answers as her thoughts filtered through the cotton that seemed to have replaced her brain.

However, she was *not* confused about how good it had been. Being with Keith had blown her mind. Made her feel special. Made her believe that he saw her for who she was. Then again, that might have been the bottle of wine they'd split, drinking it out of the stemmed glasses that were part of her collection. She found she didn't want it to be the wine, though.

In spite of lying on the floor, naked, with a man that she wasn't sure if she would have had sex with if she'd been sober, she'd rarely felt as good about herself as she did now. When she thought a little further back, it wasn't even just right this moment, but it was the few weeks since she'd met him.

While Em wished she could have stayed in school and finished her degree, it hadn't been the right thing to do. She would have racked up more student loans, cost her sisters more money out of the pool that they now shared in order to pay her tuition, and she didn't have a thesis. So she would have been in the dorm, spending extra money to be in L.A. and she still wouldn't have graduated. It would have been a semester where she floundered and felt bad about herself because she didn't do what she needed to do.

Here—while she still didn't have a thesis or even an idea—in two days she would start her new job, one that paid much better than bagging groceries or being a law clerk. She'd been able to turn down the position as the receptionist at the hair salon, and that had felt good. Em was proud of herself for getting the new position, even though it wasn't full time and it probably hadn't entirely been her own work that had made it happen.

She was a Mayfair and Harper Rose told her about the position. It was probably the last name, coupled with her sister's recommendation and her parents' reputation that had gotten her in the door. But the woman who was hiring was in the middle of an event that she'd been stuck decorating on her own. Melanie had interviewed her from the top of a ladder while hanging garland. Emma Kate had jumped in. Trading places, she let Melanie climb down and direct from where she could see everything. It was probably her recommendations for how to make a too-short garland look like it was meant-to-be that had won her the job. There had been five applicants, she knew. And Em was proud of coming out on top.

Despite being on the tightest shoestring budget she'd ever known, she liked the little house. She liked Keith—maybe more than "liked." She liked having things ready when he came home at night for dinner.

Each day was an accomplishment in and of itself, a box she could check. She stayed on budget. *Check*. She'd made a video. *Check*. She had dinner ready. She did the laundry, cleaned the kitchen. She picked up his boxes from his grandparents' house. *Check*. *Check*. *Check*. They were all tangible things that she could do.

Em didn't think she'd moved or anything, but next to her she could feel Keith coming awake, too. His voice sounded as cottony as her brain felt. "What time is it?"

"I don't know, but it's clearly still the middle of the night," she answered him in the dark. It was easier to talk in the dark, she thought.

His hand reached up, stroked through her hair and even though it was the middle of the night, a little bit of light came through the curtains that weren't quite blackout curtains. They couldn't afford blackout curtains, but she found she liked this.

The Barkers had a light on the backside of their house for security, and she and Keith had taken to leaving their own porch light on. Whatever glow came around the side of the house was filtering through the window, maybe even moonlight, it still felt just a little magical.

But she could see his eyes dark and focused on her. "How do you feel?"

She could have said *worried*, *confused*, or any of a number of other accurate words, but she settled on, "Good. Very good." It was also true.

"Me, too," he whispered into the space between them and stroked her hair again. She found her own fingers tracing the edge of his shoulder blade as though she could memorize the curve and feel of him.

His muscles rolled, responding to her touch, but it didn't stop her. Em simply touched him more. The line of his neck. The curve of a bicep. The long length of his forearm.

His fingers slid along her waist, making her suck in a breath. As the movement brushed the tips of her breasts against his chest, heat flared through her. For a moment, she'd almost forgotten they were naked. It had been comfortable, natural, normal. Now, it was hot.

She breathed in again, and as she breathed out, she felt him suck in his own breath. Keith lost the delicacy in his touches as his fingers moved to her hip and clenched there, holding her to him. They found each other in the dark again, mouths fusing, tongues searching, need building.

His fingers slipped between her legs and touched her until she cried out his name. Her hands found his erection and she stroked him until he told her he needed her, all of her, right now. Then he was inside her again, the feeling of him in every cell, reaching down to her toes and out to her fingertips. He was hot to the touch and she was on fire.

When at last she came apart, Emma was straddling him, watching his face as he tipped over the edge. His hands gripped her hips, moving them together, his mouth dropping open as he moaned out her name, until she let her head fall back and her body disintegrate into feeling.

As the waves subsided, she sucked in air and draped herself forward over him. His arms immediately came around her, holding her there, letting her know that he'd wanted her closer, skin on skin.

She didn't know how long she stayed that way, or if she even fell asleep again. But in a moment of sudden clarity, she panicked and blurted out, "Did we use a condom?"

❧ 18 ❧

Keith was laying partly on Emma Kate this time, his scrambled brain suddenly clear even though the outside world was just a buzz in his ear. Sex had sobered him up better than time or coffee could have. His orgasm clearing all the fuzz that had built.

Everything had been scrubbed away: All the times he told himself this was just an arrangement. All the times he told himself that it didn't matter how much he wanted her. All the times the voice in his head said she wasn't what he was looking for. None of it mattered. She was here, she was different from anything he'd ever expected, and she was somehow so much more. She surprised him every day. And she'd surprised him this evening too.

He'd had his fair share of girlfriends in the past, but he'd been so focused on school, it was difficult to say if he'd had anything that actually qualified as serious. Some of his relationships that appeared serious from the outside had lasted a long time but, when they had been over, they'd not left him heartbroken. Some had been short and hot, but they burned themselves out too fast for anything to get too tangled, not his life, not his sense of self, and certainly not his heart.

He was almost thirty and he could say with certainty that he'd never really been in love. He'd been more heartbroken by a girl in high school who'd never had the time of day for him than he'd been by any woman he'd actually dated. His feelings then had run deep and dramatic, but even that hadn't been love.

Still, there was something about Emma Kate that was reaching into him and planting little hooks. There was nothing he could do about it either. He was definitely tangled with her. And he felt... something that compelled him to act. It pushed him to ask her to move in with him after having been in the car with her for just a few days. It was probably what had compelled him to ask her to marry him in the first place, or at least to say "yes" if she'd been the one to ask. A Vegas wedding to someone he'd just met was so unlike him, but maybe it wasn't unlike her...

He was wondering what he would do when she decided it was time for her to move out and start her own life. That had been her original plan after all. Despite the hooks in his heart, he was a side trip for her. Though he understood that, he was finding he didn't like it and he was wondering what he could do to change it.

Keith decided to approach it the way he'd approached everything. His singlemindedness had worked in the past—set a course, make a plan, follow it. So he quickly decided on a course that he thought was suitable. He was opening his mouth to ask her, when she suddenly stiffened in his arms.

"What is it?" He was whispering, though no one else was in the house.

"Condom!" She creaked out the word, terror behind it. "Did you use a condom?"

He almost smiled. That one was easy. "Of course."

He had had them in his wallet, several condoms, in fact. Despite the fact that he told himself he was ignoring the voice telling him how much he wanted her, he wanted to be prepared if an opportunity presented itself. Like tonight had.

Or had he invented the opportunity? He couldn't quite say.

The movie, the wine, what was essentially a date—he'd done all that on purpose. But she didn't have to worry—

"Both times?" she asked, her fear not having dissipated yet.

"Of course," he replied again, almost shocked that she would even think to ask. He was just wondering if maybe she was upset about something else when she calmed that notion. Clearly, she'd asked about exactly what had upset her, because his answer made her body instantly relax in his arms.

He held onto her tighter. It bothered him how good it felt to have her there. She burrowed her face against his chest, and his hands crept into those blonde waves, enjoying the feel of her curling into him.

No, Emma Kate Mayfair was not what he'd expected, nor was she what he would have chosen. But it turned out, she was what he really wanted. He tried to start over, now that her worry was assuaged. She sighed heavily, and he opened his mouth again to ask her, only to have her beat him to the punch again.

"Do you think we slept together on our wedding night? Do you think we used a condom then?"

"You don't remember?" he asked, curious. He just assumed that—while she said she didn't remember—she meant she didn't remember the details of the evening. They hadn't really talked about it. But now it sounded like...

Her head snapped up, her eyes wide, catching glints of light in the darkness as she looked at him. "No, do you?"

"No," he answered honestly. "I just hoped you did."

"I don't have any idea. I don't remember any of it. Which is weird. I don't drink like that normally. I only know what we have evidence of—the rings, the paperwork, the pictures..."

Keith laughed. "I'm glad we don't have photographic evidence of the rest of it."

She was laughing, too, but then she quickly turned serious again. "If we didn't use a condom that night, I could be pregnant." The last words tumbled out, the fear having returned to her voice and falling out with the words.

His own hands stilled. It was a possibility he'd not considered before. He should have. He knew how all of it worked, he just simply told himself that he didn't believe they'd had sex, and so probably he didn't need to worry about it. Somehow, he'd let that be enough and he'd managed to not even consider it. "Have you been worried about this all along?"

She shook her head. "I'm being silly, I guess. I didn't even consider that it was a possibility until now. Until we..." she paused and managed to once again jump right back in just as he was getting ready to speak. "I mean, I'm not even due to have my period for another week. But..."

This time, he made it into the conversation. "Well, we're safe for tonight." He was trying to be logical. But that was the thing about this woman, she made him anything but logical. "We used a condom both times. If we had sex on our wedding night, it's been two weeks. So a pregnancy test would work. I can pick one up tomorrow on my way home from work..."

But Emma Kate was already moving.

"Where are you going?" He was still lying on the floor, wanting to hold her, frowning.

"I have to go get a pregnancy test."

"It can't wait until tomorrow? Even just the morning?" he asked, looking around for a clock. He had no idea how close or far the morning was. Where was his phone?

She stared at him, standing above him now, completely naked and unconcerned with her nudity. "Can you make it until seven a.m.," she asked, "not knowing? I won't sleep. I'll make plans for something that I'm hoping isn't even going to happen."

Looking at the clock, he saw that seven was still six hours away. They hadn't been asleep all that long. Strangely, he thought he *could* wait that long, because even more strangely, he found the thought of Emma Kate being pregnant didn't bother him on an emotional level. She might be afraid, but he wasn't. Then again, she was younger than him, not as financially stable—though his "right now" finances sucked big time. And maybe she didn't want kids at all. She'd said enough about how she didn't want to be like her "Mama," at home raising kids and making dinners.

Logically, he knew their budget sucked. They couldn't afford a baby. This house was not big enough for three. He also knew that it wasn't romantic to have a baby, that things would have to change far more dramatically than he'd bargained for. His rose-colored glasses would break and fall off. It didn't give him the sharp, cold fear he'd experienced in the past. But it clearly did for her.

So he took her hand and stood up. "Where can we go at one in the morning in Breathless and get a pregnancy test?"

"Oh God no. Not in Breathless." Her denial was swift and harsh. "We need to head over toward Cumming or Buford, some all-night gas station where I can hope no one knows me."

He didn't like the fear in her voice that someone would know she was buying a pregnancy test. It hit him like a personal rebuke, as though she was ashamed of him. But he reminded himself that she was rightly afraid. He wasn't the one who could be pregnant, that even though it was—or would be—his baby and he would support it and her, she didn't necessarily know that. How was she supposed to trust a man for the next eighteen years when she hadn't known him for that many days?

It hit him then, just how quickly he'd fallen into this. His logical brain told him to back off, even as his voice was telling her that she would be okay. Even if they were pregnant, he would be there. He would make good enough money. They wouldn't be rich, but he'd be able to support a small family before the baby came.

Emma Kate was nodding at him, but she was climbing back into her clothing and straightening her hair. He almost smiled at the thought of walking into a gas station in the middle of the night, in nowhere Georgia, with a woman who screamed "beauty queen" and looked like she'd just been good and fucked. But Emma Kate got herself together far too well for that.

She was fishing the keys out of her purse when he held his hand out and offered to drive. Keith was grateful when she said yes. He was grateful that the car warmed up quickly. Though he wished she'd talked more than just to give him directions, he was grateful an hour later when they got home and she came out of the bathroom and told him to set the timer on his phone.

He was thinking while they waited. Should he ask her now? It didn't seem right. He'd been watching her all evening, wondering if he could tell if she was pregnant. But it finally occurred to him that—if she'd gotten pregnant the night they met—she would have been that way the whole time they'd known each other. He would have nothing "normal" to compare to.

When at last the timer went off, she squeezed her eyes shut and held the little window of the stick toward him. Keith had already memorized the results options. "You're not pregnant," he offered with a smile.

But before she could even fully breathe out her sigh of relief, he asked the question he'd been wanting to ask since he'd first woken up in her arms. "So, what would you think about giving this marriage a real try?"

❧ 19 ❧

Emma Kate froze at the sound of Keith's voice asking her those words. "What would you think about giving this marriage a real try?"

It was three a.m. She'd been thinking she needed to go to bed in an actual bed rather than on a floor. She was wondering just whose bed that ought to be tonight, given everything that had just transpired, but Keith's words stopped her dead.

She was standing in the living room, facing him, the pregnancy test still dangling from her fingers. Em was still processing being grateful that it was negative and wondering if it had even been necessary, but she hadn't known. She hadn't wanted to spend the seven dollars. But her peace of mind was more than worth it, and she wouldn't have slept if she hadn't known. She would have calculated a budget, planned for possibilities, and more. She didn't even have health insurance. She had another month to pick it up through the school, but she'd have to pay for it this term as a student on a break.

Her brain was wandering, probably in shock from what he'd said. She'd only had her relief for half a second though before Keith had popped his little question.

"So," she could hear his voice in her brain, playing on an

endless loop that she didn't quite know how to deal with, "what do you think about actually staying married?"

Em had not considered their marriage real at all, but now found herself standing there while emotions roiled their way through her like a cat-five storm.

What did she think about it? She opened her mouth to answer and then closed it. She opened it again... and closed it, again. There were no words for what she thought about being truly married to Keith Lee.

She thought, "Yes." She thought, "No." She thought, "Holy crap, that's crazy," and she thought nothing had ever felt so right. Then she said the stupidest thing she could ever say. "I thought we were getting it annulled."

That had been the plan, the one they talked about, what they agreed on. But now he looked like she'd slapped him. His head pulled back and the smile disappeared faster than it had showed up. It was only then—as his expression changed so dramatically and she realized she'd hurt him—that she understood he wasn't just offering because he'd slept with her. He wasn't being nice, or chivalrous, or thinking he owed her a commitment because they'd engaged in a biblical act.

Keith Lee didn't want to get their marriage annulled. But her statement seemed to have told him what he needed to hear and she watched as he took a deep breath and pulled himself together.

Emma Kate tried to think of a way to backpedal. Her Mama had trained her in the fine art of "always having the right thing to say." Emma Kate had been the worst at being a belle. Her older sisters had taken to it easily, but she'd fought it all the way. Right now, she prayed in her head that her Mama would hear her in Heaven and tell her what the fuck to say to make this amazing man understand.

But her Mama probably didn't answer prayers that came with the f-word and Keith was speaking before she had the chance to think of anything that might help.

"I actually don't think we can get it annulled." His words were far too calm.

That was not what she'd expected him to say. She'd thought he'd readily agree and walk away. Annulment was the game plan. She blinked and looked up at him, "What?"

His shoulders pulled up in a shrug as though to say it wasn't his fault. "I think we can't get it annulled. We have to get *divorced*."

"Divorced? I don't understand. Or maybe it doesn't matter which we do. I mean, what's the difference aside from it not showing up on my permanent record?" As soon as the words were out, Em wished she hadn't said it. It was yet another thing—another thing caused by her—that made his expression turn south.

He shook his head and sighed. "To get our marriage annulled, we have to be able to state under oath that we were never really married. I'm not sure we can do that anymore. I mean, we just slept together." He absently waved his hand at the floor behind him as though to present evidence. "I'm pretty sure you can't get your marriage annulled if you slept together. Wait, I think maybe you can if one of you committed fraud against the other."

This time, she laughed. "I have not defrauded you. I couldn't have. I don't have anything to defraud you with. I didn't lie and say I was rich or anything. I'm not gay. I'm not already married. I didn't try to sell you anything because I don't have anything to offer you," she said, out of possible options for a fraudulent marriage.

"That's not true," the words were soft, and they weren't really part of the conversation, but they grabbed her in her heart. She'd as good as told him that she thought they shouldn't be married—even though it wasn't really what she'd meant—and he was still being wonderful. Before she could say anything, he moved on. "I haven't defrauded you either, so that means no annulment. We've also been living together," he said it as though there was no avoiding it. "In fact, we've been living together from the moment we woke up in that hotel room."

It hit her. Hard. He was right. Anyone outside of this little house would think they were a legitimately married couple. His grandparents probably believed they were married. In fact, even the Barkers they rented from believed they were married. They'd held up their rings—the rings she noticed she was still wearing. She'd only taken them off when she'd gone to have dinner with her sisters. And then she'd put them back on as soon as she got in the car. Em had told herself she didn't want to lose the valuable rock, that she was wearing their largest investment. But rather than lock them away, she wore them. That was telling...

Only her sisters would be able to say with absolute honesty that they had no idea Emma Kate was married, and they couldn't say that she'd said she *wasn't married* or that they believed she wasn't or even that she was acting like she wasn't.

Crap, she thought. "So we don't really have any option other than to be married?" she asked.

"We don't have to be married. Just because the paperwork exists doesn't mean we have to live like it, and that wasn't why I was asking. What the legalities mean, is that we don't have any option other than to get an actual divorce, I think," he said, "and I don't have the money to hire an attorney to give us advice one way or the other."

Emma Kate almost laughed. He didn't. She sure as hell didn't. For a moment, she thought about it, wondering if she knew any attorneys, but she couldn't think of any off the top of her head. "So is that it?" she asked. "We're just married?"

He turned away, and she wondered why he couldn't look at her. She meant it as a technical question. But that clearly wasn't how he'd taken it. He'd asked her to try being his wife. His real wife. Her heart turned again. She didn't deserve him, and he didn't deserve her hurting him.

The house was small enough that he didn't have to turn back and face her to be heard. "That's not what I meant. Technically, we're married and there's nothing we can do about that right now, but we don't have to live like it. I just thought," he paused, "given tonight," he waved his hands at the blanket, wine bottle, open, empty and on its side, everything they left where it was when they scrambled to get out to get the pregnancy test, "that it might be something we could try. We don't have to."

The downturn in his voice told her he thought she would say no. He thought she already had.

"Give me a while to think about it?" she asked.

From where she stood, she saw his shoulders drop. In life, "maybe" usually meant "no." But he nodded, giving her the time she wanted. Then he said, "I'll clean this up in the morning. Don't worry about it. I'm just going to go to bed."

But those words grabbed her. He was earning all the money. He needed to be up in several hours to go to work. And still he told her to leave the mess, that he would clean up after the date he'd asked for.

Keith Lee casually took care of her. He wasn't macho about it, because he didn't need to be. His masculinity wasn't threatened by a pink shirt or washing the dishes, because it was an innate part of him. He stood firm when he needed to, held his convictions close and didn't let anyone sway them. He was careful with every creature around him—including one Emma Kate Mayfair.

She didn't need time. In fact, it might be that all she needed was Keith Lee. She opened her mouth and took possibly the biggest jump she ever had. At least she was sober. She smiled to herself, but as his hand grasped the knob on his bedroom door, she told him, "Yes."

❧ 20 ❧

*You long-sheet the beds. And the pretty side goes face down. This
way when you fold it back, you see the trim. This means a bed is
'made Southern.'*

TWO DAYS LATER, KEITH FOUND HIMSELF WALKING IN THE
door at the end of another long day of work, but once again with
a smile on his face. He smiled even though it had been an
awkward two days.

Emma Kate had said "yes" to his question. Though he'd tried
to play it casual, at the time it had felt almost as though he'd
gotten down on one knee, held up that ring, and asked her to
marry him the old-fashioned way. Though if he'd done that,
Keith was pretty sure he would have known the answer before
he started.

He'd had no clue what she would say, and it felt like she'd
taken five hours to finally tell him yes. It had likely been under
five minutes, but he'd been counting every heartbeat. It was
almost better that she said she'd needed time, and then she
didn't take it. Her blurted out "yes" had made every part of him
soar. Unfortunately, he didn't know what exactly he'd done to

spark that turnaround. He wished he did so he could remember it, bottle it, and bring it out again later when he needed it.

The awkwardness of the past several days had come in from a variety of directions. Had he gotten down on one knee, they would have likely already made the decision to move in together, which would have included sleeping in the same bed, kissing hello, curling into each other on the couch. Those were all the normal things that happened as a relationship progressed.

Theirs had been anything but normal and they found themselves working out each piece like a kink in a wire or a contract that needed to be negotiated. Like the fact that he'd barely slept the night they'd spent on the floor then run out of town for a pregnancy test. He'd gone to work all the next day. Some people could do that, not sleep at all—he'd done it when he was an undergrad—but lately he didn't quite have it in him. Maybe he'd learned the value of sleep or the necessity of clear thinking. So he'd come home, eaten dinner, and fallen face first into bed and slept until his alarm went off the next morning... completely neglecting the wife he'd just asked for.

Apparently, his face-plant into a near coma had left his new wife trying to decide which bed to get into. Hers? Like they'd done so far. His? Since he'd asked and all. She'd chosen neither. Keith found her on the couch the next morning, saying she'd been contemplating climbing in with him, but the bed was a twin. "Basic physics says we won't both fit. It's worse than the floating door in *Titanic*. So the couch was a good alternative."

She'd smiled as though it was all okay and Keith had felt it like a punch to the gut. *Way to kick off your first night as a real married man*, he berated himself.

But Em hadn't held a grudge. She had made dinner and breakfast, went grocery shopping, and basically gotten them ready for the day when she went to work too. He had walked in the door tonight, expecting the two of them would make dinner together, since she couldn't have gotten home much earlier than he did. But she was pulling a pan out of the oven, matching hot pads in her grip. She'd hung them around the kitchen as though they were decoration. She was like that—he saw utility, she saw possibility.

"How did you make dinner?" He was startled, almost alarmed when he saw that it was lasagna. He knew the effort it took to make. For a moment he was afraid she'd gotten fired—it was the only option he could think of that got her home in time to do that kind of work—but she smiled at him.

"I put it in the freezer when I made lasagna last week."

Then Keith watched as her expression slightly turned. He was learning how to read her and for some reason she was upset. "I'm sorry I've served lasagna so many times."

"Geez, Em," he felt it again—that feeling that he'd failed her. How could she be sorry for this? "I expected to be eating Ramen noodles and cereal—possibly without milk. This is fantastic."

"Sure, but you only expected that because of me. Because we spent all our money in Vegas."

He almost laughed out loud. "Oh, no. I knew I was poor before we did that. But you're right. It wouldn't have been that harsh. I would have bought the milk."

She laughed at him, turning his insides from fear that he'd screwed up to the warm feeling that Emma Kate Mayfair inspired when she looked at him that way. He didn't know what it was. He didn't know how to keep it, but he was damn well going to try.

As he watched, he saw her thought process change. Her eyes widened and he could see she wanted an answer, but she had the tact not to ask. He knew what it was about, though. Today was pay day.

"So," he told her, "my direct deposit information didn't go through." He watched as her face fell. "But," he spoke quickly, "Housley wrote me a check. I would have loved to have told him I didn't need it, that we were fine..."

"—But we're not fine," Em told him, breaking in and finally speaking her mind. "I don't get paid for another week."

"I know. I only *wanted* to say it. I've got the check in my pocket; I'll put it in the bank tomorrow morning. I've got a client to go see anyway," he told her, "Just for the morning."

She smiled and tipped her head. "Figures. I've got an event tomorrow evening. My first one, so I have no idea other than what Melanie told me—that it could run very late."

As he understood it, she was working for a woman who ran a small, two-person company that handled charity fundraising events. Em was now the second person. The job consisted of finding and booking venues, coordinating invitations, decorating and hosting the events, and collecting the funds. Decorating and charming wealthy people into giving their money to charity seemed directly up Emma Kate's alley to him. It was his sincere hope that she loved it. He hadn't mentioned her thesis and neither had she. Though he liked the idea of her finishing the degree, he wasn't ready to send her back to California.

Despite getting the check, there was still bad news about the money. "Since Housley gave me a check and not a direct deposit, we still don't have any money tonight. At least we'll have it tomorrow." He thought for a moment that they didn't share a checking account, and he wondered if that was worth doing. Some couples didn't, but he had money now, and she didn't. He didn't think that was okay. He sighed, "I wanted to take you out tonight."

She shrugged as though it were no big deal. "We have lasagna." She even laughed about it.

He looked around the tiny house. This was not what he'd expected of his life. He'd expected the budgeted living, but by himself. He'd expected he'd eventually find someone to share his life with, but Keith had—for some stupid reason—thought those two things would happen at very different times. In his mind, he'd imagined meeting the right woman at an event or online even. He would take her out on dates, get to know her and, at some point, even realize he loved her.

Though he was well aware that was about the dumbest

expectation he'd ever had, Keith was still struggling. Because, despite the stupidity of it, everything else in his life had worked that way. He'd expected to get shipped off to Breathless to spend the summers with his grandparents. It had happened. He'd worked hard, expected good grades, and expected to get into several good colleges. It had happened exactly that way. He'd chosen veterinary school because a teacher had pointed out his aptitude for science and his love of rescuing animals. Done. He'd applied to several programs and expected to get accepted at most of those. That was exactly what had happened.

Then came Emma Kate. His orderly world was upside down and he was inside out. Keith only credited himself with the ability to see that it was amazing and he should stop questioning it and start fighting to hold onto it. But that was hard with a house barely big enough to not bump shoulders in, and a paycheck that made eating well a budgetary Olympics. Emma Kate was taking the hurdles with speed and grace and he was humbled by her acceptance.

He was going to hold onto her, he told himself. He was going to take her out to dinner. But, as he had to tell her, "It can't be tomorrow, because you're working when I'm not and vice versa. I don't think we'll even see each other."

"What about Sunday? We could go to Bobby's Pizza. I know it's not big, but I love it," she offered, taking yet another hurdle with excellent form.

He headed into his room to set down his work bag and stopped dead.

"Em, what is this?" He shouldn't have said it that way. But the house was small enough that she was beside him before he could take it back.

"It's a bed." She said it over his shoulder as though that was obvious.

"We don't have a king-sized bed." Just as he said the words he realized that was his mistake. If there was anything he'd learned in the past few weeks, it was not to underestimate Emma Kate Mayfair.

She smiled again, "No, we don't. It's the two twins, moved together. The Barkers let me into the shed for some plywood, and I made a headboard."

"You *made* the headboard?" He asked it, dumbfounded as he saw that the bed—why it hadn't occurred to him that it was the beds they already had—did indeed have a padded headboard. It had a beautiful sage green fabric, over thick padding and three matching buttons across the middle. In a spell, he moved toward it.

"Oh, don't look at the back!"

But it was too late. He saw the plywood where the fabric ended. There were probably staples—he was now absolutely certain she owned a staple gun—but she'd put ribbon over the raw edges. Jesus, she'd told him not to look at the back, but even it was done up, Emma Kate style.

"Told you," she stood in the doorway with her arms crossed as she watched him walk around the bigger bed.

The remaining space was almost entirely gone, but he looked up at her and didn't ask about sheets or whether there was a dip in the middle of the bed. Instead he said, "I love it."

And he wondered what he'd get next.

❧ 21 ❧

Emma Kate was off Monday and Tuesday, though Keith was not. She'd been granted two days for a standard "weekend" plus an extra day because of the Saturday night shift Melanie had her work. Though the shift itself was less than a full eight hours, as Melanie had said, it was worth two full days of crazy. Em agreed and was learning that was the way the events often were.

Melanie, whenever possible, liked to take two days off afterwards just to recoup. She'd "suggested" that Emma Kate do the same. Since there was no work in the office that she yet knew how to do without Melanie supervising, Em had taken the suggestion. Since the event fell on a weekend, she already had Sunday and Monday off. It was Tuesday that was now extra.

It felt a little decadent, to have a day off, even though she'd only worked the job for two. Em would have liked the extra day's worth of work, but she certainly wasn't in a position to ask for it. She was paid by the hour. Eventually, after her three-month probation period, Melanie would give her a small raise. There wasn't much in the way of benefits, but the better pay made up for the fact that it was part time. She was at least out-earning what she would make at almost full-time as grocery checker or office "Girl Friday."

Suddenly, her "routine" had changed and it felt strange being home alone again. Just the two days at work had gotten her into a steady rhythm. She'd fallen easily out of one without a job, without school, with only this little house and wherever her gas money could take her.

So, with Keith gone, she tried to be as useful as possible. Monday morning, Em headed out and did her shopping. Though Keith had gotten paid, she still wasn't ready to act like it.

He'd shared some of the money to her account, though she'd found herself in the odd position of almost refusing when he offered. But what would she buy groceries with if he didn't share? Her credit card? She had—most of, anyway—an economics degree. Emma Kate understood predatory lending and even just the ills of credit spending. She'd had enough of it in the past two weeks to last her a lifetime.

But Keith made it as easy as he could. After they'd eaten the lasagna and he'd washed the dishes while she packed up leftovers for lunches again, he'd sat her down at the table. "I don't want this to become an issue, so let's just do this up front from the start. Do we want a joint checking account? Do we keep separate accounts? Who should be responsible for paying the bills? Jesus, Em, how much have you been spending on groceries? I know you said you're staying in our budget, but I don't see how you can."

She'd smiled and told him all her tricks. She'd impressed the hell out of Keith Lee. Then he'd showed her his paycheck, with a sigh. It wasn't a manly, "Woman, I've got this! Preen over my money," issue—which she appreciated. He was making way more than she was, but he was working long hours for it.

He must have seen the gears going in her head, because he laughed and said, "Don't calculate my hourly rate! It's crap right now. This will have to steady out in another month or something will have to change. But I think it's a good time investment."

She'd asked, and he'd told her about Housley. About how some of it was old-fashioned and that was good. But some of the vet work needed to be brought into the modern era and he wasn't sure how to broach that with the clients just yet. She'd told him what she expected of her paycheck. "I mean, it's not full time. Maybe once it settles in, I can get another part time job."

He'd looked at her sideways then.

"What?"

"You can say no. But Housley and I are hiring someone to come in and be a bit of a Jack of all trades. There's some cage cleaning, some runs where I would need an assistant, some office work." He shrugged as though she wouldn't want it.

"I'm not above any of that, but I'd have to work around Melanie's schedule for me." Em figured that would be the end of it, but Keith promised to ask.

They'd worked out the money, and he'd called within minutes of arriving at work the next day to tell her she'd been hired.

"What? He hasn't even met me." She was stunned but didn't want to look a gift horse in the mouth.

"He likes the idea of family. Likes that we'd both be involved. So it's yours if you want it, though parts of it won't be pretty."

She could handle "not pretty." They just needed to watch out.

She'd headed to the store that morning with less dread and more confidence. Though it felt as though the new money was burning a hole in her pocket, she understood the importance of staying on her budget. Still, there was one thing she wanted to do. It was pretty cheap, and they'd decided each of them should have some discretionary money. Hers would cover it, so she was going to do it.

Just as she'd been unpacking the groceries, her phone rang. Bailey Ann wanted to go out to lunch, just the three sisters. They met up at Bobby's Pizza near the house, and Em didn't have the heart to tell them she'd gone to another one on the outskirts of town just the day before.

There was more she didn't tell them. She also pulled her rings off, surreptitiously stashing them in the small dash compartment in her car. She'd been disturbingly grateful no one she knew had seen her and Keith together and asked about the sparkling rock on her finger. Living out of town had its advantages.

She still hadn't told her sisters what she'd done. And why would she? she thought.

First, she hadn't told them because it wasn't a real marriage and she hadn't wanted to get crap about getting stitched into a wedding in Vegas she couldn't get herself out of. She'd not wanted to say she would have to get a divorce, later, when they could afford it. Bailey Ann would have written a check to the Vegas licensing office right on the spot, because one—Bailey Ann still used checks, and two—she simply would have undone Em's mistake. That's what a big sister did, even if the little sister wanted to handle it herself.

Secondly, she wasn't telling them about the marriage now because she didn't even know what she would say. The meal would already consist of her getting grilled about school and her thesis. A marriage out of nowhere? Em wasn't ready to defend every part of her life. So she'd stashed the rings and headed in bare-handed.

As she'd expected, Bailey Ann had hugged her, asked how she was doing, and managed to wait until the fifth sentence to ask if she'd made any progress on her thesis.

"No, it's an odd cross section of disciplines that I'll get my degree in and I want to be sure I pass on the first try." Em had hoped that would fend them off.

It hadn't. When Harper Rose had pressed her about topics, Em had cracked a bit. "What exactly should I do? I need something that straddles sociology and economics. It's the only way that my chair let me get away with taking the mix of classes that I did. But I don't have an idea that will hold water. Not yet."

Being helpful, or trying any way, Harper Rose and Bailey Ann had thrown ideas at her randomly during the meal but Em had shot them all down. Either the idea was way off base and her sisters didn't even know it, or they hit, but Em hated it.

She tried again to fend them off and close the subject. "This needs to be my thesis and I'll think of it when I think of it."

She watched as Bailey Ann's mouth set, and she could hear her sister thinking, *But you need to finish this degree. There's so much money and time sunk into it, and it doesn't mean anything if it's not finished.* She was just grateful that her sister, for once, didn't say it out loud.

She knew the issue was that Bailey Ann was afraid Em would *never* finish it, that she would get so close and quit. Unfortunately, while Em wanted to yell at them that they were all wrong, that they were being judgmental pains in her ass, she couldn't say anything of the sort. She understood Bailey Ann's irritation. And she also understood that now, with their parents both gone, Bailey Ann somehow managed to feel even more protective of her baby sister than she had before—maybe just more *responsible*. But Em didn't like it and didn't want any part of it.

It was hard telling someone she loved to butt out, but she needed to do it. Unfortunately, she didn't find the words or the strength that day over pizza. She evaded and ducked and eventually distracted them, by sharing a little tidbit that she knew. "Bobby's Pizza is getting sold!"

"What? The whole chain?" Harper Rose had been stunned and Em's plan worked. "They can't change the pizza."

Emma Kate couldn't say. She knew what her friend Lennon had gone through. She knew why Gabe was selling the successful brand—for Lennon. It was almost like a wedding present. Those two would be getting married soon, she could feel it. Her heart twisted with the hope that they would be coming back to Breathless before she left again to finish that pesky degree in California.

She and Lennon had not been in the same place together for a long time, and she felt it in her chest each time she wanted to turn to her friend and had to rely on technology to get them connected.

Lennon was the only one she'd told about Keith. Lennon was

the only one who wouldn't lecture her. Em sat through all of lunch with her sisters, eating pizza, deflecting blows about her leaving school, and practically bursting at the seams. It was hard to not tell them about Keith at all. She hadn't even had a chance to call Lennon and tell her what Keith had asked—and that she'd said yes.

When the conversation turned away from her, the lunch was wonderful. The rest of it kept her on eggshells. But she hugged her sisters goodbye, and she meant it when she told them she loved them. Then she climbed in the car and she headed to the hardware store, only realizing as she slid her rings back onto her finger just what she'd done.

She'd put Keith aside for a while. And she'd made it harder to tell her sisters about him later. How long could she hold out like this? When would be the right time to tell them she'd screwed up yet again, but this time—this time—it was working out wonderfully. Still, a dark feeling of foreboding started worming its way through her chest.

❧ 22 ❧

Emma Kate was standing in the middle of the main room in the middle of the tiny house when the doorknob turned, and Keith walked in.

She had been standing there for almost two full minutes— from the moment she heard his bike turn up the gravel driveway until the doorknob rattled. Standing with her hands clasped in front of her, Emma Kate tried to stop her nerves from jangling. She would have to go back to work with Melanie tomorrow morning. And Keith said she was expected at the vet clinic in the afternoon to meet everyone. There was no way to fix this. It was done.

So she put on her best smile and waited.

She'd bought king sized sheets for the bed, though she'd promised him she was capable of stitching the twin sheets together to make a sheet set that fit. But in their budget discussion, Keith had voted to buy them. She didn't know if it was because he was afraid she couldn't make it work, or if he was afraid there would be a noticeable seam down the middle of the bed.

But why would he be afraid of that? He was always telling her that what she'd done around here was miraculous. Em had bought the sheets and crossed her fingers that he wanted them for what she was calling the "right reasons." In her mind, that meant they had a little money and just wanted real sheets. The "wrong reason" would be that he wanted the option of pulling the beds apart and putting hers back in her room if he changed his mind.

Keith had commented on how she'd filled in the gap between the mattresses. "I can't even feel that there are two separate mattresses in here." He'd run his hand over it and even laid sideways across it.

Em had explained how she had used more of the roll of batting she had. Running a small roll down the length of the gap and then putting two more layers over it. Without a real king-sized mattress pad, she'd improvised with a large, old blanket she had, tucking the edges in tight enough to keep the bed from slipping apart. Of course, she'd filmed all of this—one piece on putting the beds together, and another on making the headboard.

Keith had also questioned how she'd moved the beds on her own. Em had merely flexed her muscles and smiled. The fact was, she hadn't done any heavy lifting. Once she took the pieces apart, the mattress just slid along the floor between the doors, and the bed frame was light-weight metal. It had taken a little geometry to get the piece through the door without bashing anything, but that was all.

The whole while she'd been working, she'd had her phone on its little tripod stand and she filmed all her tips and tricks. She'd filmed as she'd worked today, too. Saying hello to her new followers and her regulars. Showing what worked and what didn't. She had about five videos banked, which was great, because—starting tomorrow—she would be working two paying jobs.

Once she'd put the beds together, her room had been left empty. She'd filled it with a folding table from her sister's—not a video-worthy move—and pulled their laptops out of the living room. She set them up with an office in there, the way a real married couple would use two rooms. Well, a real married couple with a single folding table for both their desks. She tucked a cheap file drawer under the front corner and stitched up the edges of a piece of upholstery cloth to cover it. Her sisters' had made fun of her for loving fabric, and buying it when she hadn't known what she would do with it. Em was grateful now for her odd hoarding habit.

It wasn't beautiful, but it wasn't ugly either and at least there was now a place they could go while the other one could watch TV. Keith could file reports or check out papers online without being interrupted. She found that she liked this, as there was a possibility that she might be working from home some days. Melanie had informed her this would be an option as they went along.

The actual office where she would be working most days was Melanie's converted garage. Em had already witnessed her boss explaining to a potential client that the garage was a point in their favor. "My company's job—as the charitable host organization—is to not take any more money than absolutely necessary to create your charity event." Em had watched Melanie close that deal, mostly on her reputation. "Emma Kate and I will put as much of the donations as possible into the coffers. We do that, in part, by working out of a garage."

Em had stood and smiled, offering moral support and making a mental list of life goals. The garage was a testament to Melanie's skills. Once you were inside, you had no idea you were in a converted space. Em was hoping for that same kind of reception from Keith now, but what she got wasn't what she expected.

Keith came in the door with a grin on his face and ignored everything she'd done.

There was salmon, plated and steaming, on the table. She'd asked the fish monger if there was anything that he needed to sell quickly. Salmon had been the winner. She splurged on asparagus wrapped in bacon. At one dollar a piece, she'd bought three as a luxury. They could not have afforded it before Keith got paid, but now... now, she'd also bought minced garlic. The real kind, not the powder she'd brought from California, though the mashed potatoes were still from a box.

Keith saw none of that, nor any of the other—big—things she'd done. Instead, he walked in the door, returned her smile, and headed straight toward her. Dropping his bag to the floor with a thunk, he wrapped his arms around her.

Leaning in, he murmured against her mouth, "I missed you today." Then he proceeded to kiss her with the kind of welcome heat that let her know his words were true. Em found she could only smile up at him, her eyes wide, and she hoped he understood that he'd simply taken her breath away. He did sometimes have a tendency to misread her.

She just couldn't quite make words. She wasn't sure what she had done to deserve this guy, though she was pretty sure what she had done was get drunk and be an idiot.

He kissed her again, and only on stepping back did he take an inhale, and ask, "What smells so good?"

She pointed into the dining room, and that was when it happened. He saw it. All her work, all around them. She sucked in a breath as he let his out.

"Holy shit, Emma Kate. What did you do?"

23

Keith turned the corner into the back hallway of the veterinary clinic, winding his way between cabinets, scales, locked supply pantries, and more.

Housley smiled at him as he passed. "Did you just vaccinate that litter of puppies?"

Keith nodded with a grin. Definitely one of the plusses on this job. It had been a wriggling, squirming, adorable task. He and the assistant had to lift each one, check the puppy, hold and vaccinate it, and then place it into a separate bin it couldn't climb out of. It was necessary so they didn't mistakenly vaccinate any of the pups twice or, God forbid, miss one. Ten was a large litter.

"The mom seems to be doing okay," he told Housley, knowing that the family that had brought the dogs in were long-time patients of the clinic. The older couple had rescued the mother from a creek bed she was hiding in. She'd been underfed and once they started feeding her, they realized she was pregnant. They were now housing the puppies until they were old enough to find forever homes.

Keith suspected he'd see at least several of them with their new families for a spay or neuter within the year.

"Good thing your wife isn't working in the front today," Housley told him offhandedly, but it made Keith pause. *Uh-oh*. Em had been working here for a week now, but her sum total time had constituted only about three half-days. Housley had been very accommodating of working around Em's schedule with Melanie, saying it was more important to him that jobs stay in the family than that he actually get the help he needed, or so Keith thought of it. Someone with a more open schedule would serve the office better, he thought.

It was a shitty thing to think, and he knew it. Eighty-percent of the time, he loved having her here. But the other twenty percent, she made him nervous. She was Emma Kate, she got into everything—just look at what she'd done with the little house. But the office here didn't need paint and good china, it needed the cages cleaned out so that an animal didn't smell the past resident. It needed the files organized in a standard medical system. Housley needed his crap organized, period, which was a lot of what he'd hired Emma Kate for. But the whole thing made Keith nervous. Which made him feel like a shitty husband.

Turning, he opened his mouth to ask why it would be a problem for Emma Kate to be working out in the front today, but Housley grinned and beat him to it. "You'd be taking two puppies home with you if she were here."

As his heart stopped stuttering, Keith laughed. That was plausibly true. And he needed to stop worrying about problems that hadn't happened. Housley seemed to genuinely adore Emma Kate. "You know," he told Housley, "you can tell her, or I can if you need me to, that she needs to put the kittens in a different crate while she cleans out the one she's working on."

Em had a habit of cleaning with one hand and holding the resident animal with the other. Keith was afraid it slowed her down too much, but Housley only laughed.

"I don't know. The kittens sure like it. She's a little slower than my other staff, sure, but she caught that one of the kittens had an eye infection. Real early stages. Brought the kitten to me and saved a lot of money in treatment, and time." Housley spoke with affection in his voice and that calmed Keith's nerves a lot. He liked the old man. He liked the practice. He liked Breathless, and if his wife would venture into town with him more, that would be great. So he felt better that Housley understood that Emma Kate seemed to do things her own way, and he was grateful the old man appreciated it.

He was still waxing poetic about Keith's wife. "Emma Kate just thought the kitten was squinting too much and she caught it because she'd been playing with her the whole time she was cleaning out the crate with the other hand. I have a hard time being upset with that kind of attention."

Good, Keith thought, and decided to take a lesson from the old man. Though he saw a thousand ways he would improve the efficiency of the office and bring it into the new century, he realized he should maybe take a step back. It wasn't his clinic yet, and it made more than enough money to pay everyone. So if Emma Kate was a little slower than others, maybe attention over efficiency wasn't such a bad thing.

Veterinary work was like that, he'd found out. You loved the animals, but you also had to get the job done. Still, maybe he could relax a little bit.

"To be fair," Housley said. "It wouldn't necessarily be that Emma Kate picked out some of those puppies. It would be that some of the puppies wouldn't let go of *her*. Then again, I should have known you wouldn't marry someone who the animals didn't like."

Keith had laughed again, but he felt his chest twist a little at the thought. He wouldn't have married someone who didn't like animals, and he wouldn't have married someone that the animals didn't adore right back. Dogs in particular always seemed to be a good indicator of the kind of person that one truly was. Housley's assumptions were all absolutely valid, things Keith *would* have done if he'd *chosen* Emma Kate—and surely he had, but not in any conscious way.

"Well, I'm glad she's working out," he said, as he headed back toward the offices. Only as he turned the corner did he see that she was standing in the middle of Housley's office, and her eyebrow was quirked as she turned to look at him. It appeared she'd listened to the whole conversation.

He didn't know what she'd been doing, but she had stacks of files all over the place, though that might have been Housley's doing originally. Keith couldn't be sure.

She crossed her arms and looked at him with a blank expression and told him, "I'm glad I'm working out."

"I'm sorry," he said feeling like crap as he stepped into the room and closed the door behind him, even though it wasn't his office.

"Clearly," she deadpanned, indicating that she *clearly* did not accept his crap apology. She even stepped back as he approached.

Shit. He did not like this. Every time something came up between them, he saw it as a wedge. He would then scramble to yank it back out of their relationship before anything could come along and hammer it in further. "I just don't want to wind up in the middle of anything, and I don't... " he sighed. He was still doing it all wrong. "And I wasn't sure cleaning cages was a job you would want."

"I'm not above breaking a nail here and there." She still had her arms crossed, was still staring at him.

"Well, I've never worked with anyone I... " He broke it off. What was he going to say? "With anyone I was *with*? *Married to*?" That was a given, as he'd never been married before. Taking a deep breath, he tried again. "I want you here. But I'm afraid if things don't work out with you and Housley, it will kill me. I'm walking on eggshells here."

"Well, don't do it on my part. I can handle getting fired. I can find another job. In fact, I'll make up some lovely excuse and quit now if you want." She was still angry.

Shit. "No. That's not what I want at all. I just want to know that it's all going to work out. That you working here won't interfere with us being *us*. I actually really liked having you out on house calls with me the other day." She'd been nervous, though whether it was new job jitters or from being around the animals, he couldn't tell. She'd handled herself like a champ, though. "You don't know as much as the trained assistants do, but you have a better feel for it than most. You're good at it. But I'll admit that it felt good to hear Housley say how much he likes you."

At last, he could see the ice melt around her. Thank God. He did not want to screw this up. Despite Housley's mis-estimation of Keith's having chosen Emma Kate, he had her.

Stepping into the space she finally allowed, he reached out to hold her, then slowly kissed her. His heart might have melted a bit when she kissed him back.

After far too little time, he had to pull himself away. "Okay, I guess I'm going to be the problem, making out in my boss's office." He grinned at her. "Doesn't mean I don't want to, though."

She smiled back, but then it dropped off her face. He was reaching for the doorknob when she motioned him not to open the door just yet. "You need to look at these files. These ones on his desk? Some of them he hasn't seen in about four months. So these aren't his current files that he's documenting."

She pointed to the inbox Housley kept to review all the day's patients. He would send them back out front to get refiled once he'd done his documentation and checked them or gotten the lab results back in. Keith frowned.

Emma Kate held open one of the folders and said, "Look, he's really undercharging these people."

She was right, the numbers didn't add up. Keith had been thinking the clinic was charging prices at least five years too old, if not ten. They could stand to raise the costs a little to come in line with other veterinary businesses in the area. But this? Keith wanted to raise prices, and Housley was undercutting even what he had.

But then Emma Kate threw another curveball. "I think he's doing it for families that can't afford it. But you definitely need to check and be sure. If you're going to be a partner, this is your money, too."

He noticed she didn't say "our money."

"And if you're going to run this business by yourself in a few years, you need to know about these things." Keith nodded at her and noted the names on the folders she'd pulled aside, but then he headed out into the hallway.

Having Emma Kate in the office was definitely playing with him. Just not in the ways he'd expected.

✦ 24 ✦

Keith rolled over, his arm reaching out for his wife on the other side of the bed. He woke up as his hand encountered only empty space.

Emma Kate wasn't there.

Slowly his eyes opened as his brain became aware of his real surroundings, not the ones he'd dreamed up—the ones where Emma Kate was drowsy in bed beside him. Nope. It was Saturday and he remembered she'd gone in to work for Melanie for the bulk of the day.

Housley was holding down the vet office with one assistant and, honestly, he probably could've used either Keith or Emma Kate's help. But as big as he was on having family in the office, he was just as big on having family out of the office as well. He believed in days off, and he believed in making sure the young couple got as many of theirs together as possible.

Keith believed Housley meant it in the best way. Well, he believed that for about ninety-seven percent of the story. The other three percent of it was that Keith suspected Housley was seeing one of the clients he was undercharging. What Keith was trying desperately to hold onto—as Emma Kate had reminded him to do—was wait until he knew why. So he sucked in a deep breath and rolled over, but the bed was still empty.

Em had found two more families that Housley was charging dramatically different rates to. The good news was that the older vet had *asked* her to go through his files and sort them. He'd had too many piles around his desk, and it was easier to pay Emma Kate to clean them up. It was possible Housley hadn't been paying attention to what he left out, but Emma Kate was.

Because the old man hadn't labeled all of his files correctly, she'd taken to opening them, finding what was in them, and then putting them in their new, proper place. She'd not missed what the going rates were for procedures and visits, though Keith could easily guess that many other assistants might have.

Though he needed an answer, Keith hadn't wanted the information passing through their tiny little grapevine to wind up with him confronting Housley. He'd practically begged Emma Kate to bring it up right to Housley. Luckily, his wife had no problem ferreting out information, and she'd promised to ask the question. But she also told him she was going to use her Southern Belle charm and work it into the conversation when it was appropriate. So it hadn't happened yet, at least not that Keith was aware of.

The angle of the sun coming through the slit in the windows would have let Emma Kate get up and get ready. The tiny space wouldn't have allowed her much room, but she'd still managed to do it without waking him. She and Melanie were hosting a charity brunch this morning and he had probably until three or four in the afternoon before she returned, or maybe even later.

He'd been thinking last night. Every time he was gone and she was home, she did something special for him. It was a high bar she'd set, but he was determined to do his best to clear it.

One day, she'd put all the boxes away and organized the whole house. Another, she'd created a king size bed out of two twins, and even built the new bed a headboard. Apparently as Emma Kate was wont to do, she'd simply painted the living area on a day while he'd been out. He'd come home that night and it had taken him a while to catch on. She'd been frowning at him until he turned around and finally looked. But the beautiful robin's egg blue managed to set off the white counter, the cream stove and the blue fridge and made them look as though they all belonged together.

He'd been afraid she'd spent all her money on the paint and supplies. But, as usual, she assured him she hadn't.

Still in just his drawstring pants, he rolled out of the bed on her side, the side nearer the door, and headed into the hallway. He opened the office door and looked inside. This, he was going to do for her.

She'd worked from home three mornings over the past several weeks, making calls, recording files, and sending and answering emails for Melanie. Emma Kate had done it all from the small, cheap, square folding table made smaller by his laptop taking up part of the precious space. She'd not complained once.

He knew what he needed to do. He was going to paint the room and God help him, he hoped he chose a color that she liked.

First, he went to make coffee, only to find it was already made and waiting in the pot for him. It just solidified in his head what he needed to do today. He'd read somewhere that love didn't erase the bad times, and it didn't create the good times, but it made all the times better. Emma Kate was like that, everything she touched she just made it a little better.

It was his turn to repay the favor. They needed desks. Looking at the almost bare and definitely ugly room, he realized he needed to get moving if he had any hope of being finished by the time she came home.

Ten minutes later he was dressed and out the door. Unfortunately, while he could handle paint on his bike, he couldn't also handle desks. He quickly headed to his grandparents' house in hopes of trading the bike for his grandfather's truck. Being the kind of easy-going people they were, they handed over the keys, but it had tacked another half an hour onto his trip.

He'd first headed to a store where he could get cheap, but sturdy desks. It had taken a while to figure out the best bargain for his money and the best bargain meant he would have to assemble them both when he got home. Checking his watch, Keith calculated whether he could still make it happen and decided he could.

Leaving the two desks in the flat bed of his grandfather's truck, he headed next to the hardware store but as he was pulling the big truck into a tight spot, he realized he didn't even know what supplies or tools he needed. If he asked somebody in the store, they would likely try to sell him one of everything.

So, still sitting in the cab of the truck, he pulled out his phone and searched "Painting a room on a budget." The answer shouldn't have surprised him, but it did. The fifth link down was a video with his own wife's smiling face shining out.

Beyond curious now, he clicked the button and watched as Emma Kate came on and wished him, "Hello to my crew! If you're new here, I'll try to show you all the tricks I've learned to make things easier, or at least better."

She showed him how to pick a color, how to buy good colors on the cheap. "If you go into a hardware store at the paint section, there's usually a shelf like this. Sometimes it's out of the way and you have to ask. But it's where they keep the colors they mixed that someone didn't pick up, or maybe returned." She picked one up. "They put a dot on the lid so you can see exactly what you're getting, and it's a great way to maybe pick up some great color on the cheap!"

Picking up each can, one by one, she inspected the color dot on the lid, made a decision and then set it back down. Then a quick edit later and she had a gallon in her hand, the camera down close to the dot. "Found it!" He saw the beautiful robin's egg color of his room. Her video was of her painting their house.

Desperately wanting to watch it all the way through, he

forced himself to turn off the video because he simply didn't have the time. With the short list of tools Em had showed off in the video firmly in mind, he headed in and looked at the same shelf she'd showed off earlier.

She'd done it. She'd saved him a ton of money, because surely she had all the tools she'd showed him, somewhere in their tiny home. He only needed a new roller, more tape, and the paint itself. He was just starting to make a decision about color when he heard Emma Kate's voice and his head snapped around.

But she wasn't there. He was just beginning to think he'd hallucinated the sound when he heard it again.

"Finn, what about this one?"

He caught the voice then. It wasn't Emma Kate, but a pretty brunette woman, standing shoulder to shoulder with a man who must have been her husband. She'd called him "Finn." Wasn't that Emma Kate's brother in law's name?

Probably because he was staring, the woman look up and offered a half smile for his weird behavior.

It was the eyes. The smile, the almost dimples in her cheeks. The coloring was all different, but this was clearly Emma Kate's sister. He smiled again, wondering if he should introduce himself, and how that should go.

But the woman only looked away, giving no recognition of him at all.

❦ 25 ❦

It was slightly after five in the evening when Em opened the door to the small house. She'd been exhausted on the drive home and envisioned herself coming in and sinking into the sofa —a much nicer act now that she'd recovered it. Instead, she cautiously opened the door, a frown across her brows.

There was a truck sitting in her driveway. She thought it might belong to Keith's grandparents. His bike was missing, and it didn't make sense that anyone else would be here. Still, she didn't want to be the dumb blonde, so she held back, a little wary.

Figuring vocal contact and staying near the door was her best option—just in case something was fishy—she called out, "Hi, Honey. I'm home!" and wondered what she might get back.

Who would even invade their little house? And what would they do? Steal the folding desk? or the smushed together beds with the padded, stapled headboard she'd made with plywood?

The TV and computers were the only thing of real value, well, that and her Mikasa. Not that she'd paid the proper value for it, but...

From the back room, she heard a noise and a voice that was distinctly Keith's. It made her smile, even as it called out, "Shit!"

Laughing—no longer concerned and now very curious—she headed down the hall to where the office door was closed, where the voice had come from.

"Well, I hope you had a very fine day, too," she singsonged as she gingerly pushed the door open. Only as she looked into the mess that had once been an office did what she smelled coming down the hall actually click in her brain. It was paint. Keith had splotches of it all over him. Though if what he'd been doing could be called "painting" was anyone's guess.

A hand-print covered his heart, where he must've touched the once-white fabric, not realizing he'd previously stuck the same hand on the wall somewhere or, perhaps, into the paint can. She could almost see the gesture and the expression on his face as he would have done it. Another handprint would have been perfect on his hip if he hadn't done it multiple times. Again, she could almost see him staring down the walls, as though to tell them they had to do what he said, rather than wondering what he might have done wrong.

As she watched, he turned to her, frustrated rather than smiling. It was then that she noticed he also had paint in his hair. She wanted to laugh, but he seemed frustrated, so she pressed her lips together to hold it in and forced a deep breath. Trying to keep him from seeing, she turned away and looked around the room, to see what exactly he'd been doing. The room was too small to hide anything, but she'd been looking at her hot, frustrated husband rather than the things around her.

He sighed and held his hands up, one of them still holding a flat paint sponge. "I hope you like the color."

"I do." It was a peachy orange—bright, sunny and warm. He had three of the four walls painted, and the last was the wall that backed the kitchen, so it was a blank slate, with no windows or woodwork to have to work around. He'd already gotten most of the edges. She pointed, "You did good work, but you need to finish before you lose your wet edge."

She circled the space then, around the middle of the room

where two desks stood back to back. An office chair sat, gently tucked under each, as though someone might sit down and work here in the middle of the room. A hutch was constructed across the top of each desk, providing open shelves and small cubbies.

"Holy crap, Keith! Where did you get all this?"

"We have *some* discretionary money," he said. "And I had a little more room on my credit card. The desks and the paint came out of what I was allotted. The office chairs... not so much." She watched as his lip curled like he'd eaten something distasteful. His words said otherwise. "I really wanted the office chairs."

She laughed at him. "Did you put these together yourself?"

They looked freshly assembled given the papers with pictures and arrows and numbered steps still lying on the floor and the three leftover screws. She chose not to ask. Tiny Allen wrenches sat at various points in between the paint cans he'd opened.

"I really do love the color," she said. "It's warm and sunny, and it goes well with the color of the desks. I'm afraid you may have overspent, though."

"Oh. No, no," he shook his head and waved one spattered finger at her. "I did not. I wanted to know how to do this, so I went online and searched. And guess what video came up?"

"What?" she asked thinking that she must know where this was going, but she wanted him to say it.

"Who taught me how to paint this room *and* get a bargain on the paint, but my lovely bride." He smiled at last, wide and genuine.

She laughed at him. "You watched my video?"

"I've got to say, even for all your realistic tips, you made it seem easier than it is. Though, this is much better than it would have been without you. You might start including how long it actually takes to do these things. I thought I'd paint it and put the desks into place and have it all ready when you came home." He looked sad about missing his self-imposed deadline.

"Well, you have to let the paint dry first," she said, though he had a good point about stating how long the projects took. She was trying to make things easy for her followers and that was a good thing to know.

"But when you painted the main room, you had everything back in place before I came home. You'd even made dinner! And that room was much bigger than this one." He was gesturing with the painting sponge and she was glad he'd followed her instructions to get the plastic drop cloth. That three dollars was always well-spent.

"Well, yes, but I didn't have to move anything away from the walls. So I didn't have to move anything back. Or wait for the paint to dry. It was probably still a little tacky when you got home. I was just counting on you not actually touching the walls," she told him.

This time he laughed. "I know that now. I didn't watch the whole video at first... I was too pressed for time—" Keith held up that red spattered hand again, "I know, that's a mistake. But when I took a break, I watched the rest of it and found out."

That meant he'd watched the part where she pointed out how to paint as much as possible around the back of a large item —like their behemoth of a fridge—without pulling it out. Something someone of her size couldn't safely do.

He shrugged at her. "I'm sorry it's not all ready to sit down in and work. The computers are back in the bin by the couch for tonight."

"Well, I wasn't going to come home and do more work anyway. So you didn't miss much." Holding out her hand, she asked, "Would you like some help?"

He looked at her for a moment. "I don't know. This was supposed to be a surprise. I'm not sure it feels right if you help."

"Trust me. It's a huge surprise and I love it."

He looked at her from the side of his eyes for a moment, then picked up the multipack of sponge paint and edging tools and handed her a clean one. But he looked at her oddly until she asked, "What?"

"Don't you want to change?"

She shook her head. "I'm good." She'd done enough painting in her day, and this was only one wall, and she was only doing half the work. They'd be done in no time and then she would change.

Em found she liked working side by side with him. She liked watching his shoulders flex and thinking about what he could do with those strong fingers of his. She loved the way he smiled at her when he caught her looking. And that, when she had to bend over to get into the corner, she caught him looking at her.

She still wasn't sure quite what "giving their marriage a real try" would end up looking like. Originally, she'd thought that she'd survive anything, after all, she'd had her heart broken before. But now, as he smiled at her again, their painted areas getting closer together to meet in the middle of the wall, she thought she might not survive losing Keith Lee.

She was starting to smile at him again when his phone rang.

After fumbling to set down his paint edger and not get paint on the phone, he managed to get it onto the floor and answer it with one knuckle. Emma Kate would have laughed, but the screen clearly said, "Mom."

Looking up at her as though he had no idea what to do, Keith said only, "Hi, Mom."

But Em heard the voice clearly over the line, even though his face was down close to the phone.

"What's this I hear that you're married?"

✣ 26 ✣

Keith couldn't quite decipher the look on Emma Kate's face. Clearly, having dinner with his grandparents wasn't something she was truly looking forward to. She'd already met them when she went to pick up his boxes, and she'd done that on her own. But now she seemed tense, her face almost on the border of a frown since his grandparents had invited them.

He didn't know what to do with her. Honestly, he wasn't sure if he didn't know what to do with Emma Kate in particular or a wife in general. It could be either. Eventually, he decided that didn't matter. He didn't have a wife in general, he had this one. He liked this one and he wanted to keep her—that part was becoming more and more important to him each day.

She'd seemed fine when she came home and found him painting the office for her. She'd been smiling when she volunteered to help and had grinned and flirted with him as they finished the wall together. He'd threatened to put paint on her nice clothes and she mocked his lack of skill. He'd loved it. And he'd maybe fallen in love with her a little more.

Emma Kate had gushed about the room, about what a great surprise it was, and that the desks were an un-necessary but adored gift. She repeated several times that the color was perfect, as though she'd caught on it was something he was nervous about. After all, it was someone else's cast off color. But not getting it mixed saved just enough money to eek the office chairs onto his credit card.

After all his concerns about her, he'd been the one to break the budget rules. It figured. But Emma Kate made sure he knew his one day of surprise work—compared to her every day—was appreciated.

She'd run her hand across the top of what was basically a cheap desk. It only looked good because it was new. "This is amazing." She smiled up at him even though the desk was still in the middle of the room as they waited for the paint to fully dry. "You shouldn't have spent your money on the office chairs. I would have been fine with the folding chair." But still, she pulled it out and spun around in it almost like a kid.

It was funny, he thought. At first glance, Emma Kate came across as a pampered princess. She didn't scream "money," but she certainly screamed "class." She wore classic clothing—white button-down shirts, blue jeans without tears. He could tell from sharing a closet with her that she invested in quality pieces that would last, rather than putting her money into trendy items.

Her hair always looked like she paid some bucks to get it done. But he'd yet to see her grace a salon or spend on it. He wondered what would happen when she ran out of that high-end shampoo or needed a haircut. But he could only hope she could hold out until they had a better budget. It shouldn't be *that* far away, he thought.

Though she wore scrubs at the vet's, her hair and makeup were always impeccable. When she left to go work with Melanie, she was always put together enough that—if Keith had walked into the garage office where the pair worked—he would have wondered which of them was the boss and which was the assistant.

Yet, she'd looked just as elegant tucked up to a card table, sitting on a folding chair with her laptop open in front of her. Of course, being Emma Kate, she had a decorated pencil holder and a two-level inbox that she'd put on the back corner of the small table for the both of them.

Now, those things sat in separate cubbies on her new desk in the room he felt reflected her much better than it had before. He'd pushed the desks against the wall the next day when she was out, and lined her laptop, pencil holder, and all her desktop toys in the middle. She must have come in and seen it, for they were now all sorted to wherever they belonged. He smiled at the sight.

Emma Kate had warned him they might have to paint the walls back to their original depressing, grayish, neutral tan before they left the house to the next renters, but Keith hadn't cared. The look on her face had been worth it, but when the phone call came from his mother, she'd tensed up.

Then his grandparents had called, inviting them to dinner. Though she'd agreed to the visit with his family without any hesitation, he could tell it wasn't something she was looking forward to.

Keith hadn't made things any better for her when he brought up the hardware store. "So, when I was picking out paint, I could have sworn I heard you there."

"Were you hallucinating?" At least that had brought a smile to her face and he'd thought he should continue telling his story. Big mistake.

"I thought maybe I was, because I'd just been watching your video on my phone, but no, it was a woman who sounded just like you. She was there with her husband, a man named Finn."

Em had frozen on him, her expression going cold and staying locked. Whatever it was that he'd said—something about her sister or Finn—made her look scared. Keith did not like it. It put every cell in his body on alert.

"What did you say to them?" she asked, the words rote and forced.

It shocked him how relieved she looked when he said, "I didn't say anything."

After a pause, where his suddenly-icy wife only nodded, Keith continued, as if—by talking more—he could undo whatever he'd said. "I was in a hurry. She didn't seem to recognize me. So I didn't think it was the right time to introduce myself."

But Emma Kate had only nodded once more, the ice thawing, but only a little.

She'd hardly spoken for the remainder of the evening. They'd eaten dinner, gone to bed, and gotten up and gone to work the next day as though nothing had happened. She'd worked late hours with Melanie that night and now, they were on the way out the door to have dinner with his grandparents, having talked only what little amounts they could squeeze into the random spaces he'd found. None of it had been about his grandparents or her sister. He hadn't even brought up that his mother had given her parents a video chat system, and she would likely be calling tonight, to virtually meet his bride.

Xia Lee had not said the words, but Keith had understood, his getting married and not telling them about it was problematic. He should have alerted them *before* he'd gotten married. The fact that *he* hadn't known about his wedding before it happened was no excuse. His only recourse was to provide them with a bride they adored. Xia had married a white man, thus giving Keith his striking looks of mixed Chinese and... who knew what kind of Swedish, Irish, and Spanish ancestry. She'd also named her only son "Keith" rather than something Chinese, so he figured she couldn't be too upset with Emma Kate Mayfair and her stunningly American beauty.

The only question was whether Emma Kate would charm his parents. Not if she *could*—he knew her capabilities were a God-given fact—but if she *would*. She seemed more than a little irritated and he was afraid she felt she was getting put on display. Since he couldn't tell her she was wrong, he hadn't said much of anything.

Without having talked to her, he led her up the front steps. He had no idea if her concerns were just meet-the-family nerves, or if maybe it ran a little deeper.

Sometimes—most of the time, if he was counting—it felt as though they were in perfect sync. They laughed. She made him smile. She surprised the crap out of him on an almost daily basis. But other times she froze up, or he said the wrong thing and he felt there was an ocean between them. Now was one of those times, though he'd been driving her tiny car, and she was close enough to reach out and touch. He wasn't sure he could or whether he should.

So she stood on his grandparents' porch, the cold Georgia night painting her nose an endearing pink. She sighed at him. "Let's go do this."

Keith had no idea how the evening would go.

❦ 27 ❦

E m tensed as she heard the words she'd been expecting all evening.

Well, there were several things she'd been expecting to hear. She'd not been expecting to see the grandparents again and then immediately get told, "Let's call Xia and Ben. I know they are dying to meet you!"

Emma Kate had pasted on her best smile and instantly agreed. She turned to her husband. "Keith?"

"Xia and Ben are my parents," he offered with a smile.

"I know." She felt her teeth grind as she kept her smile in place. She should have been a damn beauty queen. There should have been a sash and a tiara if she was going to have to put on a dog and pony show. "I just meant that you should come get in the video with me."

She'd consciously unclenched various muscles as he smiled at his parents on the book-sized video tablet. His introduction made her melt and loosened some of the rigid steel holding her up.

"Mom, Dad—this is Emma Kate. She's amazing and you're going to love her."

She'd smiled and waved, almost ignoring his kind grandparents in the background.

"I wish we were there, and we could meet you in person!" his mother said it with just enough inflection that even Emma Kate's superior Southern Girl senses couldn't determine if it was a wish or a reprimand.

"Well, Mom, it was all very sudden, and you know that."

Go, Keith! She thought.

"You'll get to meet her in person later. In the meantime, you should just know that she makes me crazy happy." He'd squeezed the arm around her waist, and it wasn't just for show that she turned and looked at the amazing man holding her.

The small talk had wedged its way into the conversation then, about Keith growing up, about her childhood. Then, the questions had started coming. "Where do you work?" "Where is your family from?" and the dreaded, "And what is your degree in, dear?"

His mother's tone was kind, but it was clear there was not an option for, "oh, I don't have one." On the upside, his family clearly valued their education, and they'd spent plenty of time discussing how proud they were of Keith, his scholarships, his academic accomplishments, and more. She'd heard nothing about any sports he played, or whether he was a decent person even, so she'd expected this question. As the conversation had rolled on, she'd known it was inevitable. And—*thunk*—though she was still standing awkwardly in front of the video tablet, it landed in her lap with an almost audible dull noise.

"I'm still in progress at UCLA," she offered the phrase she'd planned, and watched as Keith smirked the corner of his mouth in a tip of the hat to her. Well, she wasn't going to say she'd quit or dropped out. She *hadn't*. She kept telling herself she would finish the degree, and she sure as hell wasn't going to put herself in a poor light with these people. Though it was tempting to do a beauty-pageant wave and say, "I'm Emma Kate Mayfair and I'm Miss Georgia!"

They asked her about her major, and she spoke around it, making sociology and economics sound like a more intentional blend of courses rather than a haphazard happening. To be fair, she'd sat in enough classes that she could speak about it with clarity and an educated tone. That seemed to be the thing that most impressed his parents about her.

His grandparents had joined in the conversation and Em realized this was going to take a while. She and Keith had been asked over for dinner. She just hadn't realized she was the meal to be served up. She smiled and hoped she was getting Chinese food at the end of this.

They asked about her family as well. In the South, it was common to ask *who were your people?* She told them straight out. "I'm a Mayfair. It's an old family name from this part of the state."

Being a Mayfair came with a long and sometimes illustrious history. The name of the town had been picked by her great-great-grandfather, and she liked to tell the story. "The rumor is that he went up to Lover's Leap and that the view left him breathless, and that's why he named the town that. Apparently, he had decided it was time it was no longer called 'Mayfair,' what with the Civil War, and all that."

Emma Kate loved talking southern crap with non-Southerners. They didn't get it. She could say things like "the Civil War, and all that" and they would have to ask her to explain. She didn't consider herself a mean person, but she wasn't going to take any crap about the fact that she'd married a guy with a doctorate degree when she didn't have any letters after her own name. So turning the conversation to something she could talk about was only self-protection.

"I don't know about the Civil War," his grandmother said, and Emma Kate believed that was fair. Only some Southerners had been around for "The Late Unpleasantness." Her family, and their town, had been here for all of it.

"Well, the town of Mayfair was very divided," Emma Kate said.

"Divided?" his grandfather asked. "I thought the entire South was pro-Confederate once you got south of the Mason-Dixon."

"Oh, no," Emma Kate corrected. Civil War history belonged in every Belle's back pocket. "There were areas of resistance all over the South. They made a movie about one of the towns, something about Jones, but there were far more than that. In many places, the brothers that left and fought for the North were disowned from their families. Mayfair went the other direction. Most of the town fought for the North, and those who fought with the Confederacy were the ones getting disowned. I have a great-great-uncle somewhere back there, a couple of them, I think, who decided they were Confederates, but the oldest brother was a staunch Union supporter. As the oldest brother, he owned the land and basically the town. So he decided that the whole town would go one way. Not all the residents agreed."

His parents were staring through the video chat in rapt fascination, and Keith's grandparents were watching her, too. Even her husband didn't seem to know any of this. It was local history, nothing that belonged only to her family. So she kept talking, though she still thought she'd earned that dinner.

"Anyway, there had been rumblings to change the town's name after that, and my great-great-grandfather was the one who finally decided it should be so. But the fact is, there are no real records on why he chose *Breathless* as the name. Still, when my sisters and I used to go up to Lover's Leap, we would run up the trails. We always said that he named it Breathless since any normal person would have been out of breath by the time they arrived at the top."

At least that got a small smile out of Keith's grandparents. She'd done it on purpose, not wanting to talk about her sisters. Already, Keith had run into Bailey Ann, and Bailey Ann had not recognized him. Keith found this unusual, but Emma Kate wondered how he thought her sister could possibly recognize a man she'd never heard of. She was standing there, on the video chat, when she realized her husband had no idea that her sisters had no idea she was *married*.

At first, she hadn't told anyone because she and Keith were going to get the marriage annulled. Even now that they'd decided to give it a real try, she hadn't told. When she looked back, though, Em had to admit she'd been wearing those rings all along. After just one day in the car, she knew she really liked Keith Lee, and that—despite the fact she'd chosen him when she was drunk enough to not remember the evening—she seemed to have chosen very well.

But now he was going to ask—since they'd decided to stay together—why hadn't she told her sisters? Was she hiding him? The scary truth was, she didn't know.

❧ 28 ❧

Em watched as her boss sighed in frustration and practically threw her pencil at her desk.

"Is it anything I can help with?" Emma Kate asked tentatively. She was the newbie here, but she'd heard some of the conversations Melanie had been having and hoped she'd get a chance to give it a shot.

Her desk was smaller than Melanie's and sat to the side of the garage, though both faced the main door should anyone come in. Behind Melanie's spot was a step up and a door into the house—Em rarely went there, though Melanie ducked in several times during a shift. However, there was a window on Emma's side, and as she looked out, she saw the day was a dull gray that insisted her good mood go downhill.

She'd been tense throughout the entire dinner the night before. And she'd been mad at Keith for taking her before a firing squad and not telling her. She'd waited until they pulled out of the driveway. She'd waved to his grandparents, who sweetly stood on the doorstep until they were out of sight, then she'd lit into him.

Her hands had gripped the wheel—she'd insisted on driving because she didn't want him to drive off the road or miss a turn when she let him have it. "Did you know I was going to meet your parents, too? Did you know about the video chat?"

"I... no."

The pause made her press her lips together and give a little shake of her head. She was not one for putting up with bullshit. And it would be better if Keith Lee learned that early. "So you did have an idea. You just didn't know the specifics?"

"That's more like it." He was nodding, though it was clear he could see her head was about to blow off.

"So you took me in front of a firing squad and didn't warn me?"

"I—"

"It's a yes or no question, Keith." She hated the sound of her voice right then, but she couldn't stop the words or the anger.

"Yes." He paused for a moment and she was grateful he at least acknowledged it. After a pause from both of them, while she waited out a light and took a left turn, he spoke again. "Can I explain?"

"Go for it." Again, her words were clipped and harsh, but she was still mad.

"We barely spoke since my Mom called. I didn't really have time to warn you."

"But you would have if you'd had time?" She wanted to hear this. Because there had been time. It only took a minute to stop someone eating her breakfast and say, "By the way, my Mom is going to give you the third degree."

"Yes."

"Because I found time to make French toast in the crock-pot for breakfast." That was snippy, but damn, he could have done it.

She heard him sigh from the other side of the car, but she didn't look over to see his expression. After a moment he spoke up again. "You're right."

All the heat went out of her. Damn him for admitting it. Her shoulders sagged and suddenly she was tired from being tense for the past two days. Painting together had been great, and the contrast of facing the firing squad that was his family had wound her up tight enough to snap wire.

"I should have said something. My family isn't like yours. But I didn't think much of it because they are my normal."

"But I'm the woman you married in Vegas! They probably hated me before they ever saw me. How could they possibly like me? And you sent me into that?"

From the corner of her eye she'd seen him shake his head. "Actually, I talked to my Mom between the call you heard—when we were painting—and tonight. I told her how amazing you were and... how much I wanted to spend my life with you."

Her heart swelled and she didn't think her chest would hold it. Damn this man. She'd almost hated him about five minutes ago. "You told her that?"

"I did."

Her eyes were wet, but she wasn't crying. At least that's what she told herself. "And that was your mom being *nice*?"

He busted out laughing then and she almost drove the car off the road. Maybe she shouldn't have driven.

"Yes. She's not wired like you, Emma Kate. She doesn't see people, she sees accomplishments. And she measures them her own way." He looked out the passenger window and away from her. "I was too much like her... up until now."

"And now?"

"You're rubbing off on me." He reached across the center console and plucked her hand from the steering wheel. Without another word, he held her hand all the way home.

It had been late, they both had work the next morning, and they'd quietly gone about climbing into bed, the argument forgiven but not fully forgotten. She was almost asleep when his hand stroked through her hair and down her arm.

"Em, forgive me," he whispered it into the darkness around him as he let his fingers trail down to her waist, over her hip, and back up. He did it again, waiting until she turned to him. When she did, she found a hot, bare-chested man ready and wanting her. Had anyone been standing outside the little house last night, they would have heard her screaming his name. She'd come into work with a smile she couldn't quite hide. And it had stayed in place until Melanie's frustrations had busted it.

Melanie looked up. "Clara Deacons wants to do a ballroom event."

Em nodded. She knew this.

"She wants to do it for half the amount I suggested, and I'm struggling to make it work. I understand she wants as much of the money as possible to go to charity. But it's not like she doesn't have the funds to do this up right."

"I know," Emma Kate said. "It'd be easier if they just put a lot of money at it, but I understand. It does seem harsh to spend fifty-thousand to raise a hundred."

Melanie nodded her agreement, but grumbled, "That woman has been in a competition against herself to make her ratios better and better. And it's not just the ratios, she wants her numbers bigger and bigger, too. She has to be able to say she raised X amount of dollars! Every time I work with her, she wants to spend less money on the event. I'm not making a real profit here. To be fair, I do pay my own salary, and I pay yours, but it's nothing to write home about. I do the work because it's good work. Aside from a little bit of overhead, there's not much wiggle room. There's no CEO with a golden parachute here."

Melanie sighed, but Em was already getting up and walking across the small space. She stood behind Melanie, looking over her shoulder at the spreadsheet for floral for the event. "May I?"

Melanie waved her hand at the budget on the screen. "Have at it. If you can figure this out, I'll give you that raise right now."

Well, shit, Emma Kate thought. If that wasn't an incentive, she didn't know what was. "Does she have a theme in mind?"

"Flowers."

"That's not a theme." She sighed. *Shit.* "Flowers get expensive. Well, we're usually busy in the several days leading up to the event anyway. Do we have time for a trip to Atlanta in the time budget?"

"I often go," Melanie said. "It's not something I haven't done before. Why? What are you thinking?"

"Well, in Los Angeles, there are wholesale markets downtown. Fabric, fashion, jewelry, and *floral*."

"We do have a market like that in Atlanta. I mean, I know it's not as big." Melanie was nodding. "It's not something I usually do for events here. But if she wants *flowers*, it's probably worth the trip."

"Now, if I could get in touch with one of the vendors..." Emma Kate knew it was hard to find direct numbers for the wholesalers sometimes. They sold to the shops directly. "I'm assuming you've worked with at least some of them in the past."

"I have some deals," Melanie said, seeming to catch on to where she was going.

"Are they aware it's for charity? Because they can get a tax break, and it looks good on their business. But that's not enough, is it?" Emma Kate asked.

"Not enough to get the budget where she wants it."

"So, when I was in school, I always won the charity canned good drives. I brought in so many cans, no other class could compete. My classmates loved me. I always won the pizza parties or the chicken biscuit breakfasts."

"What did you do?"

"I went around to all the local businesses and collected from them. It was for charity after all. I could get a full box from each grocery store and a good handful from each of the restaurants in town. It all added up."

Melanie was nodding. "And you want to do the same thing here."

"It's for charity," Emma Kate emphasized. "It's a write off."

Melanie nodded, "Go for it."

"All right. Give me a while." Emma Kate headed all seven feet back to her desk, and it took her about fifteen minutes to look up what she needed in Melanie's records. Then she started making calls.

By the third one, Melanie was smiling over at her as she talked to the floral vendor. "Hello. This is Emma Kate Mayfair. I'm with a company called Fundraising By Design. I'm hoping you can help me out." She used her best Southern Belle voice, her best professional phone manners her mama had taught her, and everything she'd learned in a handful of psychology courses that went along with that sociology degree: Be polite, give your name, open with the opportunity for the other person to become your personal savior.

She explained a little of their business model. "We work with wealthy clients who are putting together big charity events. We reserve venues, plan events, and raise money for charities of all kinds, usually determined by the person who hires us. This event is for St. Jude's Children's Hospital, and if you and your business are willing, you can get an excellent tax break. Here's how you can help."

In the end—as Melanie had found—there was no one who would provide the flowers they wanted at the price Clara Deacons wanted. But that hadn't been Em's plan. She worked a series of smaller deals with a handful of different florists on their side of Atlanta. They would get two-day-old roses last minute. They would already be open, which was bad for a floral shop, but good for an event. They would buy three quarters of their stock at three quarters of the price, and then each company would make a charitable donation of the remaining quarter of the order. It would be a handful of paperwork, Emma Kate knew, but her time was cheaper than roses.

"Okay." She turned to Melanie. "I think I've got the full order, all white roses, as requested."

"And," Melanie added, "at two thirds the price. I'm impressed."

Em just smiled her way through the rest of the short shift. Melanie promised her the raise starting the next day. It was an extra two dollars an hour. It wasn't much at the time, but it would add up. Besides, it was her first raise.

As she headed out the door, she saw that Clara Deacons was arriving for her meeting with Melanie. Em was glad she didn't have to sit through it. Though nice enough, Clara Deacons was stubborn. Who knew what she would demand of them for tomorrow?

But she passed by the woman's car—an old Mercedes, probably pushing fifteen years old. It had to have a ton of miles. But Clara waved to her, even that motion had the air of old money. "Hello, Emma Kate! You have a good evening, dear."

"You, too, Mrs. Deacons." But that old car got Emma Kate thinking.

❧ 29 ❧

Keith felt like the world was collapsing in on him—as though he had become a black hole at the center of the universe.

He listened as his wife repeated her harsh question in a tight voice. "Do. You. Love. Me?"

There was almost an exclamation point at the end of each word. Being the man he was, he had to answer honestly, but the fact of the matter was he didn't really have words for what he felt for her. He didn't know what the honest answer was, so he shrugged.

In reply, she looked at him and said, "You don't know. You don't know if you love me or not."

"I don't." That was the truth. It wasn't as if he was lying and saying he loved her when he wasn't sure he did. He'd never done this before—he didn't even really know what "this" was. "This thing between us is so new, Emma Kate. I don't know what it is, or if it will last. I do know I am crazy about you."

"I get that, Keith," she said, "but you need to get that, too."

When she'd come in the door earlier, she'd been on top of the world. He'd gotten off work and arrived home earlier than her today. She'd called to say she was staying late and cutting deals, so he'd made dinner. It was nothing on par with what Emma Kate would do, but he had hot food on the table when they got in.

They'd eaten dinner together, smiling and laughing as they talked about their day. The whole time, he'd felt like a real husband—a good one, one who made his wife happy and was contributing to his home. It wasn't his parents' marriage. They were so publicly unaffectionate with each other, that he'd often wondered how he'd been conceived. This was his marriage, and stunningly close to what he'd always imagined the ideal would be.

Only the good feeling had faded as they'd sat on the couch, watched a little TV to unwind, and he realized what was nagging at him. Unable to let it sit, he'd asked her then if she'd told her sisters about him. He knew she didn't have parents to tell, just her Aunt GiGi and Uncle Dex.

She didn't even look away from the TV as she replied. Maybe that was what bothered him most: that it didn't bother her. "I told my cousin Lennon," she said, "but no one else."

"Why?" he pushed. He'd learned early on that her best friend and cousin, Lennon, lived in Chicago. So Emma Kate could check the box that she'd told some of her family, but no one she would have to face. "Are you ashamed of me?"

"Jesus, Keith, I'm not ashamed of *you*. I'm ashamed of *us*."

It wasn't what he'd expected. He'd thought she would deny that she was hiding it, and that maybe she was setting herself up to get outed. She wore his ring everywhere she went. Sooner or later, someone would ask her about it—unless she was taking it off and putting it back on each day when she got home. That possibility had not occurred to him before. Still, it seemed she was in touch with her own feelings, and that she was being honest with herself and him, but her answer had not felt any better.

While they'd talked—or argued, actually—she'd pushed off the couch and begun pacing the room in her nice work slacks and button-down shirt. She had a vest over it, and she looked like an irate prepster, her heels punching tiny angry holes in the carpet as she moved, her manicured hands flying as she gestured.

"I'm the youngest in my family, Keith, by far. I'm pretty sure my parents didn't intend to have a third child, but here I am. I didn't get the family silver. I wasn't given any legacy. I told you, the family portrait was painted before my mother even got pregnant with me. And now my parents are gone. All I have are my sisters. I love them, but they think they know how to live my life and they tell me I'm screwing it up because I'm not doing it their way. I am the family fuck-up, Keith!"

"You're not a fuck-up, Emma Kate," he told her, his heart aching for the way she thought her family saw her. He'd love to tell her she was wrong, but since he had never met them, he didn't know, now did he? Some families were like that. Even the loving ones had their faults.

"It was bad enough before my parents died, but now my oldest sister has taken over their estate, my middle sister has moved back home. And while she's basically destitute and about two inches from bankruptcy, everyone knows it was through no fault of her own. She, at least, has three children. She managed to do the one most important thing—which was give my parents grandchildren. And me, what have I done? I went and dropped out of school again. I've already gotten an earful about that. The last thing I needed to do is tell them that I also married a man that I don't know from Adam in the middle of Vegas while I was drinking my money away."

"You do know me from Adam," he protested.

"I didn't!" Her hands waved frantically, her chest heaved with her frustration. "When I tell them what I did, they'll tell me—again—that I fucked up."

"I get that." He tried to keep his voice calm. Where she was upset, he was going to be a pillar of zen, even if he didn't feel it. If there was anything that he learned from growing up in his own family, it was that Lees don't fight. "We're not loud. We're not crazy," his mother had used to say. "You can get angry, but you don't lash out."

Now, here he was, fighting with his wife and holding it all together by sheer force of will. Because he wanted to yell. But Keith held it together and tried to calmly state, "That was then. I realize it hasn't been long, and I get that that's how we started, but we agreed we were going to try and see if we could make this a real marriage."

"I know, Keith," she said, turning and staring at him, her hands on her hips. Those were not the words that would make her change her mind, clearly. "But if you don't love me, it's not a real marriage, not yet, and it means I have to tell my sisters that I decided I was going to be married to a man who doesn't love me."

All he could say was, "I want to. I'm moving that direction, Em. You got to give me a little bit of space."

"I am!" she yelled. "I'm giving you so much space! I'm giving you space without the expectations of my uptight sisters. I'm giving *me* space to figure out what I feel for you without them constantly interfering and telling me I have to do it one way or another. That it's time that I think something or feel something or just grow up!" With a deep breath where he could see she was trying to calm herself down, she dropped the volume of her voice. "You don't get to tell me how and what to tell my family if you can't tell me you love me. I'm going to bed."

Keith was left sitting on the couch thinking about what she'd said. If he wasn't so keyed up, he'd be grateful. At least he understood that she, too, was still trying to figure out what this was between them. That she seemed okay with him not being able to say he didn't know yet if he loved her.

But he desperately wanted her to tell her sisters. He didn't know why that was such an important rite of passage for them, but he felt in his heart that it was.

Sitting on the couch and staring at the wall, he realized one thing. It didn't really matter if she loved him or not or if he could say that he truly loved her. If he didn't work this out—if he lost Emma Kate—it would shred him in a way he'd never felt before. And he didn't know if he'd survive it.

❧ 30 ❧

S *weetened iced tea is always served, even in the dead of winter.*

EM SAT AROUND THE CORNER OF THE RESTAURANT COUNTER with her two sisters. They had taken the three stools at the end of the bar in the local food trailer, Wok On In.

The place was located in a parking lot, a tiny little trailer that served deep fried wontons and chow mien to die for. It was also relatively cheap, which Emma Kate and Harper Rose could get behind. Like all good Southern restaurants, despite being Chinese, they served sweet tea.

Bailey Ann was apparently the only one with any money in her pocket, and she was working hard to get her parents' money untied from all the various places they'd sunk it. Emma Kate would bet that Bailey Ann hadn't found all of it yet. Both her sisters had left home before their Dad started talking about investing, but he'd had some funny ideas. Em hadn't thought much of it at the time, but now she wished she could better remember what he'd been talking about.

Though the money was there, it wasn't available. The three

women were sitting on a reasonable inheritance—it wasn't going to make them rich, but it would change Harper Rose's situation and Emma Kate's. Bailey Ann would likely sink her share into a retirement fund, but Em expected nothing less from her oldest sister. Sadly, the one asset that was relatively accessible wasn't worth pulling out. They could liquidate the funds in that stock account, but it was dramatically underperforming.

The three of them had decided as a unit to tough it out. If any of them got stuck financially and had to pull the trigger, the other two would decide if they wanted to save her or liquidate the fund at the low end. Luckily, no one had gotten that far in the hole yet.

Bailey Ann had her degree in economics and banking, and she always commented that the Belle's secret to the stock market was *buy low and sell high*, and this was not going to cut it. She probably would have put her own funds into saving either sister if they needed it. Emma Kate knew that had stopped her from asking to just liquidate the account on more than one occasion. But her being "broke" was a lot more comfortable given that she had a safety net.

Other money that might have come in was tied up in several timeshare condos that their parents had owned. The three sisters had voted together to sell all of them. Two of the three were worth a decent amount of money, but the third wasn't in good enough shape to resell for much. Two of the three were co-owned with friends, which caused more trouble. And Bailey Ann wasn't having much luck on the real estate market, given that it was wintertime. Houses would sell, but vacation homes at the beach? Not so much.

They could have sold the house—since their parents had left them that, too—but Bailey Ann had lived in it for a handful of months, and now Harper Rose was occupying it with her girls. Having a free place to live with her three daughters changed everything for them. The elementary school was right across the street. And Emma Kate could only imagine that after all Harper

Rose had been through, being in her childhood home was a comfort. Neither Em nor Bailey Ann was willing to pull that out from under her.

Emma Kate knew that if it was her, she would appreciate the gesture. Besides, she and Keith weren't starving, they weren't homeless, and with her own paycheck, she was doing pretty well. They'd even begun paying down their credit cards, figuring if they lived poor, they'd get out of what they were now calling their "Vegas debt" faster.

It was an odd thought, her brain wandering off into the space of what might be her future with Keith Lee. Marriage wasn't a life she'd really ever contemplated, and he'd asked if she wanted to be *married*. At the time, it had seemed like a good idea, given that they were actually already married, living together, and by then, sleeping together. But sometimes—like right then—it hit her what she'd agreed to and she stopped and thought about it.

Married meant "the rest of her life," but Keith Lee was looking like a pretty good bet.

"Where are you?" Harper Rose asked, waving her hand in front of her little sister's face.

"Oh, just thinking about work," Emma Kate lied through her teeth.

"That must be some nice work," Bailey Ann commented from the other side of her.

They'd put Em in the middle seat, almost as a place of honor. She hadn't really wanted to be there, but she'd volunteered to pick up the check today, and they'd stuck her in the middle as a thank you.

"Does it have anything to do with the hot new vet at the office?"

Em almost choked on her shrimp fried rice. "What?" she sputtered out, suddenly back in the conversation. *Did they know?* "What?" she asked again.

Bailey Ann just grinned. "You said you were working at the vet's office, and Jane told me she had seen you out on a house call, riding around with one of the vets. Some dark-haired, dark-eyed Calvin Klein model looking guy."

Emma Kate had laughed to cover her gaffe. "That would be Keith, and yes, I mostly work with him."

"Lucky girl," Bailey Ann commented, though Emma Kate still wasn't sure if her sister had even seen Keith or just heard rumors about her riding around with him. She hoped Bailey Ann hadn't heard rumors of anything more.

Surely, someone would hear something—maybe even just see her ring and ask—and word would get back to her sisters if she didn't fix this mess, and soon. Under the edge of the counter, her right hand immediately reached toward her left, as though to twist the rings she wasn't wearing. As soon as she touched her finger and felt it missing, she almost jolted, until she remembered she'd hidden them in her purse.

It was the perfect opportunity, she thought. Just speak up, say, "I don't actually just work with him. I'm married to him too," but it didn't come out of her mouth. Instead, a fried wonton went in. It was hard to tell her sisters these things, especially when they'd walked into the restaurant, hugged her, and immediately asked about her thesis. At least this time Emma Kate had simply told them, "I have several ideas. Now, we need to stop talking about it," and she didn't know how it had happened, but they'd stopped.

They talked about Bailey Ann trying to find more of her parents' assets, about her combing through the bank accounts. Harper Rose had interrupted. She had her youngest, Holland, in daycare, because she'd recently started a job. So she talked about working the front desk. Harper Rose had her degree in psychology and communications, but it only apparently allowed her to keep the schedule for actual licensed therapists.

Her sister seemed involved in the work. "One of the doctors is running several experiments. She's just one practitioner and is part of a larger overall study on a new pharmaceutical. We have to follow exactly the same protocol as a handful of other offices around the US." Harper Rose was explaining what the experiments were in far more detail than a front desk clerk would probably know, but Emma Kate smiled. Her sister was happy, and she had income.

When she asked how she was enjoying it, though, Harper Rose replied, "It puts groceries in the fridge, and it's at least enough it covers Holland at daycare. That takes the bulk of it."

"Is she at daycare today?" Emma Kate asked after her sister's youngest, a two-year-old who actually most resembled Emma Kate, at least more than that asshat of a father.

"Actually, she's with a friend. She goes to her daycare Monday, Wednesday, and Thursday. But on Tuesdays, she stays with a friend of ours, and on Fridays, I take Carson, my friend's little boy. That's been a lifesaver."

"I'll bet." Emma Kate didn't know about children like her sisters did. As the youngest, she'd never had a younger sister running around, never had a baby in the house. She'd had no one to really take care of or play mommy to, aside from a few odd babysitting jobs that really hadn't been her cup of tea. Still, she knew one thing. "Having two of them is easier than one, isn't it?" she asked.

"Absolutely. If I have Holland by myself, I'll go crazy and start breaking things."

Harper Rose rolled her eyes, and Em laughed. Still, she was thinking, *I should just tell them now,* when Bailey Ann finished her meal and said, "Well, I have a surprise for y'all."

She reached into her purse and pulled out two envelopes. "I finally got into that odd little goal savings account Daddy had. I have no idea what it was for, but it's for us now. I divided it evenly."

"You can take more for yourself, Bailey Ann." Emma Kate wished her sister would take an extra portion. She'd done all the work.

"Nope." Her older sister shook her head. "I'm the oldest now. I feel responsible, and I want to take care of you guys."

Harper Rose hopped up from her seat and ran around Emma Kate so they could both hug their older sister at the same time.

Bailey Ann was smiling. "Besides, I have Finn. I have a safety net. So, I'll be yours."

Emma Kate hugged her harder. Her first thought was that Bailey Ann was wrong.

I have Keith.

But she couldn't make the words come out of her mouth.

❧ 31 ❧

Emma Kate had worked late with Melanie again that evening. Keith stayed out running a last-minute emergency call for Housley. They managed to drive up the driveway at the same time, Em in her little silver car and Keith looking like a badass in his leather jacket and gloves on his bike.

She knew that the leather jacket and gloves were because he was cold—he'd not thought such a southern state could get to freezing temperatures, and he'd not been prepared. She also knew that, under the biker jacket, he was wearing a white thermal shirt and his blue scrubs top. She didn't care. Her husband looked like a badass.

She'd been the first up the stairs to the little porch and she turned to watch as he took off his helmet and tucked it under his arm. Then she put the key in the lock and held the door for him, accepting a soft, lingering kiss as he went by.

Once inside, she'd walked through her ritual of hanging up her coat, stuffing her gloves into the pockets and setting her purse on the floor just inside the door. There was no entry way table nor coat rack, and she was grateful the Barkers had installed the hooks just inside the door.

"So how was your day, dear?" He asked it with a sarcastic

tone, but that was for the "dear" part. Keith always really wanted to know about her day.

"We went out to the Forsythe house—"

"You really have Forsythes here? I thought that was just on Dallas or whatever those TV shows were." He was raising one eyebrow as if she needed to explain herself. When it came to "normal" in the south, she often did.

"Where do you think the TV shows got that name?" She raised an eyebrow right back at him.

"Touché," he conceded, "So you went to the Forsythe house..."

"Mrs. Forsythe wants to do a charity ball, in her own ballroom—"

"Because, of course, she has her own ballroom."

Em could almost see him looking around their tiny house and knowing it would fit in the Forsythe ballroom ten times over. "Yes, she does. But what grabbed me is that the furniture in the living room is threadbare. The floors are worn along the pathways people have walked—probably for more than a century." Em flopped back on the couch. "Her grandchildren are running around, weaving in and out of these priceless antiques, and she doesn't think anything of it."

"But how is she throwing a charity event—don't those things cost money?—if she doesn't have it? I mean, you said the house was worn." He'd peeled the scrub top, usually not willing to wear them inside the house, before he leaned back on the couch with her. Both of them splayed out, feet in front of them, her in heels, him in sneakers with his top balled up in his fist.

"She does have it. That's the thing. Clara Deacons drives a twenty-year-old car with paint chips and dings."

"What's your point?"

"That's what old money is. Mrs. Forsythe doesn't care that the furniture is worn. She doesn't need to prove to anyone that she has the means. She knows it. The furniture was probably in her family. And honestly, when I first saw it, that's what I thought: *antiques*. It wasn't until I really looked that I thought, actually, it's *old*. You and I aren't classy enough to have a worn hardwood floor."

He laughed at her, but Em continued.

"And I drive an old car, but I'm nervy about it. I can't afford to replace the muffler or get another car if anything happens to it. Clara Deacons loves 'her Benz' and if anything happens, she'll be sad, but she's not worried about buying another car. Not like me. That's old money."

"You have class. I don't know if you have *old money class*, but you have real class, Emma Kate." He looked away and then looked back. "I've thought that since I woke up next to you in Vegas."

She almost bust a gut, she wanted to laugh so hard. "I was stalking the room, waving my hands around, ranting like a madwoman who'd just married a man she didn't know."

"But with *class*." He grinned, then he rolled onto one hip, facing her. "Seriously, you had just woken up—in heels—and you didn't miss a step. Your hair and makeup were just a little worn, but not like most women the morning after... whatever that was we did. You asked your questions and demanded your answers, but you didn't yell and you didn't blame me or anyone else for our predicament. I think that's why I put my bike in your trailer and got in the car with you." Then he smiled again. "You have that kind of bred-into-the-bones class that you're talking about. Even if you can't afford a new muffler."

"Actually, I can." With a deep sigh, grateful for the heat in the small home, Em realized she didn't even feel like moving, let alone reheating anything for dinner. If she remembered correctly, they didn't have any leftovers to reheat, except maybe some oatmeal. "We should go out," she said.

Keith's answering sigh wrapped the air beside her. "We don't have the budget to go out anywhere."

"Actually, we do. Look what I got." She dragged herself off the couch and headed to where she'd left her purse and pulled the envelope Bailey Ann had given her. As she headed back to plop in the couch—*class, my ass*, she thought—she held it up for Keith to see.

Only as she did it did Emma Kate realize that the envelope itself meant nothing. So she pulled it open and showed him the check inside. It was written to her, *Emerson Kate Mayfair*, and signed by *Bailey Ann Mayfair Malloy*. Apparently, Bailey Ann had dumped all the funds from this one small account into her own checking and written out the checks to her sisters from there.

"That's over a thousand dollars" he said, his expression going wide. "Not too shabby. From your sister? What did you do for her?"

"Inheritance from my parents. Remember I said it was all tied up? The vast majority of it still is. But this—this little bit— is something Bailey Ann found. And she liquidated it without hurting any of the value. This is my third." She waved the check back and forth, liking the feeling of money in her hand. Or maybe she liked having a cushion. Finally.

"What on earth did she find that was worth three thousand dollars?"

"Some little 'goal savings account' my father had stashed away. She went to close out his accounts at the bank months ago. She closed them, and used that money to fix up the house to sell it—"

"But she didn't sell, right?"

Em shook her head. They'd changed their minds, and Harper Rose and her girls had moved in. "She also used that money to cover the funeral costs and all that. And we all thought the cash in my parents' accounts was done. None of us imagined it would take this long to deal with their affairs. But, anyway, Bailey just got a letter from the bank a couple months ago stating that he had this other account, and she needed to move it, close it, or feed it more money. So she went in again, and it took two months to get them to release it, to accept the death certificate that they've already seen three times—" She sighed. *As though the* sisters had forged it or her father might come back from the dead. Though she would have loved that, it wasn't going to happen and the bank was being ridiculous. "She had to re-prove that he had passed, that she was the executor on all his accounts, all that crap. But she did it and I have a check." Then she corrected herself, "*We* have a one thousand dollar check."

"No, *you* do."

"I want to put most of it in our savings," she told him, basically ignoring his counterpoint. "And I really would like to get a stand for the TV. I searched my sister's house, but there was no coffee table. We could use one. So that would be a big splurge. But I'd like to put the rest in savings, and I'd like to go out to dinner tonight. We've worked really hard to stay in budget."

Keith cringed, but she laughed at him. "The office chairs don't count. I know you only kind of violated the budget on that and it was really nice."

"This is *your* money," he told her, pushing his hand out as though pushing the check away made it so.

"I know, but it's *our* money."

"It's an inheritance from your parents. It's not anything you earned since we've been married. Your parents didn't even pass after we were together. All of that happened before we ever even met. That's your money," he repeated.

Nodding, she tucked it back in her purse and said, "Well then, can I take you out for dinner tonight?" It felt positively decadent, having gone out for lunch and now going out again for dinner. But there was nothing but oatmeal in the fridge.

For the first week or so when she'd been home, they'd gone straight through their food, eating a meal one night and the leftovers the next because they had to. Now they were banking the leftovers for nights they were both late. Cooking was happening more occasionally, when one of them had a chance to actually cook a meal, but they still couldn't afford to be eating out all the time.

To be fair, Emma Kate didn't really like spending the money, but she'd gone a long time without a nice sit-down restaurant and table service. "Change out of your scrubs," she told him as she peeled herself off the couch. She was more ready to go than he was. Keith was still in the white thermal shirt and the scrubs pants he'd worn all day, but still looking sexy spread out on the couch.

She watched as he pushed himself upright and headed down the hall, calling back, "Do you want pizza?"

When she said no, he threw out one chain restaurant in town and then another.

"No," she repeated, "I want to go in toward Atlanta and sit down and have seafood."

"Em, that's a lot of money. We're still on a budget."

"And I'm buffering up our savings," she told him.

"No, that's your money." He repeated it firmly, and it was starting to piss her off.

It took a second to figure out what bothered her so much about that. "Are we married or not?" she called to him through the open doorway of their bedroom.

He poked his head out the door, his bare shoulder showing as he slid a clean shirt on and frowned at her. "Of course, we're married."

"I don't mean *legally*. I know we're legally married, but you asked me if I really wanted to do this thing."

Keith paused, nodding. "Yes, I mean we are *really* married. If we break up, we're going to have to get a full divorce." He sighed and his eyes darted away as he came up close to stand in front of her, draping his arms around her waist. "If we get a divorce... it'll kill me. I'm crazy about you, Em."

How did he do that? She was pestering him, trying to make a point, and he was melting her like butter in a hot pan. "I don't understand. If we're married, then this is *ours*. If this was you, would you keep the money to yourself?"

Keith was shaking his head at her before he even thought about it. "No, of course not—"

He caught on as she said it. "No double standards, Keith. I'm a contributing member of this household—"

"Yes, you are." He was kissing her, killing her argument.

"Don't! Don't distract me." She was pushing at him. "If you would have shared your money with me, then you have to learn to let me take the brunt of some things too. Do you think I'll break?"

"No." He was staring at her, and the admiration in his eyes was almost better than the heat. "I know you won't."

"Then be a man and learn how to take something from a woman." She swatted him away. "And put some pants on. No decent restaurant will let you in without pants."

❧ 32 ❧

K eith was standing in the doorway of one of the patient rooms when the front door to the clinic flew open. He'd thought he was done for the day. But it was five minutes before closing and a Friday. He should have known better.

A woman backed in through the door clutching a large cardboard box in her hands. That didn't mean anything alarming to Keith. As a vet, he often saw people bring their pets in awkward cardboard boxes. *Whatever worked*, he thought. It could be a rabbit, a turtle, or a rabid possum. Who knew? So he waited, calmly, even though as the woman turned around, he could see she looked frantic. He wasn't going to let her panic brush off onto him.

He smiled and waited as her eyes darted around the empty front office.

When she spotted him, her smile softened. "There you are."

He had never seen her before in his life, but apparently his blue scrubs were sufficient. It was exactly the reason the clinic color coded their staff. Blue for doctors, green for assistants, and purple for office workers—like Emma Kate.

The woman knew at least that she was giving the box to one

of the doctors, but as she shoved it into his hands, he looked down inside. He spotted, amid the folds of a tragically old and dirty towel, three far too tiny, far too skinny kittens.

As she blurted her story out at him, the woman did not look down into the box. "I found them on the side of the road on my way home from work. I don't think they belong to anyone. It was on the side of the freeway."

She let go, leaving the weight of the box in his hands. He had simply been handed these three kittens without agreeing to keep them, and she was already heading back out the door.

"I'm sorry, are they yours?" He meant *did she want to keep them*, but it hadn't come out that way.

"No. I found them," she reiterated, "and I have to go to my daughter's recital. Please tell me you can take care of them." But she was out the door before he had a chance to answer.

One of the office staff, Sissy, walked back into the front room just then and looked at him. "What was that?"

"Drive by kitten drop?" He shrugged. That was the best explanation he had since he wasn't truly sure what had just happened, though it wasn't the first time he'd seen it.

"Oh, kittens!" Sissy came over closer to peer down into the box. "Oh, my God. They are tiny."

"Too tiny," he said. With the woman gone, and the box now firmly in his grip, he headed back into the patient room he'd just had cleaned and called for an assistant.

This was the kind of thing vets often wound up doing. The kittens didn't belong to anyone, so there was no one to bill for their care. It would cost the clinic staff time and medication from the looks of these guys, in addition to the usual list of supplies abandoned kittens needed. He and Housley would ask for a donation to cover those costs when the kittens were adopted out to forever homes. But those donations sometimes didn't happen. And when they did, they almost never covered the real cost of fostering.

As he looked into the box, he wondered what the odds of

forever homes happening were for these kittens. They should still be with their mother, and the woman who dropped them off said she found them on the side of the road, which could mean anything.

Looking up at Sissy, he asked, "Did you recognize her?"

She shook her head, ponytail bouncing. "Didn't get a good enough look."

"Shit," he said. "We need the mother."

"No hope of that now," Sissy replied in a tone too cheerful for the condition the kittens were in.

Resigned to finding a foster home for kittens that would need to be fed around the clock, Keith smiled at her. It was the only option. "Our best bet is to take care of them ourselves."

One of them looked up and offered a tiny mewl at him. "Get me some formula, please?" he asked her without looking up. They were cute.

"On it, boss."

He liked that. The staff sometimes called him that to be funny. They did the same to Dr. Housley, too. But sometimes it was just an acknowledgment of his position in the clinic, and it felt really good to legitimately be called "boss." He'd worked hard to become a vet. He'd done residencies at local veterinary offices in Berkeley before taking this job and heading out to Georgia and Breathless and the "apartment" that Housley had found for him.

Even though Keith had only been here a while, Housley was doing his best to make Keith into a full-fledged partner—asking his opinion, taking his advice on new techniques and how he did it on the west coast. The older man wasn't rude about it nor did he play the *I'm older than you, son, and I've seen a lot more* card.

Keith did not know how this clinic handled abandoned baby animals, but pausing for a moment, he entertained a thought. Maybe he did know. It was *his clinic*, and *he* handled baby kittens by taking care of them.

Sissy came back with formula, but immediately left. "Getting charts, boss."

Yes, they would also need charts. Somebody had to track what was happening—feeding times, weight gains, medications and so on.

He should have expected as much. Baby animals were a huge draw. So—given that there were no paying customers in the shop —even though it was closing time on a Friday, he had three staff members appear, ready to help, within moments. "I'll feed a baby kitten."

When at last he had each kitten weighed, all three had found a human willing to snuggle them. He would have said the kitten was "in someone's arms," but it was more accurate to say, "cradled in a hand." These little guys were *that* tiny. But each was with a staff member, making sure it was getting fed, so Keith looked around at the assistants. "Who's taking them home for the weekend?"

"I've got a test on Monday," Garrett replied. He was getting an associates degree at the local community college. Keith understood.

"I have toddlers. They can't handle this," Sissy said. Keith agreed, that wasn't safe for toddlers or kittens.

One by one the assistants fell away, some excuse or other to not take home a trio of tiny foster kittens for the weekend. He should have expected that, but just then the door opened again and in came Emma Kate. "We can take them."

She smiled, and he loved the shape of her mouth, the curve of her cheeks when her smile reached her eyes, the way she crossed her arms at him as though there was no other option.

But he shook his head at her. "Do you know what you're in for? These guys are so young. They need medical attention and feedings every few hours."

"I figured." She didn't uncross her arms, didn't back down from her offer.

He warned her again. "They might not make it. Can you handle that?"

"I don't think there's another option." She held her hands out and took the closest kitten from Garrett as though to defy them both.

Keith only knew that he *didn't* know what he'd gotten into and he *wasn't* sure he could handle it.

❧ 33 ❧

Keith sat on the living room floor beside his wife. Because of Emma Kate, he was sitting on a thick knitted blanket propped up on some very comfy throw pillows they now owned. She said she'd pulled them from a closet at her home and recovered them.

But even the comfy floor set up couldn't quite change the odds of the little creatures. Between them, they had the three kittens cradled in their laps sucking on syringes. It was time-consuming, feeding them every several hours. They were outnumbered—more cats than people—and that made feeding them even more time consuming.

Still, right now—before their stomachs growled and they needed to see to their own dinner—the kittens were cute and so was his wife. She talked softly to the tiny creature as she gently pushed down the plunger. It was the third feeding since they'd arrived home.

He was aiming for a feeding every couple hours, given that it didn't look like they'd eaten any recent time before they'd been dropped at the clinic. Despite his desire to find the mama cat, he was relatively sure that she wasn't around—whether she was hurt or gone or had forcibly been separated from her babies was irrelevant now. There was no way to get them back to her, and he and his new wife were left with "children" possibly even more demanding than a human one. These kittens weren't hungry as though they had missed a feeding, they were hungry as though they had missed an almost fatal amount of feedings.

"Flopsy, Mopsy, and Cottontail," Emma said to him.

He replied almost immediately, "No." The harshness in his voice may have been dialed up a tad too high.

Em frowned and looked at him. "We're not allowed to name them? I know they're fosters, but they need names."

He wondered about that, were they really going to be fosters? Or had they just adopted three kittens? Fosters often stuck. He knew. They didn't really have the budget for a cat, let alone three. In fact, this whole fostering thing for the weekend only worked because he'd managed to scrape all the supplies off the shelf at the clinic.

He and Em had gathered what they needed into a big bag and brought the box of kittens home. If they'd had to pay for everything themselves, well, this charitable act wouldn't have been in the original budget and Em surely would have blown her new inheritance from her sister. Though he'd enjoyed going out for seafood the night before, he was still hoping that check didn't disappear before it had a chance to be appreciated.

"You can't give them three names that go together," he told her.

"Why not? Three little kittens who are obviously from one little litter should have a set of names. How about Hope, Faith, and Joy?" she tried again.

"No," he repeated.

"At least tell me why," she sighed, pushing the plunger ever so slightly and adding a few more drops of thick formula into the infant's mouth. It mewed just a little and licked. *A good sign*, he thought.

"They're too tiny," he told her.

"Too tiny for names?"

"Too tiny to name them as a set of three. What happens if one of them doesn't make it? Or two of them? Then you'll have Flopsy and you'll always know there's no Mopsy and no Cottontail."

"That's morbid." She looked almost horrified, but he had to face the reality of the situation. These little guys did not look good.

He and Em had been late leaving the office tonight. The first thing they'd done was gotten the kittens fed, and the second would be to try to find somebody to foster them. The first had worked, the second had been an epic fail, though Em hadn't seemed to mind.

When everyone else had gone home for the weekend, he and Em had stayed late, defleaing the tiny critters. It had broken his heart to test them for parasites. Giving them medications was almost contraindicated but feeding them would be all for naught if he didn't get them medications to get their systems clear.

He wasn't sure the kittens would make it through the night, let alone the weekend. He didn't want Emma Kate getting her hopes up or losing Mopsy and winding up with just Flopsy and Cottontail. She stared at him like she didn't understand and he waited for her to speak. Em usually had a point.

"If I lose, I'll lose," she said. "And it won't hurt any less because the names don't go together."

"Yeah, I get that. To be fair though, it's harder to adopt out Flopsy and Cottontail if Mopsy's missing."

She frowned at him. "Don't say that about Mopsy! No bad vibes."

He laughed. After changing out the dirty towel in the bottom of the box for a fresh one at the office, he'd brought home a heating pad, too. He discussed making dinner, and Em pointed out she was exhausted, but they had leftovers from seafood the night before.

"*You* have leftovers." He'd eaten everything on his plate. "I'll grill a sandwich and make some soup," he said. It felt good having a few extra cans of soup as well as bread, meat, and cheese in the fridge. Having the pantry built back up again allowed him to let go of a stress he hadn't known he'd been holding. It was always weird moving somewhere new. But despite Em's efforts to settle them in quickly and beautifully, it had taken him a little while to feel at home.

They watched TV that night, or Em did. Instead, he watched Em as she cradled the kitten close to her, trying to keep it warm. One by one giving each of them individual attention.

For all her claims to the contrary, she would be an excellent mother, he thought. She was gentle, did what was needed, offered extra, sweet touches. It was clear that she would love the little kittens back to life if she could.

He didn't know when he fell asleep, but his eyes blinked open as his hand grabbed for the kitten on his chest. He froze and carefully tapped his hand around as he found the tiny thing was missing. That was when Keith realized he was still leaning back against the couch, still on the blanket on the floor, but Emma Kate was shaking him awake.

"I moved the kitten, you don't have to worry about him." Opening his eyes, he looked up at her. If the kitten was okay, why did she look so worried?

"It's the yellow one. He's not breathing!"

❧ 34 ❧

E m woke, once again, to the mewling of tiny kittens.

She tried to pop up and be cheery, but one eye felt like it was glued shut. She forced it open anyway. She'd told Keith they should bring the kittens home. She'd pushed for this, so she should walk the walk.

Besides, what other option had there been for the kittens? Housley? She didn't think the older vet and his wife were willing —and maybe not able—to be getting up every several hours all through the night, all weekend long.

She and Keith and the kittens had made it through the first two nights, and she was counting that as a huge success. Star and Lucky had even managed to gain a little bit of weight over the weekend. The ounces were small, but percentage-wise they were packing it on. Already she couldn't see their ribs quite so clearly. Once they had been washed and their fur had dried, they were quite adorable, not looking quite so mangy. But Peanut, because he'd been the smallest when he came in, still wasn't gaining weight anywhere near as rapidly as his brother and his sister.

As Em pulled herself up to peer down into the box, she noticed it was Star and Lucky who were mewling at her. Peanut lay unmoving. Her heart froze for a moment, and she reminded herself that this was not the first time that Peanut had scared the crap out of her like this.

Unfortunately, she had to ignore the two slightly more healthy kittens, and she reached in, picking up Peanut and cradling him in her hands. He was so tiny, a wisp of dandelion fluff, really. As she rolled him over, she saw that he was in fact breathing, the movement so small it had been hard to see. Her heart began beating again. She was not going to lose him, she promised herself.

She and Keith had both slept on the floor with the kittens on Friday night, but yesterday they'd begun sleeping in shifts. If this is what parenting was like, at least they were getting prepared, she thought. Then she wondered where the hell that thought had come from. She was far too young to have her own children. Maybe she should just be glad that she and Keith worked together well in stressful situations, because this was certainly that.

She'd shaken him awake in the middle of the night Friday, thinking that Peanut had passed. Yet, the young kitten struggled and held on. She'd done the same thing Saturday morning, and by the afternoon she'd felt confident enough about the tiny kitten to risk her own sleep. Emma Kate had slept a good five hours straight yesterday evening, while Keith stayed out here watching over their tiny, fuzzy charges.

It was Sunday, late afternoon, the sun coming in through the windows and the two of them had not left the house all weekend. She'd watched far more TV than she ever had since she turned twelve and was finally allowed to stay home by herself when she was sick.

She and Keith hadn't slept in the same bed, or had sex, since they brought the kittens home. He'd kissed her like he meant it once, but he'd practically fallen asleep right there, with his mouth still pressed to hers. Now, it seemed funny. At the time, not so much.

She stroked Peanut and talked softly to him. The way he

responded—little sighs, more movement—made her think he liked it. She was wondering if she needed to wake Keith. Opting against disturbing her husband's sleep over something the kitten had done many times before, she headed into the kitchen and opened yet another can of kitten formula.

As small as the cans were, the kittens didn't go through it that fast. The quantity they ate at one setting was so tiny she thought of it as virtually immeasurable. She loaded up three separate syringes, each one labeled with the letter of the kitten's name. The syringe wasn't big enough to hold the whole name, just the letter. Jesus, they were tiny.

Keith had laughed at her when she'd gotten out a Sharpie and put a scroll S, P, and L on the syringes. He'd smiled as he said, "Even the medicine droppers are pretty."

She shrugged at him. "Hey, anything that can be pretty is nice. We don't have a ton of money, and I like doing it. It makes the whole thing a little better."

Now, Emma Kate did all the prep with Peanut still in her hand. It wasn't as though he was going to squirm much and fall. She wasn't even forty-eight hours into this foster-kitten-mom thing and she decided she was handling it like a pro. Em headed back out into the living room, while Lucky and Star mewed incessantly, waiting for their food. She offered Peanut whatever drops he would take.

A few minutes in, she frowned. She could handle the noise from the other kittens. In fact, she was grateful for it. They'd been relatively silent when they arrived, and that was a little bit scary. Their noise was a welcome sign.

Peanut, however, was still quiet, and despite the fact that she was dropping food directly into his mouth, he didn't seem to be taking the formula. More of it was dribbling out the sides of his mouth, and down his adorable, fluffy little chin, than was getting in.

An hour later, Emma Kate had set Peanut aside for a while and fed Star and Lucky. Each of the bigger kittens had sucked at the syringe, trying to get as much food as possible, until they had been too fat to take any more and fallen off. Each had curled back into the towel when she set them back into the box with the heating unit underneath it. She'd picked the smaller kitten up and tried again.

Another hour after that, Em had started watching yet another TV show and was still trying to feed Peanut. She'd slowed her pace, hoping to not overwhelm him. She was giving him one drop every minute with the wish that he could keep the tinier amount down. As she watched him struggle, her heart grew heavier and heavier, and she wondered again if she needed to wake Keith.

A few hours later she'd fed Star and Lucky again and was still feeding Peanut one drop at a time, though he was moving less and less. She was on the verge of getting her husband, when he came out of the back room on his own, one hand scratching the back of his head. "How long did I sleep?"

"About six hours."

"Oh my God. You could have woken me," he was looking at her, his head tilting one way or another, as though that might clear the sleep from his brain. "How's it going?"

"I don't know," she whispered. "You tell me."

Suddenly alert, he quickly crossed the space and took the kitten from her. Instead of trying to feed him, Keith immediately placed Peanut on the scale they'd been weighing the kittens with. He'd made them a chart with three columns, and she'd taped it to the countertop. They were recording feedings, amounts, weights, and more.

Keith looked up at her, his expression not comforting. "He hasn't gained any weight. That's not okay for a kitten."

❧ 35 ❧

Em boiled her third pot of water in as many hours. In the original plans, she and Keith would have been sleeping in shifts right now. In fact, right now, she'd be in bed. But in the original plans, all three kittens were doing reasonably well.

Given the state of things, Emma Kate couldn't sleep. Peanut looked worse. Keith had listened to his breathing. It was difficult, she noticed, to hold the frail creature and get the bell of the stethoscope into the right spot on his tiny chest.

"Do you think it's his heart?" she asked.

But Keith shook his head, and in the moment that she'd found relief, her husband shattered it. "I'm listening to his breathing. He sounds pretty bad, Em."

"Oh." It was all she could say. She hadn't thought about that.

Keith wasn't done. He told her, "I can hear his lungs rattling. There's fluid in them and he's struggling just to get air in."

Em had jumped to ask what they could do to reverse that and, sadly, Keith's immediate response had been, "Let him pass peacefully."

But Em wasn't ready to give up. She wasn't a vet like her husband, but she was stubborn as hell. So she demanded action. "No. Give me something I can do."

Keith nodded and set them up with a plan. Together they created a tiny tent with a damp tea towel. They placed Peanut into a small tupperware with a soft washcloth in it. Even that made him look small. Next to the container, under the small tent, was the steaming pan of water.

"It's like a humidifier, turned up by a hundred." He told her. Em was pleased to have action but disliked that she couldn't see the kitten.

"It might open up his air passages, help him breathe better." Keith told her. It didn't look like her husband held out much hope, but Em did, and in spite of the fact that she should have been in bed, she stayed up.

She checked on her tiniest charge every few minutes, setting a soft timer on her phone. She fed Star and Lucky who reached up for the syringes as she pushed formula into their waiting mouths. Their behavior only served to contrast Peanut's lack of effort. But Em kept boiling water and looking under the edges of the tiny tent, watching Peanut as he struggled. She stroked his soft fur, encouraged him to fight, tried to feed him. It wasn't working any better.

"Do we need to go into the office?" she asked, thinking there might be better supplies or a medication they hadn't brought home. But Keith shook his head. She didn't like that. She knew he wasn't trying to stop the kitten from surviving; he would do everything he could, but the fact that there was nothing in the office that would help made Em afraid that there was nothing more that would help, period. So she decided she had only her own dogged persistence and she began boiling the water twice as often.

Eventually Keith looked at her and said, "Give him to me, Em. I'll feed him."

"I've been doing one drop every minute. It seems to help him keep more down."

"I know," was all he replied and she didn't know if that was better or worse.

Watching as her husband put a hand under the heat tent, she held her breath as he pulled out the small kitten. She watched as he gently maneuvered Peanut into position against his chest and began trying to get formula into the tiny mouth. She didn't think she'd ever felt her chest swell with pride like this at the same time her heart was cracking and dripping out between the gaps. She sat on the couch, picking up the two other kittens, knowing that no matter how bad Peanut got, Star and Lucky still needed attention. They weren't out of the woods yet, either, and she wouldn't lose one of them for neglect.

It was a little while later her eyes fluttered and she realized she'd fallen asleep with the kittens on her chest. As she looked around the room, though, she saw at least that Keith was still awake. "How long was I out?"

"Maybe an hour," he said. "I don't think even that long." But the look on his face concerned her. "Em, you need to come say goodbye to Peanut."

"Is he...?"

But Keith shook his head no. "But I don't think he has much longer. He's struggling to breathe."

She nodded, as though she were an adult and she could handle it. But she couldn't. The pressure mounted at the back of her eyes and the world went blurry as the tears formed. Keith had left her with the other two kittens while she slept, so they now squirmed as she began to move, interrupting tiny kitten dreams. It was all she could do to set them into the soft towel and let them sleep on their own. She wanted to hold all three close and never let go. But she couldn't. So she focused on Peanut.

Holding him, stroking his head, saying his name and telling him how much she wanted him to stick around were the most she could do. But fifteen minutes later, he breathed his last. Keith, who had been sitting next to her and occasionally petting Peanut as she held him now moved to take the tiny body out of her grip, but she shook her head "no" as the tears began to flow freely.

"He's gone, Em." Keith told her.

"I know," she replied, the sound harsher than it needed to be. She reminded herself that Star and Lucky were back in the box, doing all right. But she knew she wasn't. Her mother hadn't wanted pets in the house. Em had goldfish as a kid and she'd always told herself she'd have dogs and cats when she grew up, when she had her own place, when she got married. But now, she was wondering about that decision. She'd had kittens for less than two full days and she was in tears, devastated from loss.

"This is why I didn't want to bring them home," Keith said softly as he watched her, tears running down her face making damp splotches on the front of her shirt.

"Why?" She said. "What would've happened to them if we hadn't brought them home?"

"We would've found someone. I didn't want this for you."

"I'm sorry you have to watch this. You can leave." When he didn't respond, she fought the tears but it didn't work. So she spoke through them. "Do you think I can't handle it?"

He waved his hand up and down at her. "Is this *handling it*?"

"Yes!" she almost yelled it, gripping Peanut's tiny body a little bit closer. "It *is!* I knew this could happen, but now I can say I did my best. I'll get through it, but don't shut me down. Hell," she paused, not wanting to admit the truth as her eyes darted to the box where she still had two tiny charges to look after. They weren't out of the woods yet. "It could happen again. I know it. You don't have to protect me, Keith." She was getting angry now, maybe from real irritation, but maybe from lack of sleep. Em couldn't tell. So she sat on the couch with her tears and her grief and she watched her husband pace the room.

She was just about to tell him to take his judgment and at least go where she couldn't see him, when he spoke.

"You're right. I don't need to protect you."

Something about the way he said it made her wary. Was he

acknowledging that she was a full person, adult, and capable of her own decisions? Or was he saying that it wasn't his place? As mad as she'd been, she understood he was still her husband and she wanted him to think about her that way.

As her anger began slipping into fear, he spoke again, shattering her world just a little more.

He had a sheen of tears in his own eyes as he stood over where she lay across the couch, the tiny kitten still clutched close. "Maybe I wasn't protecting you. Maybe I was trying to protect myself from seeing you hurt."

❄ 36 ❄

Emma Kate sat at her desk in Melanie's office feeling more than just a little out of sorts. It took her a while to figure out why that was.

It wasn't simply that she was wearing her nice work clothes again for the first time in days—she'd spent the entire weekend in yoga pants and pajama tops. And it wasn't that she was out of the house—something else she hadn't done since Friday evening. No, it was that no one was mewing for her attention. It was that she wasn't constantly looking at her husband to see if he'd fallen asleep or checking to see if maybe she had.

Em almost laughed. Children were exhausting. Then she almost cried. Peanut was gone.

She couldn't tell if it was a male versus female thing or just a Keith versus Emma Kate thing, but while she had sat on the floor and cried, Keith called the Barkers and explained what happened. It occurred to her then that she and Keith hadn't asked their very kind landlords if they could have kittens on the property, but in that moment, she was very afraid that it would turn into an issue.

She reminded her beating-too-fast heart that the Barkers knew from the first moment at least that they were renting to a veterinarian. They didn't know they were also renting to his wife, but she was probably the much bigger surprise than the fact that there were foster kittens in their tiny house.

But Keith didn't seem to have those same concerns—that they wouldn't be allowed to have the kittens and she would have to sleep at the vet's clinic for five weeks—and he simply asked if they could bury Peanut under a tree in their backyard. Not only did the Barkers agree, but they showed up.

Mr. Barker—despite his arthritis—brought a shovel and helped Keith break the hard ground. They went a couple of feet deep and buried Peanut in the friendly spot. Emma Kate found a rock and a second sharper rock which she used to scratch a P onto the first. It was simple and seemed to fit in with the fact that, when she looked over Peanut's grave, there was nothing behind it but open land.

It was sad but heartfelt and seemed appropriate for a kitten who had yet to reach half a pound in weight. As they started to shovel the dirt back over the tiny body, Keith had only said "Peanut, you will be missed. You were loved by me and by Emma Kate."

Emma Kate had not been able to say anything as she was practically in tears again. She hadn't known the kitten for two full days, but she was certain she would grieve him much longer than that. In the meantime, she and Keith had work to do. There were two more kittens that still needed their attention almost every moment of the day. She would have brought them into work with her, but they would've mewed in the background of what should be "professional" phone calls.

She wasn't confident how Melanie would have reacted and Keith was a veterinarian. So taking his box of kittens back into his office on Monday morning was probably what they expected of him. They may have been shocked that it took three weeks for them to wind up fostering kittens, but Em was glad they'd at least had that time. She'd gotten almost nothing done that weekend—not on the house, not cooking, not just playing around. And, since the vet's office was where the kittens had originally been dropped off and they were getting professional care, that's where they belonged for the day, even if she felt a little bereft.

Emma Kate, for one, was grateful not to have to give them medications they didn't like. They would go to work with Keith every day this week and she wouldn't have to contend with their pills again, not until Sunday, though she would be spending her nights waking up and rotating feedings with her husband. She'd organized their schedule and posted it on the fridge with a pen so they could each check off what was done and see what was next. She even managed to arrange it so they could both get enough sleep. So she was here at work, all put together and ready to go, and so was Keith.

She wasn't sure what was distracting her more from her job today, the fact that she lost a kitten, the fact that she'd made up a schedule almost hour by hour for the care and feeding of their remaining tiny furry children—children she'd not expected to have—or whether it was the memory of Keith's kiss as she dropped him off at work today.

She'd had to drive him to work since he couldn't very well put kittens on the back of his bike. She'd head home from here after lunch, take a short break and maybe even grab a quick nap. But then she'd change into her scrubs and head into the clinic for a few hours of extra work. It was an odd set up, but for right now, it was paying the bills. And she would bring Keith and Lucky and Star home after their shifts were finished.

But as he had turned to climb out of the car, the kittens cradled in his lap, he'd paused. Then he'd turned back toward her, his expression one she hadn't been able to figure out. Reaching out toward her, Keith had softly threaded his fingers into her hair, gathering it loosely into his fist—not holding her in place but holding *onto* her as though he was struggling to let go.

Then he'd kissed her so softly and so sweetly and said "I—"

and he stopped, then started again, and told her, "I'm proud of you."

She wasn't sure what the pause meant, but it had made her heart stutter. When she looked at him, tilting her face, questioning with her eyes, he added, "You're strong. You did what needed to be done even though you were clearly grieving really hard. You got me to sleep, you made a schedule, and there are two little kittens who are alive now because of that. I'm impressed."

She'd smiled as her heart melted and said only, "Same goes to you. We got this."

He'd grinned and then her hot, and wholly unexpected husband, had hopped out of the car and wished her a good day as though he hadn't just turned her inside out.

So she'd spent the day making calls for Mrs. Forsythe's catering services and tried to find a venue for the weekend Clara Deacon wanted her event hosted. She was poring through albums Melanie kept of venue options, room size, location, parking, entry and more as she tried to find what would work best. But her mind kept drifting to the old cars and tattered antiques.

When she looked up, she asked Melanie, "Do you mind if I take a personal break for a call? It might be anywhere from five to fifteen minutes."

Melanie tapped at her screen for a minute, and then nodded. "It should be fine. Go ahead. Do you want to go into the kitchen? No one is in the house and you'd have some privacy."

"Thank you, that would be great."

Em could see her boss was curious, but she wasn't quite willing to share it yet. So she headed behind Melanie's desk and up the two stairs into the kitchen. Closing the door behind her, she stared into the silent house for a moment as she screwed up her courage. Then she scrolled through her contacts and dialed up her thesis advisor.

🎐 37 🎐

Keith was still having heart palpitations. He'd almost told her he loved her. Right there in the car as he'd kissed her. It had seemed so natural and almost necessary, then he'd frozen as the words started to tumble out of his mouth.

He'd known how he felt for a little while now. Even when he'd been saying that he wasn't quite sure, he'd been questioning it. But, this weekend when he held her while she cried, he felt it. And when she yelled at him for not giving her the appropriate space to grieve and that she was handling it just fine, he'd almost smiled. Not because she was crying, not even because she was right, but because he'd *known*.

He'd originally read her tears as weakness when she was simply letting out her grief. She'd gotten right back up, made the next feedings on time, and even cuddled the tiny kittens while she cried. It was a mistake he wouldn't make again.

The kittens needed that attention, he knew. In fact, though it shouldn't have surprised him, it did. They were getting more attention at home in the evening from Emma Kate than they were getting in the office during the day from the trained, professional veterinary staff. His only concern now was how he was going to convince Emma Kate to give them to other, real, forever homes. How could she send them off to be adopted when the time came?

Then, Keith decided to quit lying to himself. It was going to be just as hard for him to send the kittens off to other homes as it would be for her, and that was even if it was for her. He didn't know. He hadn't seen her in action on that front yet. But the fact of the matter was, almost four weeks into his marriage, he was sold. He had no idea how he'd gotten so lucky—or so smart—to find the perfect woman in the middle of Vegas. She was nothing like anyone he'd ever dated before, and that was part of what made her perfect.

Keith Lee would never have chosen a Southern Belle. Though Emma Kate flatly denied that she was one—calling herself a bit of a rebel and a wild child—her love of sweet tea and home décor and her lilting southern accent belied her heritage. She was the embodiment of what he had always heard about Southern belles: Spines of steel in the face of adversity.

He headed out of the surgery suite, peeling his gloves and dropping them in the biohazard bin. He'd done a tough spay on a large female pure bred who'd had too many litters already. He was grateful the family who'd found her was making her life better from here on out.

There would always be puppies in the world, he thought. Mixed breeds tended to live longer and have better health over-all, and that's what most of the feral puppies were. So he was always grateful to see a mother dog taken out of rotation, pure bred or not. He'd change his stance when the puppy supply started running low. It was too hard on the dogs.

Cleaning up in the surgical sink, Keith gave his hands a thor-ough scrub while his assistant and two volunteers took the large dog back to a resting room where she could recover and be watched carefully. He'd checked to be sure she was coming out of the anesthesia okay and he set a timer to check back in. He had to set the timer because he knew how easy it was to get distracted with new patients, emergencies, and just the general talk around the office.

Sure enough, once he was in the back hallway, he encountered Housley. "Keith, you've got to come see this."

Uncertain what kind of "see this" Housley was talking about, Keith held his breath as he followed his partner down the hall. Stopping at his office door, Housley flung it open and beamed with pride. "Your wife reorganized everything. Emma Kate is a charm."

Keith knew that, and he released all his worries and smiled. "She got you organized?"

"Not only did she get me organized, she got me so organized that I can't get unorganized again."

Keith frowned, but Housley kept waxing poetic about Emma Kate's good work. "She seemed to realize that doing two steps was one step too many for me—maybe even *two* steps too many. So now, if you look at my desktop, I have a clearly labeled *inbox*, *outbox*, and *right now*. She told the front office to come pick up the outbox, so I don't even have to return them anymore. Which is good, because part of the problem was that I wasn't returning the files properly and they were getting mixed up with the old files."

Keith was opening his mouth, when the old man added more. "She also left a pen attached to a stack of post-its here. Because I was wasting time not knowing why certain files were left. She got the front staff to agree—because it makes their lives easier too, not to have to hunt me down and see if it was done—that they will just put a note on the file when they leave it. Everything is already getting done better. I can find things and the staff is happier, too!"

Keith knew just how good his wife was. He was just surprised Housley now knew it, too. "Good," he replied. "I'm glad she's been a help."

"She's been a freaking godsend." Keith grinned at the older man's almost awkward use of "freaking." But once again, Housley beat him to the moment. "Speaking of, can I get her to take those kittens of yours home tonight? I just got a call for the Garrett Farm. They'd like us to come out ASAP."

"What do they have?"

"Horse is lame, and it's happened before. He's making me concerned. I'd love if you go out with me. We haven't seen them yet and I'd like to introduce them to you personally. Get you up to speed on Sovereign's Dubloon and his lameness issues."

Sometimes the way Housley talked made Keith afraid the old man was going to retire much earlier than in the proposed "few years." He was working very hard to get Keith introduced to as many clients as possible, face-to-face with Housley there, and Keith appreciated that effort. It didn't have to be done. But it also made it hard to say No.

He'd expected to work long, late hours this first year or two. But when he'd made those plans, he hadn't known he'd have Emma Kate in his life. He'd thought that if he was dating someone—a big *if*, since he didn't have time to date much at all —she'd have to understand what he was doing. Never in his wildest dreams had he thought he'd have a wife when he was just starting the job.

"I'll drop you at home after," Housley sweetened the deal, and Keith found himself agreeing.

When Emma Kate showed up a few hours later Keith was afraid she wouldn't have any work, but Housley didn't hesitate. "Can you, please, rearrange the medicine cabinets?"

"Oh, thank god," one of the assistants almost shouted it as she walked by. She even punched her hands into the air. Keith knew the medicine cabinets were a source of constant irritation for the whole staff. Though they'd originally been organized, as new medications had hit the market, they'd gone where they fit and not where they really belonged. When they added in the issue that many needed to be refrigerated or required special handling, where a specific kind of medication would be shelved was now a game of rote memorization.

But Keith was glad Emma Kate was being appreciated. Still, Housley didn't tell her that she was taking the kittens home and managing the feeding by herself. Keith had to do that.

He found her in the hallway, later, when they were alone. She was up on the lower counter on her knees, her head inside the upper cabinet. Keith looked up and down the hallway, making sure everyone was somewhere else and not watching him ogle his own wife's ass. "Em?"

"What?" She never said "huh?" or anything that wasn't a real word—his Southern Belle in denial. For all her rebellion, she was right back where she'd started. When he didn't answer right away, she carefully tipped back and pulled her head out of the cabinet. "What do you need?"

"Housley is taking me out to the Garrett farm tonight. They have a horse that has come up lame again, for no known reason."

She only nodded.

"Can you take the kittens home and get them fed by yourself?" He was cringing as he asked it.

Em frowned back at him. "Of course. Why are you looking at me that way?"

"Because I hate to ask you to do this."

"It's your job." She said it matter of factly and stuck her head back into the cabinet, because apparently organizing the medications wasn't enough. She was scrubbing out the cabinets and making labels. She'd put the allergy meds together and the antibiotics on another shelf and he could see she'd researched all the medications and had extra labels to say what could be used in more than one way. Because that's what Emma Kate did. In her rebel heart, she was just a fixer.

And her statement that "it was his job" was eating at him. Because visiting the horse was his job, but he was starting to feel like it was his job to ask her to do more and more for him. But he wanted his job to be "Husband."

He had it bad. Luckily, he was already married to her. He just had to figure out how to make it work. However, telling her he loved her when she had a white bleach sponge in one gloved hand and his eyes at about the same level as her ass was not the way to go about it properly. So he said, "Housley will drop me at home tonight. I'll see you then."

He walked away and began plotting.

❦ 38 ❦

Emma Kate was shocked. She'd logged into her channel and found her online numbers were up again. She had, in the last week, gained half again as many viewers as she'd had before, a massive increase.

Though the number of views on the dorm room videos had gone up, that was pretty clearly caused by new viewers heading back through her old material and catching her early videos. It was the videos she'd posted from the tiny house that were catching everyone's attention.

Comments abounded that "I would never have thought of hanging the potholders as art. Now I have to look around and see what I already have." More comments added "I have nails and a hammer, if I can find a grouping of something, I can make a wall display for free!" Emma Kate had specifically mentioned several other objects that could be used that way and she encouraged her viewers to do something different from her potholders. A few had even posted links she followed to their own pages elsewhere on the web, with pictures of what they'd done.

They bore a hashtag one of the viewers had shared, #InspiredByEmmaKate.

She almost teared up. She wasn't bringing cash or the kind of

Martha Stewart level of dedication that led to projects like washing your pine needles. But her creativity was her sweet spot.

It had taken well over a year of continuing to post videos even though almost no one had been watching. And it had taken getting stuck in a tiny house with no style to start making a name for herself. It felt good. She clicked the page.

Her episode of painting the walls in the main room had garnered more and more thumbs up. And more comments.

"Thank you for the tip. That explains why my last job went so far awry, and it will keep it from happening again on the next one."

"I didn't know about the returned color shelf! I'll have to try it."

One guy even proclaimed that he'd gotten his full house painted for under twenty dollars of paint by buying on the mismatched color shelf. "I picked walls based on square footage and how much I had of that color. So not all the walls are the same but it looks damn good!" he said. Emma Kate had cringed. Usually there were a few good colors on the return shelf, but a lot were returned because they were unattractive or because the peppermint green, a hot trending color, had come out more olive. And Olive had been over a long time ago. Still she hit the link.

On his own webpage, titled: Man on a Mission, he chronicled being a Christian stay at home dad on a tight budget. Apparently, like her, he had time but not money. He'd hit three different stores. And Emma Kate had to admit, the two blues in his sons' room looked amazing.

Em was smiling, but in the background, she was being mewed at. She'd only spent a few moments checking her information online, but it was too long for kittens. While she'd expected Keith to be home with her tonight, he was now going to run late.

Knowing the kittens were hungry but trying to be efficient, she opened two cans of soup, added water, and put the whole thing in a pot on the stove to sit. She didn't turn on the heat. She next pulled out slices of bread—four for Keith, two for her—and built sandwiches. She stacked meats and cheese and buttered the outsides of the bread. Em even set them in a pan, ready to be grilled. She had no idea when he'd make it back but she was hoping they could have hot food in a matter of five to ten minutes whenever he did finally arrive.

Once that was done, she had an idea. She knew the kittens were hungry and waiting to be fed, but she made them wait another five minutes. For a moment her thoughts swerved. Unlike Peanut, they were healthy and could wait just a short while. Keith had pushed her to not feed them the moment they mewed, every time they mewed. Since she was still on schedule, Emma Kate changed out of her scrubs and into clean jeans and a plain sweater. She redid her makeup, grabbed her lights and her tripod, and all of the equipment she needed.

Putting the cardboard box up on the table, she surveyed her scene. Though she wanted something better, shinier, flashier to put the kittens in, she always thought it was better to tell it like it was. So she turned on the camera and said, "Hello, everybody. We have a very interesting episode today. I'd like you to meet Star and Lucky." She pointed to the cardboard box, and then, one by one, pulled out each kitten, pointed to the little white dot on Star's forehead. "This is the mark that inspired her name. These are my foster kittens, so they're getting relatively simple names. I'm assuming they'll get changed when they go to their forever homes. Now, we got these guys because my husband is a veterinarian."

Em paused. As soon as the words were out of her mouth, she knew she was going to have to go back and edit that out. Her sisters sometimes watched her videos. If they saw her comment on her *husband* being a veterinarian she would be up shit creek without a paddle faster than she could snap her fingers. So she made a mental note about editing and not mentioning her husband, and started over. "These guys were dropped off at our

local veterinary office. They need to be fed every several hours."
She held up one of the spare cans of milk. "You can get this
kitten formula at your local pet store. This is a high-end brand
because it's from the veterinary office, but—" She'd almost said
my husband again. "You can buy other formula that's really just as
good, at your local big box store or maybe even at your grocery.
So if you're thinking about fostering, it doesn't have to be crazy
expensive."

Next, she held up one of the feeding syringes for the camera.
"See how tiny this is? This is about how much they're eating.
They're probably right around three weeks old—that's the
assessment from the veterinarian, not me. There were three of
them but we lost Peanut yesterday," she told her online crowd
even as she felt the tears well up. "I've been up every several
hours and catching sleep when I can. And crying..." She leaned
in toward the camera. "It's really hard losing a kitten, even a
foster. If you think there aren't dark bags under my eyes, be
aware that is due to the miracle of a heavy dose of concealer."

She went on to show her viewers how to feed the kittens,
that they had the box with the towel and the heating pad underneath. She showed the small toys in the box and discussed how
long they slept in each cycle.

The door opened while she was in the middle of the
sentence. She kept going even though Keith came in and spotted
her working and waved. At least he didn't yell out. Em made a
low motion for him to stay back, and he caught on quite quickly,
coming in and sitting on the couch when he normally would
have checked on the kittens or kissed her hello. However, seeing
that both she and the babies were on camera, he stopped where
he was, leaned against the sofa, folded his own arms and
watched.

Emma Kate paused to give herself a piece she could edit
from and started her last section over again. "Once these guys
reach eight weeks old—which will be in about five weeks from
now—they'll be available for adoption. If you're interested, you

can PM me. And here's my email." She pointed downward into space to where she would edit in her public email across the bottom of the screen.

Off in her peripheral vision, Keith's eyebrow rose, but she didn't acknowledge it. She'd explain later that she had a separate email. "Now, be aware, if you ask for one of these kittens, I'm going to be checking out every aspect of your background. I'll know if you were a third grade bully or not, and I'll try to find the best homes for the kittens. That may have to do with travel, so please don't be disappointed if you don't get a kitten. I suspect I'll have more fosters in the future, so feel free to ask to be put on my list and, next time, I'll let you know first."

Picking up Lucky, she held him belly first toward the camera and couldn't help herself from smiling at his on screen cuteness. He was a natural. She waved his paw goodbye as she noticed Star starting to peek over the edge of the box. She caught herself turning to look at the tiny cat even as she clicked her remote to turn off the camera.

At last she looked up at Keith and smiled at him. "Thank you. That will be much easier to edit without you calling out as you came through the door."

He came over toward her and ignored the tiny kitten for a moment while he kissed her hello and turned her world upside down. Her head swam and she made sure she didn't drop Lucky while she swooned.

She still wasn't quite sure what to do with Keith Lee. Emma Kate had not seen him coming.

"So, you're really going to give them away to new homes? I was sure we were going to wind up with two cats."

Smiling, she shook her head at him. "If we don't give these guys away, how will we be ready to foster the next ones?"

❦ 39 ❦

K eith smiled over at his wife. He was sitting at his desk, and she was at hers. They faced different walls, basically sitting back to back. Once the desks had been assembled it was clear there wasn't enough room to put them side by side.

He wanted to add a bookshelf or anything else to give them more usable space and make the room seem like more of a real office, but it wasn't in the budget yet. He should be mad that he was paying off a Vegas wedding he didn't even remember, but it was hard to be upset when that bill had gotten him the sweet, fierce, surprising blonde sitting caddy-corner behind him.

She was tapping at her keyboard for a moment before she spoke over her shoulder at him. "I have no fewer than a hundred requests for kittens who won't be available for several more weeks." Turning smoothly in her office chair, feet up as she swished around, she smiled at him. "A lot of people are requesting to take both of them. Do they need to go together?"

He, too, pushed off and rotated to face her as he shook his head. "Cats are often solitary. If you're willing to split them up, you can make two people happy. It probably means we wind up delivering two different kittens in two different directions, but..."

She was nodding along as he spoke, clearly considering what he was saying. "What am I even looking for in a good future cat owner? I mean, I know I'm looking for nice people who don't have any criminal histories. But do I want people who will keep the kittens indoor or outdoor? Should the person have other pets? I don't even know. Will you help me?"

"Of course." He smiled and nodded at her and wondered if he could say no to her for anything. "Are you doing criminal background investigations?"

"You know I am," she smiled, and he thought, he did know she was. That was Emma Kate. She had taken to these two little kittens with a fierce form of motherhood even though they were fosters. Furthermore, she'd impressed him by making sure that everyone understood that they were, in fact, fosters, and would not be staying with them. Whether or not they would be hers forever, she was not going to let them go anywhere she did not feel was the best possible place. Em would probably drive two or three hours to meet up with someone for a kitten exchange, and send them off with a personal homemade pack, full of kitten toys, a favorite blankie, and treats. All wrapped up with a bow. Keith had no doubt.

"Well, once they pass your criminal background check, forward those emails you like on over to me." He then mentioned a few other flags she might want to look out for.

"What? Are you serious? People do that with kittens?" Her mouth was open, her eyes wide with horror.

He wished he hadn't said anything but wouldn't want her to find out later she hadn't known what to look for. "Yeah. You have to watch out. Puppies and kittens can both get taken advantage of that way. It's probably best if you charge a re-homing fee—"

"I didn't say that on my video. Crap." She was looking around the room, thinking.

Keith thought it through, too. "But you didn't say you'd give them for free either. Anyone who's good for the kitten will understand, and probably a bunch will expect it," he told her.

"For a small reason, it's insurance that the people who take the kitten have enough money to take care of it. For the bigger reason, the fee makes it a lot less likely that your happy couple is actually taking your kitten to become a bait animal for a fighting dog ring."

He watched as her face fell while she absorbed all that. She was probably thinking that she could keep these kittens out of the fighting ring, but that she couldn't save them all. Keith wished he hadn't told her, but anyone giving away puppies or kittens needed to know that handing them over for free often meant some of them would wind up in bad places.

"Why don't you read me some of your best candidates?" he suggested, hoping to take her mind off the horrors of the underground dog-fighting world. He listened as she tapped her keys and she moved her face in a little closer to the screen. Her voice didn't sound so horrified by the world as she started reading a couple of them out loud.

"That last one sounds really good," he offered. "They sound *normal*. They sound like they've wanted a kitten for a while, and like they're ready for one. That reads like they know what a kitten's going to do, too."

"It's going to tear up the house." Her voice was wry from experience.

He nodded. As Lucky and Star had gotten older, they'd first shown they could escape their box by mewing from the tops of the curtains in the living room one morning. Em had rolled over and shoved his arm asking, "Why are they crying like that?"

They'd both found out once they located the two, clinging for their lives at the top of the curtain rod. They'd gotten up, but down was apparently harder. Neither he nor Em had even realized they could escape their cardboard box on their own. He'd brought a crate home from the office that night. Two kittens had not been amused.

And Emma Kate had already had a couple moments where she'd had a kitten ripping small snags into the pretty cover that she'd put on the couch as one or the other decided that claws were too sharp and old covered couches were just too pretty. He'd expected her to get angry, but she'd handled it beautifully.

In a few more moments of reading off candidates' emails to him she seemed happier, and he stopped worrying that he'd given her nightmares. As he watched her though, she didn't seem to notice.

Somehow, he'd made it another two weeks without telling her how he felt, and he was done with it—done with holding back, done with pretending they were going along with how things were. He wasn't. He knew what he wanted now, even if he'd had no clue a mere six weeks ago. Things had changed and he'd be a fool if he didn't grab life by the tail. Still, it had been hard to just come out and tell her.

Whereas the last time a chance had presented itself, he'd fallen back on the old "he was crazy about her" and not used the L word. This time he was ready to shout it. Only no one had bothered to ask, or even get into a sticky situation where he'd have to say it or back off. It simply had gone unsaid, resting at the bottom of his chest, waiting for the right moment to burst forth.

Most likely they hadn't been getting enough sleep. But this last week, the kittens had passed a mark where they were at least able to sleep six hours in a row. The problem was, either he or Emma Kate was stumbling into bed two hours later than the other, having stayed up for a last feeding. The other one was getting up two hours earlier to feed the kittens again.

It didn't leave much time at all for the two of them to just be together. It must be what parenting was like. So Keith decided that the house was quiet right now, and that might be all he got. Dialing up his playlist, he tapped the key and let the music pour out of his speakers.

With a wide smile that sparkled in her eyes, Em turned around again. "What's that?"

"Romantic music playlist?" He didn't know why he said it

with a question. *No questions*, he told himself as he held out his hand toward her.

Though she clearly had no idea what was going on, she put her hand in his. That's what it was all about, he thought. Reaching for the other one, for no reason, simply because you trusted them and wanted to see what could happen.

Tugging her to her feet, he marveled at how easily she slipped into his arms to dance with him. The room was too small for anything showy, but he didn't need showy. He needed close.

When the first song ended and slid easily into another sweet, low, heady song, he thanked the gods that he'd made up this list earlier. His gratitude only lasted a moment though, as Emma Kate pushed up onto her toes, pressing her lips softly to his.

He didn't mean to do any of it, but he couldn't help it. One move from her and he just reacted. His hands slid into her hair, cradling her head, holding her close. He sucked in a breath as she clutched at his waist and moved closer to him. The feel of her changed everything in his world, there was nothing beyond this room and the two of them, nothing that mattered anyway.

He leaned into her, into the kiss, his tongue searching and finding hers, finding *her*. They were reaching for each other and he couldn't tell if he was moving against her or if she was pressing herself into him. He sighed into the kiss, wanting it to never end even as his hands moved, over her shoulders, down the front of her shirt, quickly popping buttons open.

When her fingers found his waist again, he felt flesh on flesh and turned his head as she peeled his shirt upward. With one arm, he pulled her closer, while the other chucked his shirt and then hers into a corner somewhere. She was wearing a short skirt and leggings, and he was peeling them down her legs. The feel of lace on his fingertips telling him he was successful in getting her underwear down with the leggings.

She'd gone for his belt buckle, soft fingers plying the leather until it opened. For a moment, he'd fleetingly thought about the condom in his wallet and then his whole body relaxed at the memory that she'd gone on the pill. For him. For them. He'd never had sex without a condom before her, and it felt he belonged here with her.

Em pushed his pants down, leaving him naked as her mouth roamed across his chest. The flick of her tongue on his skin made it difficult to do something as simple as step out of his jeans. So when she pushed him down into his office chair, he went willingly.

His eyes glazed, Keith watched in awe as she climbed over him. Her shirt was gone, her bra straps hanging low and exposing her breasts to him. She held her skirt up in one hand, as she moved to join them together. It was the sexiest thing he'd ever seen.

But he sucked in a breath and found the strength to say, "No!"

❧ 40 ❧

Em froze. She'd been hot, so hot, wanting Keith. She
needed her husband when they hadn't had a chance to
touch each other for days.

But now she sat across his lap, basically naked and open for
his touch... and he wasn't touching her. He'd even said, "No."

With a deep breath, she stepped back. Though her legs were
shaky and her heart stuttered as her eyes filled, wondering what
she'd done wrong, Em turned away and tugged her bra straps
back up.

"No." He said it again, and she couldn't even process it. Then
his hands were on her shoulders and he was turning her to face
him before she even got her second bra strap back up. She was a
mess and she didn't understand.

"Not in here." He was kissing her, whispering to her as he did
it, melting her all over again.

His hands roved her still bare skin, igniting her again.

"I need you, Emma Kate, but I want something more. Not
fast in the office chair. I want you." The words came out like
breath, feather light across her soul.

She nodded as she kissed him back and fought the tear that
fell from the corner of her eye.

"I'm sorry. Don't cry. I didn't mean to scare you."

"It's okay," she whispered back to the man standing so close in front of her. But in a flash of a moment, she was in his arms again, warm and held tight.

She gasped as he tugged her upward, lifting her feet and kissing her quiet with a whispered, "Shhhh," as he carried her out the office door and into their bedroom.

Keith set her gently on the bed, across the comforter, and then leaned back and closed the door. There was no one to lock it against, but maybe keeping the sounds in here would keep the kittens quiet. She was reaching up for him when he shook his head again. Only this time she trusted him and waited.

Slowly, he peeled her bra away and flung it behind him without looking. She would have laughed, but his hands were already tugging at the waist of her skirt and she was wriggling out of it, his touch lighting her already hot skin on fire.

Keith peeled the fabric slowly down to the tips of her toes then pushed her knees apart and kissed his way up the inside of her thigh. She couldn't breathe, just watched as his mouth closed over her and felt his tongue tentatively touch her, then again with more force.

Her head fell back and she breathed his name over and over until the feeling of his touch spread everywhere and she arched her spine and called out with her orgasm.

He climbed up on the bed beside her but didn't move to join them together, even though she wanted that, wanted to feel him inside her. Her hand reached out to his shoulder, hoping to pull him closer, before she could find words, or trust that any words she found would have actual meaning.

But he resisted.

For the first time, she had the clear thought, *What is he up to?*

He'd never pulled away from her before, but now, as she rolled to face him, a question in her eyes, she saw the tentative look in his. "Keith?"

Em watched as he took a breath and she wondered again what this was about. It only took a moment.

"I love you." He paused a moment and said it again. "Emerson Kate Mayfair, I love you."

This time the words gushed out of him as though he couldn't hold them back any longer, the heat in his eyes leaving her no question that he meant it. He didn't want anything in return, just to tell her how he felt. It washed over her and tugged her under, stealing her breath and robbing her of the right words in return.

This time, when she reached for him, he fell into her arms, willing and strong. His belief made all of it headier and changed her escape from reality into a new reality. One where the man robbing her of breath as he pushed inside her *loved her*.

She chanted his name as they moved together, lost in the feeling of the two of them. His fingers clutched at her hip and she wanted a bruise there, shaped like his touch, as though that would help her come back to this moment later.

Holding onto him for everything she was worth, Em had no idea if she raked her fingernails down his back or screamed loud enough to be heard beyond the walls of the little house. She only knew that she reached, trying to get deeper and closer to this man than she ever had to anyone before.

"Em!" He was practically yelling her name as his hands framed her face and held her where she looked up at him. She was watching as he came apart, as he moved one last time, then once more. He was watching as she did, her hands twisting at the covers beneath her as though that would anchor her to earth.

Her breathing was labored as she came back into her own body. It was harder still because Keith was crashed on top of her, but she liked that, and wrapped an arm around him to keep him there. Her head was hanging off the edge of the bed and she could only guess they'd scooted their way across and almost off the other side when they hadn't been paying attention.

Well, she'd been paying attention, just not to her position on the bed.

It wasn't heat that flared in her at the sudden and clear thought that he'd said he loved her. It was satisfaction, contentment, some kind of fire at being loved—really loved for just what she was—for the first time in her life.

As his breathing evened out, Keith's hand came up and combed through her hair. She turned her head at his touch, leaning into it and practically purring.

"You good?" he asked softly, his mouth finding her temple and pressing a soft kiss there.

"Better than good," she murmured back. Surely he felt her sigh, they were pressed so close.

She had no idea how long they laid there, entangled in so many ways, but she offered a real, put-out sigh when she heard the mewing of a kitten.

Keith laughed. "No rest for the weary." But he rolled up and off the bed and headed out the door with a smile and an, "I'll get them."

"You better put some clothes on. Kittens are dangerous against naked men!" She hollered out to his retreating—and very fine—backside. But as she watched, he slipped across the hall and disappeared into the office, presumably to get his clothes.

"I'm the only one who gets to scratch your back," she whispered it to herself as she flopped back on the bed.

In a few moments, she heard him opening the latch of the crate and talking softly to two little kittens who were still mewing at him, not satisfied until they'd been fed to the point of fullness. If she hadn't already known she was in love with him, she would have known it in that instant.

She would have loved for him to stay in bed with her, but he wasn't wired that way. He was a veterinarian because he automatically took care of every creature around him. Including her. He changed all his plans for her. Eventually, when they'd shared their bank accounts, she'd seen what space he had on his credit cards. He hadn't needed her. He could have done fine on his own, but he had a new wife, even if he wasn't sure how it had happened, and he'd saved her as surely as he was saving the little kittens, one step at a time.

Em rolled out of bed, wishing she could climb back into it with Keith for a repeat performance. But she promised that she would do that later—soon. As soon as possible. But she also promised that her own performance would be better next time.

So she pulled her pajamas out from under her pillow and climbed into them, then she walked out into the main room where Keith was sitting on the couch. Lucky was walking on his shoulders, back and forth and clearly using his claws while Keith focused on feeding Star. She was on her back, still fitting into his one hand, even though she'd outgrown Emma Kate's palm a while ago. He was using a bottle now to feed her, as they'd finally graduated from syringes and needing to measure every drop that went into them.

He looked up as Em entered the room and from the look in his eyes it was clear he spotted that she wasn't wearing a bra. It was clear he was thinking back to just fifteen minutes earlier when they'd been yelling each other's names and crashing back to earth in each other's arms.

She sat down on the couch next to him, tugging her feet up under her. Then she touched the side of his face, pulling him to her for a kiss that had her reeling. When she finally pulled back, she looked him in the eyes. "I love you, Keith Lee."

"You don't have to say it back—"

"I know." She cut him off and smiled. "I love you."

Then she almost screamed as Lucky walked from Keith's shoulders onto hers, his tiny claws like needles. She reached up and tried to pull him off. She tried to ignore that Keith was trying not to laugh. "Give me that second bottle," she sighed to him and began to feed the tiny kitten.

❧ 41 ❧

E m rushed in the door at Bobby's Pizza, hauling her purse strap over her shoulder. She hated to be late. It only added to her ongoing reputation as the family screw-up. Couldn't even show up for lunch on time. Part of it was because she was the baby and was behind her sisters the whole time she was growing up. She'd wanted to be like them and had gotten into a heap of trouble just trying to keep up. The other part of her reputation was well-earned.

Emma Kate was aware that she'd have to be hyper vigilant if she was going to fix everyone else's perception of her. She knew it would take time for them to realize she wasn't the screw up anymore. If she was persistent, one day it would happen. But today was not going to be that day.

Melanie had needed a few extra calls, and since Em wasn't coming back in the afternoon, she'd needed to stay late and finish up before she left the office for lunch. Bailey Ann had been doing an excellent job of getting the three sisters together for lunches. And they'd kept up an almost weekly schedule.

Though Harper Rose and Bailey Ann still asked about school, they limited it to one question each and then turned the subjects. For the first time, her sisters were starting to treat her as an equal and not as the little tagalong who couldn't keep up and didn't understand where they were in their lives. Emma Kate hated missing their get-togethers or even being late, but she pushed her way in through the swinging door then stood there scanning the busy restaurant to find her sisters.

Em had missed the last lunch because of the kittens, though she believed Bailey Ann and Harper Rose had showed up without her. That had sucked. But now, she was here, and she wanted to get to the table. Though her afternoon was open, Bailey Ann's wasn't. Even so, Harper Rose was on the tightest schedule. The three were choosing restaurants near where Harper Rose worked so she could spend the most time at lunch and the least time traveling. Otherwise, they would have to postpone these meet ups until the weekends. That meant the girls would be around the house, and that would change the conversations dramatically. Em still wasn't ready for that, still wasn't quite ready to show her sisters what was really going on with her.

Besides, what she and Keith had was too new. She didn't have the words for it yet. Didn't know how to take them from zero to sixty in one conversation.

Mostly, she lived her life beyond the edge of town. Though, Aunt GiGi and Uncle Dex had invited her to Sunday dinner, she hadn't said yes. How could she go and not take Keith? If she did take Keith, the word would get back insanely quickly to her sisters. She was still swimming from Keith having told her he loved her the day before.

She thought it would be hard to say it out loud. Even though she'd known for a while how *she* felt, she still hadn't known how *he* felt. So she'd tried a handful of times to push the words past her lips to see what he said. It was her turn after all, wasn't it? Keith was the one who had asked her if she wanted to stay married. But she told herself that she hadn't had the opportunity to say it to him. She realized yesterday that what she'd been lacking wasn't opportunity, but courage. Keith had it. And she'd never been so happy.

Just then Harper Rose spotted her, popped up from the table where she and Bailey Ann sat and engulfed Em in a huge hug. But as Emma Kate wrapped her arm around her sister's back, she caught the glint of light off her rings. Rubbing her fingers together, she worked them around so that the large center rock in her engagement ring was at least tucked under her hand as she hugged back. "Hey, Harper Rose! You look happy."

Bailey Ann waived, but stayed put, pragmatically holding the table. As Em slid into the booth beside her, Bailey Ann smiled and gave her a one-armed squeeze as she announced, "We ordered for you."

"Thank you." They knew what she liked. The whole family had been coming to Bobby's for years. Sitting down and taking off her jacket, Em tried to carefully pull off her rings as she reached around behind her. Using the move of pulling off her sleeves as cover, she stripped the two rings down her finger and secretly stashed them into the zipper pocket of her wallet.

Though she wanted to tell her sisters about Keith, even more so now that she had a better grasp on how he felt, today was not going to be the day she said anything. She was already running late. She needed to think about how she was going to tell her sisters that not only was she married, but she had been married for almost two months.

Bailey Ann frowned and glanced sideways at Em's hand, as Emma Kate rearranged the silverware and napkins at her place setting. She thought she had done a pretty good job of hiding the rings, but maybe she hadn't. Luckily, Bailey Ann didn't say anything and it was always possible that frown was for something Em just didn't know about.

As the pizza arrived at the table, Harper Rose was telling them how her middle daughter, Hailey, was doing in school. Kindergarten had been a big transition for the little girl, but come spring, she was finally settling in and it was a load of stress off Harper Rose's shoulders. "I feel like I can go about the business of settling in, now that the girls are fitting in and getting used to things. I finally feel like things are going to be okay."

"That's good," Emma Kate reached out and grabbed her sister's hand for a moment. "That makes me happy for you."

She understood the feeling, but Harper Rose wasn't done. "I have to thank the two of you the most for that feeling. I know you're starting a new business, Bailey Ann, and I know—Emma Kate—you came back and you're working your jobs and you don't have any money to spare."

Emma Kate was frowning. It was all true, but she didn't get the point. Was it just to point out that she was struggling the most?

"And I know that's because of me and my girls," Harper Rose said. Bailey Ann and Emma Kate looked at each other for a moment. As Em understood what her sister was saying she saw that Bailey Ann was wearing a mirror expression of her own frown. She almost laughed. If Harper Rose hadn't been so serious, she would have. It was good to have sisters and she owed them more than she was giving them.

"We can't sell the house because of me and my girls and I need to start paying you two rent so that you can collect some of the money you would have gotten if we'd sold it."

"No, no, no, no." Just like their expressions, their voices were almost identical and both of them held their hands, palm out in front of them, waving their middle sister away.

"I'm okay," Emma Kate said. "I'm doing just fine. I mean, it's not the road to high riches, but I'm good and I want you and your girls to have the house." It was the perfect opening. "In fact, I intended to stay at the house with you and mooch a room, but I..." She was starting to say, *Fell into something* or *Got lucky, and got married*. But Harper Rose jumped into her hesitation, "You're always welcome. We can put the three girls in one room. They won't mind."

And Emma Kate's moment was gone.

❧ 42 ❧

"Lennon, what do I do?" Emma Kate could hear the worry in her voice but she couldn't stop it. She was sitting on the couch in the tiny house, clutching her phone like she wished she could clutch her friend.

She needed Lennon to be here with her now, to give her advice face to face. To sit up all night with a bottle of wine, and some bad decisions that led to good ones. Len had found Gabe, even when everything told them they shouldn't be together. It had been hard leaving all her prejudices at the door, but Lennon had done it. Surely, she could coach Em through telling her sisters she was happily married.

It had been almost two weeks since Keith had said he loved her. "He asked me about it a while ago—why hadn't I told my sisters? So I told him that I didn't tell them because I didn't know where the relationship was going."

"You hardly have that excuse anymore." Lennon said wryly through the phone line.

"I know. I need to tell them. But it's not easy and I keep ducking out." She knew she was being a coward. Em just needed an impetus to change that. "I'm supposed to have lunch with my sisters again on Thursday!"

She'd still not come up with a way to tell them that she was married, and Lennon was being no help other than emotional support. "What exactly is it you need to tell them?"

Em thought about it for a minute. "I don't know. Just that I'm married and that it's a good thing."

"Okay, what do you need from them?"

"I need them to be okay with it and be good to Keith and let us come around and be a married couple without all the 'you got married in Vegas' and 'it's another crazy thing Emma Kate did!'" Though Lennon wasn't telling her what to do, she was at least forcing Em to think through what was most important.

"What do you need to tell them to get them to stay off your back and let you be happy with Keith?"

That was the million dollar question, she thought. When she said she didn't quite know, she and Lennon agreed to think on it, but Lennon had to go. She was handing in another stage of her thesis. Her *masters* thesis.

After hanging up so Lennon wouldn't hear her, Em sighed deeply. She and Lennon should have been on similar tracks. But no. Len would get her masters before Emma Kate would even get her bachelors. Ha! At least she'd gotten married first. But Lennon would be getting married soon, too, and Gabe would be welcomed into the family long before Keith was.

Em felt bad about that. It was no fault of Keith's that he was going to be considered "Emma Kate's mistake."

The kittens were at work with her husband, so she'd come home to an empty house after finishing early at Melanie's. Emma Kate had rearranged three-quarters of that veterinary clinic, and she was about to put herself out of work.

Now that she'd completed the most pressing things, Housley was only bringing her in once or twice a week. Some of the places he wanted her to restructure meant she needed to do the work during the hours when no one else was there. She couldn't very well tear apart the front office while it was in use. So, she was going to put in a handful of hours on Sunday, figure out what needed to happen and let everybody know how she was going to rearrange it. That way she could ask what they thought of her plan and tweak it as needed. Sometimes people needed things to be the old way, not because it worked better, but because the comfort of the familiar was better than the discomfort of change.

That was maybe part of the problem with her sisters. There was a natural order to the three of them. It was Em who was shaking things up by showing up in Breathless, by supporting herself. By staying out of their hair and not needing them, she'd already shaken things up quite a bit. She liked her new elevation in the family. It would be nice to just be "sister" rather than "baby sister."

When she thought of it that way, it was easy to see that she was afraid telling them about her marriage would mean a swift demotion back to "fuck up." She wished there had been more time to talk to Lennon about all of these things, but they had spent too much time just catching up. They had to do that now that they were further away and talked less. Another bit of change that Em wasn't thrilled with.

But Gabe had gotten Lennon an apartment with a view in Chicago and Lennon was loving it, though she felt a little decadent. So for the first part of the conversation, Em had heard, "He's at home all the time. I come home to study, and I can hear him on the phone. He says things like *you can do better than that.*"

And Emma Kate had laughed at Lennon's impression of Gabe's deeper voice.

"*That's chump change Marcus* or *I need a bigger share of stock if you're going to screw me over like that.*"

The laughter had felt good, and she'd needed it. But she'd needed more time in general. She needed more advice about the serious aspects of her life, not just getting up in the middle of the night and finding the kittens had gotten out of their crate and onto the stove. Not just the time that Star had crawled under the couch and meowed each time they sat down until they figured out where the kitten was.

Lennon was the only one Emma Kate had told about Keith—about their marriage, about his proposal to not get it annulled, about the words he'd said to her and that she'd finally said them back. Em was grateful that Lennon had graciously not told Aunt GiGi or Uncle Dex about her predicament.

In the end, Lennon's only advice was, "Em, maybe it's better if you just blurt it out, like you did to me. It took me a moment to understand, to realize that this was a good thing for you. But I did. And then it was over."

"Do you really think it's going to be over that fast with my sisters?" If anyone understood it was Lennon. She and Emma Kate were roughly the same age—and being a cousin was much like being a sister—so when she was over at the house, Lennon had always gotten the same treatment from Harper Rose and Bailey Ann. Though Lennon had an older brother, Jackson, it wasn't the same thing as what Em went through.

Lennon hadn't been expected to follow in Jackson's footsteps the way Emma Kate had with Bailey Ann and Harper Rose. And Lord knew, the two of them were in each other's pockets so often, they really were almost like sisters growing up.

"I don't know," Lennon said. "You're right, it's not the same as telling me. If you make a big to-do out of it, how would you do it? Would you just show up at the doorstep with Keith in tow? Seems the simplest."

"It does. But is it fair to Keith to throw him to the lions like that? I don't know," Emma Kate replied to her own question as she thought about it. It meant instead of her defending her decision, Keith would have to be the one to defend her decision. "It would mean he would see all the outrage and all of them thinking what an idiot I am. I don't know if I want him to see that."

"Maybe you do," Lennon offered. "Maybe you want him to believe you when you tell him how your sisters boss you around.

That, even though you're in your mid-twenties, they sometimes seem to believe you're still twelve."

Emma Kate laughed. It wasn't quite that bad, at least not most of the time. And less so lately. Bailey Ann had, of course, asked about her thesis when they met for lunch the last time. Though Emma Kate actually had a working idea and had talked to her thesis advisor, she'd taken on foster kittens. It hadn't left any spare hours to work it out. Or to start drafting her outline. She was not going to get her proposal approved and have her thesis written, examined, and defended by the end of spring term. She wouldn't graduate until summer. But at least that gave her some buffer.

Still, she sat on the couch and tried to figure out all the moving pieces. She tried to solve everything from getting her thesis finished, to winding up with more foster pets, to figuring out how to tell her sisters about Keith. Alternately, she considered a path to convince Keith it wasn't worth her family knowing.

Another option she had to consider was damage control—what if someone saw her with her rings on? Or someone else brought a pet to the clinic, someone she knew? Word would get around fast and her sisters would be devastated if they heard it from anywhere else first.

Leaning her head back against the couch, Em realized she'd been lucky to make it this far without them finding out. She needed a plan.

She needed a nap.

Her breathing evened out, and the nap won.

❧ 43 ❧

Keith had followed Emma Kate into the clinic, trailing slowly behind her tiny car on his bike. He was covered in leather and protective gear from head to toe, and he wasn't quite as badass as he looked. In, fact, he was nervous as hell.

He didn't like the roads. They'd gotten icy, and people were shitty drivers around here as soon as anything went wrong, be it rain or snow or even high wind. It was the natural consequence of generally good weather.

To be fair, they weren't driving on *snow*. Northerners understood snow, but down south, you got just a little bit of it and then the sun warmed it up during the day, and then overnight—when everything froze again—you wound up with a fine layer of ice on everything, including patches of black ice. They were hideously dangerous for cars, and worse for his bike.

So he'd followed her, driving slowly into the office. Emma Kate said she needed to go in today when no one was there. The job required the office be empty and she needed the hours. Thus, Keith wanted to go along with her, just to be sure everything was okay. Instead, he was finding she was the driver most competent on the bad Georgia roads and he was the one slipping around.

She was going to take apart the office and restructure the front station in hopes of making everything more livable and workable—her words. She'd talked to him before about some kind of triangle that she needed to see that wasn't there. He had no clue what triangle she was talking about, but since she understood it, he hadn't commented further.

Though she'd clearly said she didn't want his help, he understood. She needed to clock the hours, and any time he spent helping her pull down files, move around the furniture, or anything he took off her plate became hours she didn't get paid for. Ironically, the money was coming from the clinic, which was going to be his bread and butter for the coming years, and thus, *theirs*.

He found he wasn't looking forward to her finishing the office. Likely, she'd be finding another job once Housley ran out of things for her to do, and he liked having her there. Hell, at the rate things were going, she'd organize her way out of the job before the end of the month. Maybe they could recommend her to another office, or maybe she was going to become an internet star.

He'd told her the other night that it was time to monetize the video channel she had. Emma Kate had agreed and even dove right in, signing up for various options the platforms allowed. She'd already received three different emails to plug several products during her program. They were offering her reasonable amounts of money, too, but Emma Kate had turned them all down.

"They're cheap products," she complained. "I have no issue advertising things that work and are helpful... as long as I can say I was paid to do it. But I hate these suggestions, because clearly these companies think my reputation is for being cheap. But I want my name to be synonymous with not spending a lot of money, and the two are *not* the same. I'm not telling my viewers to use things that are going to fall apart. It would ruin everything!"

He'd smiled as he agreed, loving her passion. As far as he knew, she didn't know any of her viewers personally. Well, except him and her family. So these were all strangers, but she was hell bent on keeping her good name. He had to admire her integrity because they could have used the extra cash in their pockets.

Still, she was earning her money with this job and he'd wanted to come out with her this morning. Maybe because he just wanted to spend his Sunday with her or maybe because he told himself he had a stake in her work. He would be living with this front office re-design far longer than Housley would.

The more he talked to the old man, the more he'd thought his new partner had been using "several years to retirement" as a long-term projection. As a backup if maybe Keith didn't work out. The longer Keith worked the shorter Housley's timeframes got. He'd been saying things like, "Next year when I'm sitting on my patio," and "This summer when I'm fishing." Keith hadn't asked outright, but he was starting to believe it was going to be his veterinary clinic very soon, and that meant he was going to need to hire another veterinarian, but he liked the idea of that.

He watched as Emma Kate gingerly took the right-hand turn into the parking lot at the clinic. She climbed gingerly out of the car and stood on the ice, hopping back and forth, one foot to the other in the cold, and he hoped she didn't slip on anything in the parking lot before they headed inside.

Once inside, she turned on the coffee pot and got straight to work. Standing in the center of the space, she turned a full circle, slowly examining every part of the office before she sat down in each of the chairs and touched all the equipment.

Keith had no idea what she was doing and asked, "Why are you touching everything?"

Em smiled up at him from the reception seat behind the counter. "I'm trying to test all the functionalities that this position requires. The person who sits here has to answer the phones —quickly. They have to greet the guests that come in the door."

She stood up and looked over the counter at the front door. "They also have to take credit cards, print out receipts, and do filing. I don't like it."

Obviously, she didn't like it. Housley seemed to think Emma Kate could work magic on it, even though to both Keith and Housley's minds, it had been working just fine all along.

"Look at me," she said.

"Okay?" He stood there like any pet owner would, his arms crossed on the high counter, peering over at her.

"See? That's the problem right there." She grinned up at him. "Unless I'm doing nothing and just sitting in the middle looking out, I'm not at a position where you can easily see me. The counters are way too high over here."

"We're not going to remodel the entire interior," he cautioned, not liking her concerns.

"Exactly, but this section here—" she pointed to the cut out. "This low portion of counter, this is where the stations need to be. This is where people need to be sitting to greet the customers. We can tuck the computers over here where they're out of sight, and credit cards scanners are small enough to tuck away rather than taking up counter space..." She stood and turned again, "and the phones need to move, too. The floors are a good tile, so that's nice." She looked up at him again, explaining. "That means you can roll the seats back and forth—get to things easily. Right now there are no stations and no triangle."

He had no idea what she was talking about, but she wasn't looking at him. One day, he'd ask her about that "triangle" but now was not the time.

She kept talking. "So we've got two people up here. If we divide the front in half..." She started moving her hands around as if to demo something she could see but he couldn't. She sat back down. "If I sit here doing the charts, then I need the phone on this side because I need to be able to answer the phone no matter where I am. And if I stand up..." She headed to the wall behind her where the files were. "This really can't be moved, but we need an additional system because y'all have more files than space. So we need at least another shelf. I'll have to figure out where to put it."

"We can trim the files down." Keith told her.

"How?"

"What we need is to take out full files and additional paper-work on any animals that have passed more than six months ago and move them to another filing system."

"That's a pretty big job."

He nodded at her. "It is, because a lot of the animals that have passed are going to still have their files inside file folders."

She was nodding. She'd worked here long enough to under-stand that the files were by family last name and all the pets were in that one folder. "Because many of the deceased animals are from families who still have pets they bring currently." She nodded as he did. "Do we want to do that?"

"I think we need to. We need a system to put a note in the chart—basic info about the deceased pet but take the bulk of the files from that animal and put them separately with a binder or a data file. The note or page that's still in the chart should provide info that tells us where to get to them if we need them."

"Do you want to digitize them?" she asked.

He realized then that the decision should be his. He would be living with it. If the animal was deceased, there was no reason to keep the files on paper. "Hey, if Housley's willing to pay you to do that, then yes. Yes, I do." And it would keep her around the office a while longer. He had to admit he liked that.

She nodded absently. "Well, that's a job for another day. First, we'll need to put them into a separate filing on paper, and then we'll digitize."

"Sounds like a plan." He'd watched for a while, but with her insistence that he not touch anything, he was useless. So, he'd left and headed home. The kittens needed to be fed, and he needed to figure out what he was going to do about the fact that his wife was definitely under his skin and definitely now his wife.

And she still hadn't told her family about him. What did that say about them?

❦ 44 ❦

Emma Kate didn't pull down all the medical files on all the pets. Instead, she sat at the front desk for a good twenty minutes, figuring out what the staff most needed to do—what was most important and what had to happen the most often or the fastest. Then she had to decide where to put things to try it out.

She did initial rearrangements, changing one station, but leaving the other as it was for comparison. She couldn't, however, simulate an actual workday. That was the real test. Her memory would only suffice so far, and she hoped it was far enough. The new arrangement—with one changed, "testing" station—would allow anyone working at the front desk to try out the new set up for a day. It would take a little while to get used to things. It would suck not being able to find things for a while, but she hoped the change would be worth it and, in the end, the space would be more user friendly.

She'd noticed that the front desk staff were always getting up and running across the space to answer the phone. So fixing that was one of her priorities, as well as making sure that the person at the desk could both see and be seen by a patient coming through the doors. It was good manners, and that meant good business, but—maybe more importantly—people sometimes came through with emergencies. She'd seen it happen, and the ability to find a friendly face, fast, was paramount in those situations. So she let those things become the priorities of the desk.

Next, she addressed finding a section of counter space where a person could have several files open. The staff needed to add pages into the files as necessary for any animals coming into the clinic. Emma Kate had seen them working with the files stacked because there wasn't enough counter space to prep them before the patients went into the exam rooms.

So she moved the phone over, tucking it into the space under the lower countertop since it didn't need height like the computer screens did. Next, she slid the computer the other direction. There was a small tablet with a chip for reading credit cards and it was sitting in the middle of the counter. She'd have to ask about getting a second one, because if they each had one, it would fit neatly under the edge of the computer. She thought originally the one reader had been in the center, but it had been a much bigger piece of equipment. Over the years, the readers had gotten better, smaller, and cheaper. But when the office got the new ones, they had likely placed them right where the old ones had been. Once again, it left staff hopping up, walking around and running to fetch receipts.

The printer was also sitting on the counter, and it was a massive use of space she'd like to free up. She'd watched them use it. They needed to be able to first pull a printout from the tray easily.

Heading into the back of the building, she hunted through the back closet, certain she'd put a small rolling table back here about two weeks before. Em then rolled it out to the front and found that it was a little lower than her dream-table, but the wheels were nice if anyone needed to move it in a hurry.

It took several hours, but once she had everything arranged, Em sat at the desk again checking whether or not it actually worked. Done for the day, finally, she realized she'd have to come back and do the other side, maybe next week. With a big sigh, she closed everything down, locked up the clinic and climbed into her car.

Aiming for home, Emma Kate took a deep breath and had a Come-To-Jesus moment with herself. It was well past time to decide what to do about Keith. Well, it wasn't Keith that she didn't know what to do with, it was her family knowing about Keith. If she didn't do this herself, and soon, someone would see them and just offhandedly say to someone, "I saw that Emma Kate out with her husband. You know, the hot veterinarian? Oh yes, she was wearing a big ole rock. Trust me, they're married."

That would be the end of it. So Emma Kate had to get out in front.

Lennon had been right, asking her what her goals were. Em had thought about it and she knew that she wanted the meeting to go well for everyone. For her, but mostly for Keith. So no yelling, no craziness, no deciding that her marriage was a mistake —she and Keith certainly no longer thought that.

Deciding there was safety in numbers, Em thought the best thing would be to host dinner for everyone. Lennon and Gabe would be back in Breathless two weeks from now. Uncle Dex's birthday was coming up and they'd be here for that. Em didn't want to do her big reveal on his birthday. That would steal the old man's thunder, and Dex was nothing if not dramatic. But she knew Lennon and Gabe would be coming home several days early. That made the regular family Sunday dinner the place to pull back the curtain on her big secret. It gave her two and half weeks to get ready.

It was just a nice bit of breathing room that she would have two and a half more weeks that she didn't have to face the firing squad. But that was the date that met all her goals. Uncle Dex and Aunt GiGi would naturally be very excited for her. They'd never worried about how she was going to pay the bills and whether or not she'd grow up. So, they would just be thrilled and

Em could only hope some of it would rub off on anyone who doubted her.

If Harper Rose came and brought her three daughters, and if Lennon's older brother Jackson was there with his girls, that would provide numbers. Then, everyone could get together again—a few days later, when the dust had settled—and celebrate Uncle Dex's birthday. It would be another chance to get to know Keith, but she and her husband wouldn't be the center of attention. In her perfectly planned coup, Uncle Dex's boisterous personality would draw much of the drama away from her and Keith.

She sighed into the car as she kept her eyes on the road. At least the daylight was good. Grey days made her feel cold and cranky. Swerving around a patch of ice she could see on the road, Emma Kate mentally patted herself on the back.

Even her thesis advisor had also finally emailed back, approving her idea. She was on a roll.

She had it all worked out in her mind. She would tell Keith her plan as soon as she got Uncle Dex and Aunt GiGi to agree to host. Reaching toward the dash, she hit a few buttons, carefully keeping her eye on the road.

"Emma Kate? How are you!" It wasn't a question but an exclamation. It was how Aunt GiGi started every conversation.

"Aunt GiGi! I'm doing so great. That's why I'm calling."

"Then tell me what's going on, girl." She could almost see her aunt, cradling the handset as though it were still tethered to the wall.

"That's the thing, I'd like to plan a surprise dinner to tell everyone, but I don't have room at my tiny house to fit everyone—"

"Well then, you'll have to do it here. You just let me know what you need and when."

Em felt her heart swell. She wasn't sure if there had ever been anyone that loved as unconditionally as Aunt GiGi. And maybe no one in her life had loved her as unconditionally as her aunt had. Her parents had worried that she was the family screw up. Her sisters were... her sisters. They fussed and took care of her and then fussed about the fact that they'd always cared for her. It was what sisters did.

But Aunt GiGi had never stopped a moment to worry. She'd always told the others, "Emma Kate will be fine. She's got her own little light, but it's bright." Em reminded herself to give the woman a hug the next time she saw her. Aunt GiGi loved a good secret. And the good news was, if she told anyone, she would swear them to secrecy. Which meant that she and Keith might walk into that dinner with some people already on the downlow, but they wouldn't be able to say anything. Em liked the idea more and more.

So she opened her mouth and said, "Aunt GiGi, can you keep a secret?"

"You know I can!"

"You've got to keep it for two and a half weeks."

"I can do that. Now you have to tell me what it is, girl!" Em could hear the smile in her aunt's voice.

Though she was grinning, Emma Kate was still watching the road. So she saw the car coming at her from the other direction as it slid slowly across the road and into her lane. She didn't manage to tell her secret. She only said, "Oh, shit."

🏵 45 🏵

Keith looked at his watch, not liking his growing feeling of unease. It was five o'clock and the world was starting to turn to dusk.

He hadn't liked the shape the roads were in on the drive out, and he'd expected Em to be home well before now. Keith reminded himself it was more than possible that she'd just gotten wrapped up in the work and was only now realizing she needed to head home. He certainly hoped she would drive in the daylight, which meant she needed to already be most of the way home. The tiny house on the Barker property was cheap and it was warm, but it wasn't close to the clinic.

He'd called more than once to check on her, but she hadn't answered. To be fair, he hadn't really expected her to, but still he called both the office and texted her cell phone several times and received no answer.

That was truly what was bothering him. He knew she could get involved in something, and there was every possibility her phone wasn't ringing because she'd set up all the lights and was filming a video about rearranging the office. But he'd been texting and calling for almost two hours. Surely she would have checked her phone sometime during that span. He fed the kittens again. Star and Lucky's mewing was like an alarm reminding him that Em had been gone far too long with no word.

Deciding that safety was the better part of valor, he dialed the front office staff on their cell phones. One by one they answered and said they hadn't been into the clinic, so they had no idea if Emma Kate had gone home yet. Eventually, when the kittens were fed and put back into their crate with the heating pad underneath, he bundled up and headed out.

By then, the fading daylight made him truly nervous. It took far too long to get into his jacket, his gloves, his warmest pants, his boots, and his helmet. In his best case scenario, he would find her car at the clinic—and Emma Kate along with it. Maybe she'd just lost track of time, though that wasn't like her.

There was nothing else he could do but go find her and assure himself that everything was okay, and it was a long, cold ride to the clinic. He didn't pass her on the way out—which had been his hope—and when he arrived at the clinic, there was no one there. In fact, it looked like she hadn't been there for quite some time. His chest twisted in tight and his breathing stuttered even as he told himself she had to be okay.

It was dark by then. Dusk had passed while he was riding, and as he looked around the area, everything was lit only by streetlamps. Snow was starting to fall, and he watched the flakes in the cones of yellow provided by the old lighting. It would have been beautiful if he wasn't getting scared.

Reminding himself to keep calm, Keith peeled his glove and called the house, dialing the land line that went to the phone hanging on the wall that he and Emma Kate had never really used. But given that it ever-so-rarely rang, he hoped she might answer.

No one picked it up. Not even a machine he could talk to and tell her how worried he was. He called her phone again, this time leaving a fully frantic voicemail to add to the other two calmer ones he'd left earlier. As soon as he hung up, he texted her with, "Call me as soon as you get this. VERY IMPORTANT."

He drove home slowly, trying not to become an accident himself. It would be very Romeo and Juliet of him to kill himself while out making sure that Emma Kate hadn't killed herself on the slippery roads.

It was only because he was going slowly that he saw it. In the ditch on the right-hand side of the road was a mangled car. He slowed, glad that the car was red and not Emma Kate's silver. But as he went by, he almost spun the bike out. Behind the red car was a tiny silver hatchback. It too was mangled, and looked like it had twisted and ripped open. His heart stopped dead as he fought to control the bike he'd ignored for just a second too long.

He told himself it couldn't be hers, but as he spun the bike around far too fast for the conditions, he saw that it was the exact same make and model. Slowing down, he aimed his head-light at the tangled mess. He heard himself then, saying out loud, "She's okay, she's okay, she's okay. This isn't her car. It's a common model. She's okay."

Pulling over onto the gravel, he aimed the headlight, looking for clues in the accident. The only thing that gave him any solace at all was that both the cars were empty. No one was here help-ing, but it looked like they had been.

Tire tracks marked the gravel and mud in every direction. His brain told him there would have been ambulances and firetrucks. The silver car confirmed much of that. When he hopped off his bike and headed down into the ditch, he could see that it wasn't as twisted as he'd thought at first, but it was cut open. Someone had brought out the Jaws of Life.

But as he repeated that her car was a common model and... That was *her* license plate.

His heart plummeted. His breath soughed, taking in the cold and freezing him from the inside out. He sat there for a minute, knowing he couldn't possibly drive with his adrenaline spiking the way that it was.

It didn't matter if he could get back on the bike and drive to her, because he didn't know where to go. For all he had grown familiar with the town of Breathless, he suddenly realized he didn't know the important things. He knew where the farms were, he knew where the big animals were, he saw the addresses from the patients, but he didn't know where her sisters lived and he didn't know where the hospital was.

Unable to sit still in the cold any longer, he knew he had to find her, even if that meant he drove to every hospital within a hundred miles and demanded to know if she was there. He pulled out his phone and opened the maps, looking for the nearest one. Once he found it, Keith tipped his bike up and climbed on.

He raced off, driving far too fast for the conditions. But he told himself it didn't matter. He only needed to get to Emma Kate.

✴ 46 ✴

The appropriate response to 'I'd like a coke' is 'what kind?' In the true south, 'coke' refers to any soda. For example, you could answer with 'I'd like an R.C. Cola please.'

EMMA KATE SLOWLY CAME AWAKE TO THE SOUND OF A regular beeping noise. It took her a moment to figure out that the noise was her heartbeat, and another moment to realize why her heart was beeping.

Her head hurt in exact cadence with the beats. *Squeeze, release. Squeeze, release. Beep beep beep.* So then she had to figure out why her eyes wouldn't open.

Em started to lift her arms, but found they were heavy, too heavy to lift really. They were weighted, that was the only explanation, and she must still be dreaming. She decided to take stock of the dream—beeping, squeezing pain, and talking in the background. At least she was warm.

She was starting to drift off again when she recognized one of the voices mumbling in the background. *Bailey Ann.*

Emma Kate's eyes still didn't want to open, but her brain was slowly coming around to being fully awake. She wasn't dreaming

—that was actually Bailey Ann's voice, suddenly coming through like expertly cut crystal.

"Harper Rose, *no*. Don't bring the girls down here. She's pretty bruised up, but the doctors say she's okay... There's no need to pack everyone up in the cold to see her sleep... Yes, it was horribly nerve wracking and she looks awful. Bruises and small cuts everywhere, but the doctors say she was lucky... We're just waiting for her to come around. "

Hmm, Emma Kate thought. She was waiting for herself to wake up, too, or at least get her eyes open.

Another voice came to her left. "Bailey Ann! I think she's waking up."

It was *Finn*. Her new brother-in-law had a deep comforting voice that still carried a hint of lilt from his Irish homeland. He was laid back, creative, and just driven enough to give her sister plenty to do.

Bailey Ann was the design eye behind their house flipping business. She picked the tiles, found the best deals, and put together color combinations that would not mark the house as a trend from this year. Finn was the perfect counter-balance to Bailey Ann—an architect with an eye for classic lines and historical preservation work—and a good solid sound to come around to.

Interesting, Emma Kate thought. She'd not believed that she and Bailey Ann were much alike in the past. But she could see now that Bailey Ann had redecorated their parents' whole house last year. Now, here she was, doing the same in the tiny house on the Barker property. She could even admit she'd taken some cues from her older sister's color choices.

Maybe they were much more alike than either of them had thought. But Bailey Ann had always aspired to be just like Mama, and Emma Kate had always aspired to be nothing like their mother. Yet, somehow they'd met in the middle.

With a deep sigh, Emma Kate set to the work of prying her eyeballs open, but it didn't happen. She felt it then. Her arms under the blanket, heated, weighted. The beeping sounded like hospital equipment and she wondered who might be in the hospital.

"Harper Rose," Bailey Ann's voice was crisp and clear, cutting through the muck and the background noise of the hospital again. "She's waking up now, I'm going to give you a call back in just a few minutes, okay, honey?" And then, knowing Bailey Ann, her sister had clicked off the phone. No matter what Harper Rose had said, Bailey Ann had a plan and it was getting executed.

Emma Kate smiled at the thought.

"She's smiling at you," Finn said, and Emma Kate began to laugh.

"Never mind, she's laughing at you. She's going to be okay."

Emma Kate only laughed harder, though why Finn was having to tell Bailey Ann that she was okay was still a mystery. She still didn't fully understand what was going on.

One by one, she fluttered her eyelids until her eyes opened all the way and she looked around.

"Hey Finn," she tried to offer a smile, but instantly regretted it, the pounding in her head having changed to a vice like grip. "Shit."

"No swearing in hospitals," Bailey Ann said.

"Fuck off," Emma Kate told her through the rust that clouded her voice and watched as her sister—for once—laughed at her swearing.

"You gave us a scare," Bailey Ann told her as she reached over and took Em's hand. *Oh, there it was. Good. Still attached and not actually having any lead weights on it.*

Then Em looked around the room and suddenly realized *she* was the one in the hospital bed with the rails pulled up on the sides so she couldn't fall out like a child. *She* was the one everyone was talking about.

When she thought back over her sister's words and Finn's, it made perfect sense. Now. But...

"Why?" she asked, again feeling the vice grip on her head that punished her for words.

"Car accident."

Emma Kate blinked up at her sister. "Who?" It was worth the punishment. Something was off here, and she was uncomfortable not knowing what it was.

"You. A car hit you head on."

Em must have made the strangest face, because Bailey Ann rushed in with an explanation. "Your car is totaled, but don't worry. Finn and I will get you another one. You're banged up, but miraculously nothing is broken. You'll come live with us until you're ready to go back to your own place. We worked it all out. And the accident wasn't your fault. It was very clear the other car hit you, on your side of the road."

Her head spun, the words winding the vice down tighter and tighter. She wanted to fight back, to rail against her sister making plans for her. She didn't need the two of them to take her in and care for her, though her brain stuttered as to why that was. Still, she couldn't fight back. It was enough effort to squint her eyes as though that would block out the onslaught of Bailey Ann making plans for her.

Eventually, when her sister had laid out everything—definitely trying to keep Emma Kate from worrying, but having decided everything without her—Em got her head on a little straighter. Slowly, snippets of the accident came back to her. The red car crossing the road, her voice saying "oh, shit" to someone... Who?

"Bailey Ann! Bailey Ann!" She was reaching out, grabbing her sister's sleeve as she turned away to get something. Her brain flashed to a memory of being very tiny and reaching for her sister this way. Though Bailey Ann planned everything to a hair breath of its life, she was learning that she couldn't, and Emma Kate was slowly seeing that it was at least done from love and not power or disappointment.

Bailey Ann turned back to her, "Baby, what is it?"

"I was on the phone with Aunt GiGi! Tell her I'm okay!"

"I already did." Bailey Ann offered their mother's smile to her and Em felt her sudden onset of panic ebb. "She called me as soon as you had the accident. She didn't know what it was, but we were able to get here right behind the ambulance because she alerted us. She knows you're doing okay. Finn texted her and Uncle Dex just a moment ago to let her know you were awake."

Finn held his phone up at her as though showing her the screen was proof, but Emma Kate took it. Letting her head fall back, she tried to let the strain fall away, but it didn't quite work. Her brain still wasn't functioning. Though everything seemed all right, she was missing something major, she knew it.

Finn saw her and misread it for exhaustion. Reaching out, he grabbed her hand and gave it a slight squeeze. "Bailey Ann and I are going down to the cafeteria to get something to eat. Can we bring you back a soda?"

She nodded and would have laughed at the fact that he'd never come around to calling every soda a "coke," but her head was hurting again. God, a good fizzy coke sounded good.

Bailey Ann looked at her husband with a quizzical expression. "We are?"

"She needs a moment," he whispered it, but Em heard. "So yes." He turned back to his sister-in-law. "We'll be back in a bit."

They headed out the door, hand in hand and it hit Em hard. *Keith*. She needed *Keith*.

She needed to tell him where she was. That she was okay. She needed to curl up in his arms. Emma Kate was scrambling around, frantically searching for her cell phone, when he came running in the door.

❧ 47 ❧

Emma Kate's heart both settled and soared at the same time. Keith was here.

She had no idea how he'd found her in the hospital after a car accident and her brain wasn't up to the task of figuring it out. As her thoughts finally cleared, she realized her sisters would not have even known to call him and let him know what had happened. But he was here, and everything was all right now. She felt it in her bones.

Reaching up, she hugged him and in return, he looked at her for a moment, before suddenly holding her tight and kissing her. She could feel him sighing in relief, the sound soothing her even as he let out his own stresses.

He had practically skidded his way into the room, holding the corner of the bed and sliding around to get to her. She could tell by his expression that he needed to see and touch her, to know that she really was all in one piece.

This man loved her.

"Thank God you're okay," he breathed the words out and just as quickly questioned them. "You are okay, right?"

She heard the worry creeping right back in. "According to my sister—who has managed to solve all the world's fuel problems in the two hours since I arrived—I have bruises and cuts everywhere. But that's all. I'm very lucky, but that's all."

"I found your car," he whispered.

"Yeah, it's totaled, huh?"

The grind in his voice told her the harshness of what he'd seen. "It was cut open, Em. The body of the car didn't collapse, so that was good. That's probably what saved your life, and definitely saved you from any worse injuries. But it looks like they couldn't get you out through any of the doors. So there's a big cut in the side, and the car was pried open like a tin can. It was so scary to see that and not know where you were."

"Holy shit," Em replied. "I don't remember any of that."

He shook his head, once again coming down from the hit of adrenaline. "It's okay. It's not surprising, honestly. Most people don't remember accidents like that," but he stepped in closer again, his hands touching her hair, feeling the bones of her head and her shoulders. Though it set off pangs from all of her bruises, she let him check her out.

The doctor came in then holding out his hand. "Hello, I'm Dr. Jergenson and I'm on rotation for the next twenty-four hours." Luckily, the doctor didn't have Keith's need to touch every bone for security. He asked a few questions, and said, "I think we'll be letting you out by late morning. As long as nothing goes wrong, you can go home."

Keith smiled at the comment and then the shift nurse came in through the door even before the doctor left and said, "I thought your sister was here. Do you know where she went? She signed your intake forms and we'll want her signature again if we can get it."

Em nodded. "She and her husband went to grab drinks." She pointed out the door as though the nurse might need directions to the cafeteria. That was dumb, but to be fair she'd bumped her head and it probably wasn't the worst the nurse had heard.

Expecting Keith to be laughing or at least smiling at her, she looked up to see he was surprised by the news. "They're here? You didn't wake up alone?"

She shook her head no.

"Oh, thank God. How did they know to come?" he asked. His voice soft and a strange little current of suspicion ran underneath it.

"I was on the phone with my Aunt GiGi when I got hit."

"Oh my God, that must have been terrifying for her."

"I'm guessing so. She called Bailey Ann when the line went dead. And she and Finn apparently managed to find me fast. They arrived while I was still in the ER." At least, that's what her sister had told her.

Keith nodded, his eyes darting away but his hand reached out and found hers. Softly, he linked their fingers together under the warm blanket and she held onto him. There was a slight clink as their wedding rings contacted, and she thought about what she had planned to introduce him properly to her family. The accident may have screwed everything up... or maybe not.

She remembered now the call with Aunt GiGi, the idea of having dinner with everyone in just a few weeks. She was opening her mouth to say just that to Keith, when Bailey Ann and Finn suddenly turned up in the door.

Emma Kate watched as her sister barreled through at a relatively high speed—probably expecting to come back and rescue her baby sister from the loneliness of a hospital room—but she suddenly drew up short. Finn nearly smacked into her back while balancing the extra coke for Emma Kate. She could see the looks on both their faces as they spotted Keith.

Em had no idea what to do but Keith pulled his hand out from where their fingers were tangled under the blanket and reached across over Emma Kate's bed.

"Hello," he said. "I'm Keith Lee."

Em's heart stuttered. It was the first meeting between her husband and her sister, even if Bailey Ann didn't know it. Her sister seemed to have calculated the whole situation and figured it out, given the smile on her face. So Em wasn't all that surprised when Bailey Ann replied, "Oh, you must be the veterinarian that Emma Kate works for."

Em was already working her rings off under the covers. She didn't want to take them off, but now was not the time for a big reveal. She had this all planned out and she wasn't going to let the car accident ruin anything more than it already had.

Keith looked down at her with a frown and Em looked back up at him from her position on the bed, a warning shot in her eyes. *Please don't do this now.*

Leaving her rings tucked under her hip, she held her hand up to make the introductions, "Yes, this is Keith. Keith, this is my sister, Bailey Ann Mayfair."

Bailey Ann, ever the consummate southern belle, took that ball and rolled with it. She smiled and shook his hand as though it was a parlor and not a hospital room. "It's nice of you to come all the way out and check on Emma Kate."

"I was working in the office this morning," Emma Kate rushed to fill the space and insert the story she wanted to tell today.

"*Yes.*" It was all Keith said, and Em breathed a sigh of relief, glad that he'd understood and gone along with it. She would have to convince her sister that she could go home alone... even though she wouldn't be alone. Keith would take good care of her. But she had two more weeks to get this right and she needed every second of them now.

"I just wanted to be sure everything was okay. We like to take good care of our employees." The undercurrent to his tone froze Emma Kate. From the side of her eye, she could see Bailey Ann start to frown, as if she picked up on it. Her sister would never break a social smile, but Finn had no problem letting his brows drop.

Keith reached out and held her hand for a moment, his smile hard. She felt the warm heat of the metal ring. "Well, now that I know Emma Kate is in good hands, I'm going to head home. I have foster kittens to feed."

He smiled wide, though she could tell it was fake. Maybe that was just what she saw through the lens of her heart breaking. Keith just kept going. "It was nice to meet the both of you. Good to know Emma Kate has such a caring family."

He didn't turn back and look at her as he headed out the door, leaving her clutching his wedding ring.

❧ 48 ❧

K eith rode his bike home in the biting cold air. He was
grateful he hadn't been ticketed. He was certain he'd
parked it illegally, ditching the bike and running hell for leather
to the front desk... all for a woman who couldn't even admit that
she was with him.

The kittens needed to be fed, he reminded himself, thinking that
the ordinary things should be a comfort. Or at least they would
keep him upright and moving forward while he tried to figure
out the remaining pieces of his life. He was working hard to
ignore the stunned hit to his chest.

He was halfway back to the tiny house on the Barker property—it was hard to even think of it as "home" since she
wouldn't be coming back—before he realized he hadn't put his
gloves on. He was bare-handing the bike, his knuckles freezing
into the curved shape of the handlebars.

Not being completely stupid, and with the roads still icy and
his attention pulled fifteen ways, he pulled over. Clearly, he
wasn't fit to be driving, but he had to get back and feed the creatures who were counting on him. He pulled his gloves on, and
almost laughed at the absolute southernness of it when two
different cars stopped to be sure he was okay.

He tried to find a kind smile as he told each of them, "Yes," even though it was a lie. They were likely asking if he was having bike trouble. The good people of Breathless and the surrounding rural areas wouldn't want to leave a fellow citizen stuck out here in the cold weather in the middle of the night with the temperature dropping. "I'm okay," he lied to each of them a second time.

His bike was okay, so that much was true. But it wasn't his bike that was broken.

He thanked them both with whatever smile he could muster and wondered if it looked as fake as it felt. Driving the rest of the way on autopilot, he arrived with his only memory of the ride that of the cold wind searing his lungs despite the helmet. The freeze felt stunningly appropriate.

When he opened the front door, the mewing of the kittens reminded him just how long he'd been gone. He'd gone first to the clinic to see if she was there. When she was gone, he'd ridden around slowly until he found her mangled car. He'd ridden faster after that, but she hadn't been at the first hospital he tried. So he'd driven to a second one before the kind person at the front desk said, "Yes, we have an Emma Kate Mayfair who was just admitted for observation."

Then he'd stayed in the room talking with Emma Kate for a while. It only occurred to him on the ride home that no one had called him when his wife had been in a car accident because no one knew she was his wife.

When she was working in the clinic, he would hear people say, "Oh, Hello Emma Kate," and "I didn't know you were back in Breathless!" They recognized her even though the clinic was a little ways out of town. Had she hidden her rings then too? He didn't know.

His left hand felt cold, but the feeling was strange. The ring had felt cumbersome when he first wore it, but now the loss of it was a weight heavier than wearing it had ever been. He couldn't just put it back on either, couldn't pretend that nothing had happened, not since he left it tucked into Emma Kate's hand.

Her stunned expression looking up at him was the one frozen in his memory. But he'd said goodbye to her family as politely as he could—as politely as her employer would—and he'd walked woodenly out the door. He'd aimed down the hall, not seeing the people who came at him and slid past. He was out the hospital door before he knew where he was going or what he was doing.

Keith told himself he knew—he *knew*—she hadn't told them. He hadn't admitted it to himself yet, but her betrayal wasn't a shock—he'd seen this day coming. He'd said he loved her. He'd figured it out, and he had been man enough to voice the words. She'd said the same to him more than once. It had even become the normal daily thing that newlyweds said. They made love looking in each other's eyes, and he'd realized he couldn't live his life without her, and yet here he was, walking away.

The kittens mewed harder while he put his coat and helmet away.

"It's okay. I'm coming." But the words didn't have anything behind him. They were just words. Just a promise of an action, not a feeling. He was numb.

As he got the bottles ready for the kittens, he would have normally pulled Star and Lucky out of their crate, let them crawl around the house. This time he did all of the actions completely by rote. The kittens' tiny cries unable to break through the cold shell around him.

As he poured formula and wet food into impossibly small dishes, he remembered what Emma Kate had said. She had told him that when she knew they would last, she would tell her family. She told him she loved him and she wanted to stay together and be married. Wasn't that forever?

Keith didn't see any good options here for what she meant by her actions. He put down the tiny dishes and watched as though from a distance as the two tiny cats trotted over and began eating with gusto and joy he couldn't feel.

It was possible Emma Kate knew this would happen. She

knew that he wanted them to stay together and that she would truly be his wife, but she'd lied.

She hadn't told her family, because she wasn't going to. Maybe she'd had no real intention of telling them. There'd certainly been plenty of opportunities, and he imagined it was hard to hide her marriage in a town where she was practically royalty.

The other option he could think of was that maybe she really did love him, but she still didn't intend to stay with him. Maybe she hadn't understood that he meant marriage forever. Maybe she simply meant she loved him *for now*, and she would see how it went. Maybe it hadn't been worth telling her sisters and her extended family in town.

That possibility hit him harder than the idea that she'd lied. Had he so horribly misread their situation? Maybe her love didn't mean what his did, and that was a harsh pill to swallow.

Reaching out, finally, he stroked the kittens while they ate their tiny dinners. They were used to being handled now, tummy rubs, cuddles, sweet southern lilted words about how big and strong they would grow up. But he was no Emma Kate.

When they finished, they wandered around with full tummies, more resembling drunken sailors than well-fed cats. They climbed the tiny ramp Em had built them to get into and out of the litter box. And their adorable antics would have amused him if he hadn't been so broken. He should have put them back in their crate, but he turned the TV on and let them play.

In a short while, both found their way into his lap and curled up to go to sleep, and he'd never felt more alone.

49

Emma Kate limped down the hall at Bailey Ann and Finn's house. Bailey Ann had insisted that Em stay with them rather than in their family home with Harper Rose. Harper Rose had her own hands full with her three daughters, and while Em understood that, she liked the family home better.

It was home. This wasn't. She needed home. Nursing a broken heart hurt worse when there was no one to tell.

Bailey Ann and Finn had bought this house almost three months ago. Their intention had been to remodel and live in it themselves. They were partway through some of the work. The main upstairs bathroom currently had plastic sheeting hanging across the door. Though the tub worked it was the only thing left in the room. The toilet and sink were just holes in the floor. The walls were stripped bare, and the room was dusty.

Thus, Em was sleeping downstairs. Though the upstairs bedroom would have been nicer—bigger and already remodeled, and *warmer* in the middle of winter—that room only had access to the gutted bathroom. If she stayed upstairs, she would have to use the downstairs restroom or walk directly through the master bedroom to get to the one functioning upstairs bath. She did not need to walk by her sister and her husband in the middle of the night to pee.

So she'd stayed downstairs, used the hallway bathroom there. No one else was in the house. Just the happy couple and Emma Kate, third-wheeling it. At least at night she didn't have to share it, and she didn't have to climb stairs, but her feet were cold. All of her was cold, but that probably wasn't due to being downstairs. She cried herself to sleep for three nights straight, the only upside being that her face was already so bruised and puffy that no one had noticed.

Despite numerous calls and texts in which she begged him to just respond, Keith wasn't speaking to her. Though it broke her heart, she understood and knew he had a right to be that angry. She'd told him so. She'd apologized. He'd still not responded.

She'd strung both of her rings and his onto a gold chain that she'd clasped around her neck and tucked down the front of her sweater. The rings stayed warm there and felt close, but no one saw them. It was the kind of symbolism widows used, and she thought it fell far short of what she needed right now.

She was stuck in this house for at least a week. Unable to drive, she wasn't fit for work anyway. Em had called Melanie the next morning and explained not only why she was late but that she wasn't coming at all. She hadn't been checked out of the hospital until almost noon that day. Melanie had assured her there was no problem with the missed days and that she only hoped Emma Kate felt better soon.

While she was glad Melanie had no problems with it, Em sure did. It sucked being stuck in the house all day. It sucked hurting everywhere, inside and out—though the inside part was her own fault. She was trusting Keith to explain where she was to Dr. Housley and the workers at the clinic. It didn't seem right to call in and have to explain that not only had she been in an accident, but that her husband had left her... and that it was not his fault. She didn't call.

What she needed right now was to tell her sister what was

really going on. Em needed something to go right. She missed having the kittens to take care of. She missed helping to create charitable events, and she missed the paycheck that she was now not getting at all. She wondered what Keith would do without her additional income, but the more she thought about it, she figured he'd probably be better off. He had been the one bringing more money into their little household.

She headed into the kitchen, still featuring dull, cream-colored laminate counters that Bailey Ann had already told her would go. Her sister had given a glowing tour of what the place would become in the future. While Emma Kate could fully see the vision, this house, unfortunately, was going to take a while to fix up to what they wanted it to be. Because it was for them, and not for profit, they had to do it in their off time, Bailey Ann and Finn had told her. But they looked at the old walls with smiles on their faces and a glow in their eyes, and Emma Kate felt just a little more like crap for not telling them what was going on.

Now, she didn't just feel bad that she hadn't told them about Keith because Keith needed to be accepted into the family, but also, for the first time, she felt bad about keeping such a big secret from her sisters.

Limping the last few steps into the U-shaped kitchen, she held her phone in one hand and her twisty tripod in the other. Em figured at least the lighting in the old house in the kitchen was good, and on the other hand, it didn't matter. Her face was bruised up as it was. Lighting wouldn't change that.

Setting her phone up and aiming the camera at her, she checked the background and then started filming.

Bailey Ann was asleep and hopefully would stay that way. She'd slept late most mornings that Em had been here. Finn had gone out early to do an estimate on a house they were considering buying. So, hopefully, Em had the space to herself.

She smiled into the camera as best she could. "Hello everyone! First, let's address my face. Yes, my face looks terrible. I was in a car accident just under a week ago, and that actually has inspired today's video. I'm fine. Please don't worry about me. I'm going to heal right up, but I'm in my sister's home and you can tell that she and her husband are remodeling it." Em panned the camera around, "Given my current state, today we're going to talk *good food*. I'm going to make a very simple breakfast, the kind that's really good if you hurt everywhere. The doctor said I needed protein, but my jaw hurts, and I don't feel like chewing or chopping a lot, so this is easy and good for me. It's my Mama's secret scrambled egg recipe."

Em proceeded to scramble the eggs with garlic pepper and showed off her secret ingredient—a dollop of mayonnaise. "I promise you'll eat the whole thing, so you'll get all your protein. Don't forget to add wheat toast for carbs. Jam is optional, but this meal took all of three minutes to make, and—luckily—not a lot of movement." Holding up her arm, she showed off small cuts and big bruises to her audience. "Seriously, everyone, wear your seatbelt all the time!"

She promised to be back with more videos once she healed up and signed off.

Just as she turned off the camera, she heard Bailey Ann behind her. Turning, she held up the pan of eggs and said, "I made enough eggs for you too."

Her sister smiled, said half of "thank you," then immediately turned green and ran down the hallway. Limping behind her, the pan left on the stove, Emma Kate followed to where she found Bailey Ann hugging the toilet bowl.

"Are you okay? The eggs are great. It's Mama's recipe."

Bailey Ann shook her head and wretched up her last night's dinner one more time. Then Em dove to hold her sister's hair, though she already had it clutched in one hand like a pro. Em was getting a cool washcloth ready when Bailey Ann smiled and said, "I'm fine."

❧ 50 ❧

Emma Kate stepped out into the hallway as a wave of jealousy hit her with a tsunami-like force. She'd simply moved out of the way before it knocked her backward.

"Oh, my God, you're pregnant." She felt the words roiling and rolling out of her with her sudden recognition of her sister's expression.

Bailey Ann smiled up at her, even though she still looked green, even though she immediately leaned over the toilet and tried to lose more of the breakfast she hadn't eaten. Eventually, her sister sighed heavily as apparently the feeling passed. Then she closed her eyes and leaned back against the opposite wall. Nausea was hard work.

"How can I help?" Emma Kate said, swimming through the harsh tide of envy. Her sister was not only happily married but expecting a child. Though she was truly excited for Bailey Ann, it was hitting her just how much she'd fucked up with Keith. It was hard looking at a picture of what she'd thrown away.

"I just need to go upstairs and brush my teeth," Bailey Ann told her. Em offered a helping hand to get her sister off the bathroom floor and watched as Bailey Ann headed down the hall. As her sister swayed just a little, her fingers trailed along the old, faded wallpaper, as though touching the wall helped keep her upright. Having been sick before, Em imagined it actually did.

Heading back into the kitchen, she plated the eggs onto two plates, added the toast that had popped up, and slathered jam on her own but not Bailey Ann's. Listening to see if her sister was coming back down the stairs, she set out glasses of ice water for both of them.

When Bailey Ann joined her at the table, she looked less green and more openly happy. At least looking at the eggs didn't make her vomit again, and she ate the toast.

Em scarfed down her whole breakfast. She would have liked to add diced tomatoes, ham, and grilled onions, but watching her sister slowly chew dry toast, perhaps it was better that she'd not been up to chopping a lot of things. Em decided to broach the subject.

"How far along are you?" she asked.

"Nine weeks," Bailey Ann replied.

"Did you tell Harper Rose?" The jealously hit her again. She'd always known her two older sisters were closer to each other than they were to her, and she'd always attributed it to the age difference. But now she was an adult, wasn't she? Shouldn't they share with her, too?

It felt a little too good when Bailey Ann shook her head. "Finn and I are the only ones who know. We didn't tell anyone. Not his sister, not Harper Rose, not you. We wanted to get to twelve weeks first."

Emma Kate nodded. That wasn't uncommon, and as long as she had Keith by her side she wasn't sure she'd do anything different herself... not that she would have Keith by her side. She fought the tears that were welling up in her eyes at the thought. But her sister must have attributed them to the conversation at hand, because Bailey Ann only smiled.

"How is it going?" Em asked, trying to turn her attention somewhere other than her own fuck-ups.

"Honestly? It's a little shaky," Bailey Ann told her.

"Oh, no." Well, her question had worked. She'd stopped eating and turned all her focus to her sister, worried now.

"Part of the reason we didn't tell even y'all early, was because we've been to the hospital twice already. Each time we thought I'd miscarried."

"But you didn't." Emma Kate slapped her fork on to the table, not sure if she was asking a question or making a demand.

"No," Bailey Ann said. "But unfortunately my risk is really high."

"My God. I'm so sorry. Do you need to be on bed rest or anything? I can help out with the business if you need a second set of eyes. Let me know whatever you need." It was a legit offer. She was going to lose her work with the clinic soon, if she hadn't already. And her sister didn't yet know it, but she'd lost her lease... Keith was living there. If she wanted to live in her own place, she'd have to set out and find it herself. Just thinking about it was like plunging a knife into her chest over and over.

She wound up making her sister an extra slice of toast, even though Bailey Ann commented that she was actually okay, and was supposed to be taking care of Emma Kate. "Rest doesn't help. I'm supposed to stay healthy and wait. It sucks!" Bailey Ann was clearly frustrated. "I guess it's a lesson in letting go of control."

Em didn't comment. Bailey Ann was big on control, but instead of thinking anything snarky or mean, all she could think was how hard that must be for her sister.

"All I can do is wait!" Her sister let out an un-Bailey-like sigh of disgust. "If we lose the pregnancy, we do. There's nothing I can do to help or hurt it apparently. Well, except I can't drink or bungee jump or ride roller coasters or..."

Laughing, Em picked up her plate and took it into the kitchen. "You didn't do those things in the first place." All those things actually sounded a lot more like Emma Kate than Bailey Ann.

"I know! But now I *can't*."

Em let Bailey Ann clean the kitchen counter and stack her dishes into the washer, her bruises suddenly hurting less in the face of her sister's concerns.

"No worries," she told Bailey Ann. "You just see if you can eat any eggs. You need protein. I've got this."

She left her sister sitting at the table, refilled her ice water, and brought a third round of toast. It wasn't much, and there was no variety, but at least her sister was eating enough.

As she wiped the last of the counter, her hand came up toward her neckline. It was time, she thought. Hell, it was *well past* time. She needed to tell her sisters. With a quick thought, she decided she couldn't wait any longer. She would tell Bailey Ann because she was here now. And she would tell Harper Rose as soon as it was physically possible. Waiting for the right time, waiting to get everyone together and make a formal announcement was what had gotten her in so much trouble in the first place.

With Keith gone, she supposed she could just let the story slide into her history. Just the thought of that hurt so deep that she vowed it wouldn't happen. She would have to get Keith back. To do so, she suspected she would need the full force of her sisters behind her. It was time to confess and beg for help.

With a deep breath for courage, Em called out to her sister, "Bailey Ann, I have something to tell you, too."

"Oh!" came the startled reply from the other room. But it wasn't a question. It had an exclamation mark at the end of it, and Em didn't know how to interpret that. So she turned and walked through the door into the dining room—the door was definitely something Finn would want to knock out, and probably make it into an arch or something.

But as she turned the corner and saw her sister's face, she had to ask, "Is everything okay?"

"No." Bailey Ann uttered the one word, short and sharp, and Em noticed her hands were on her stomach.

"Bailey Ann, are you okay?"

"No." Her sister looked up with tears and fear in her eyes. "I need to go to the hospital. Now."

K eith set out food for the kittens. He'd taken to mixing
their formula with more and more wet food. They no
longer required him to hold them or feed them with bottles like
little babies. In just a few weeks, they'd grown up so much. They
were still tiny, still underweight for their age, but so much
improved. Even in this last week.

Emma Kate had been gone for that week, so she hadn't
seen it.

With her gone, Keith had less and less around him that
needed him. With the kittens' development, they'd needed more
time out and about. He'd been letting them run free more often
than not. He watched as they hopped up onto the table, walking
carelessly across Emma Kate's nice linen tablecloth. Their antics
should have made him smile, but he didn't have it in him.

As he let them roam free more and more, he'd found them
climbing the curtains more than once. They were learning to get
down on their own. It helped that he no longer took pity on
them and plucked them off, setting them back on the floor.
They'd learned their way around out of necessity.

Though he didn't notice from a distance, when he looked up
close, he could see tiny pulls in the fabric from where they had

climbed. He wondered if Emma Kate would notice that he had let the kittens harm her handiwork. He wondered if she'd be upset, or if he'd even care.

He wasn't sure if he was depressed or not. Not prone to clinical depression, he could only guess that his flat emotional level was something close. He no longer got happy or sad about much of anything. Except for the nights he'd curled up in a ball, alone, in the middle of the big bed and wondered where she was and why she hadn't loved him as much as he'd loved her. Then, he'd felt *everything*, and every last moment of it had sucked. *Flat* seemed to be his better option these days.

For a while, he'd eaten reheated leftovers that remained in the fridge from when she'd been here—from before the accident that hadn't destroyed her physically, but had destroyed his life just as effectively. Some of those leftovers he had helped to make. However, now on his own, it became clear that the artistry was all hers. She was the reason they ate fish fillets and asparagus. She was the reason there was oatmeal or French toast casserole waiting in the crock pot for him in the morning.

The pots and pans stayed in the cabinet now. The fridge held more beer and less food. On his own, it became blazingly clear that he was not responsible for any of the wonderful things that had touched his life lately. On the coffee table, there was now an empty pizza box and two beer bottles right where he'd left them. Normally he was far too touchy about cleanliness to leave it that way, but now he just glanced at it as he sat down.

Sinking into the couch without even the TV on, Keith watched as the kittens roamed away from their food, and then came back to it to take tastes, or reassure themselves that it was still there. He had set out two separate bowls even though he knew better. The kittens didn't have a preference for one bowl or another and they would still clunk their heads together trying to eat out of the same dish when there were clearly two options.

He was working at mustering up a smile for them as the knock came at the door. It was probably the Barkers. So he didn't think anything of it as he got up and opened the door without checking at the peephole.

But it wasn't either of the Barkers.

Emma Kate stood there on the porch, looking at him with her own flat expression.

Not sure what to say, he didn't even say hello. He stood there in the space of the open door, letting the heat out, until she asked, "Can I come in?"

It hurt him that she had to ask if he was willing to let her into her own home. But she hadn't been here for a full week.

He wasn't sure if he'd say yes, so he just looked at her. He was still heartbroken, utterly gutted by her actions. It didn't seem to matter. She pushed past him and stopped in the living room. She turned to look at him, but her expression hadn't changed.

Standing there, she peeled the gloves from her hands and opened the buttons on her coat because it was too warm inside the house for all the layers she was wearing. He waited for her to take it off to hang it on the coatrack, but she didn't.

She must not be planning to stay very long.

Em stood silently before him in her beautiful wool coat. Gloves in her hand, her hair perfect, she looked just like his Emma Kate. But her heart shone in her eyes and she said the two words he desperately wanted to hear.

"I'm sorry."

Keith waited for more. But no other words came out of Emma Kate's mouth. Eventually they would be at a standstill if he didn't say something. So he asked, even though he really didn't expect there was an answer he would like. "Sorry for what?"

"I'm sorry that I didn't tell my family about us." She looked away, then back at him. "I should have told them. I meant to. I wanted you to know that I had called my aunt GiGi and set up a family dinner so I could introduce you to everyone."

She paused for a moment. "I had Aunt GiGi and Uncle Dex signed on to host a big family meal so I could show you off to everyone." She sighed, the kind that caught in the back of her throat, and he almost fell for it.

"When was this going to be?" Keith asked, curious because she seemed to think that the plan alone was enough.

"It's still a week and a half away. Lennon and Gabe will be here for Uncle Dex's birthday, and I was going to do it a few days before then. For Sunday dinner." She offered the details as though they were proof of her intentions. But she looked off to the side, watching as the kittens leapt up on the chairs and then the table.

Their antics didn't make her smile either, and Keith found a moment's satisfaction that she seemed as unhappy as he did. But her dinner plans weren't enough for Keith, he thought, and still too far away. He didn't need *plans*. He needed *action*.

As he watched, she broke down. "I'm so sorry, Keith. I have your ring. It's on me," she pulled the gold chain at her neck, showing him the three rings she was wearing.

But she was still hiding them, he thought, and the anger surged through him even as she spoke again.

"...and want to give your ring back to you. I want you to wear it, and I want to wear my rings again."

"But your dinner isn't enough, Emma Kate!" The words and anger burst out. "I need to know that you're proud to be with me. I needed you to *want* to tell them."

"I did!" She was almost yelling back at him. "I had the big dinner planned, but being home with my sister this week, I told her. And then I called Harper Rose and I told her as well. They know everything now."

"Only because you were in an accident! Only because it was too hard to hide it or explain why your *employer* showed up in the hospital so worried about you."

"You can call my aunt GiGi," she said, though her voice was smaller now. "She was on the phone with me when I had the accident. That's what I was asking her about."

"I'm not calling your aunt GiGi to see if you made dinner

plans, Em! I don't care about that. I care about who you turn to. Who's your emergency contact in your phone, Em? Who?"

She knew what he was asking, and her eyes welled up. It wasn't him. That's what it meant.

She whispered, "Bailey Ann," as she nodded, finally seeing his anger, that her plans weren't enough. "I understand."

"*No*," he yelled, "I don't think you do understand. How can I trust plans for two weeks away when you don't finish anything, Emma Kate? You didn't finish your degree. You made plans but didn't finish telling your family about me. You don't finish your dinners. Hell, you don't even finish your own damn name, *Em*!"

He took a deep breath, the emotions pulling into his lungs and he hated it. He wished he could shut down again, but he couldn't. So he yelled one more time. "How can I trust you to stay when you don't finish *anything*?"

❦ 52 ❦

Emma Kate was finding a way to get through her life. It wasn't easy, but she was doing it. It had been two weeks since she'd spoken to Keith.

Keith, unfortunately, had made some very solid points. Though he'd yelled at her when he said them, he hadn't been wrong. He was right to be mad about her plans to tell her family. Though she'd initially chalked it up as a win, it was truly "too little, too late." Despite her intentions, she hadn't actually *told* them, not until she was forced to. Not until her words no longer meant what they should have.

Though she'd managed to hide her marriage from her sisters, even while she was in the hospital, it had cost her far too much. The one thing Keith hadn't asked her—while he'd been asking if he could trust her or if she would finish anything—was whether it had been worth it.

The only answer was *It hadn't*.

She wished now that she'd just opened her mouth months ago and told them. She wished she'd shouted it out loud. She wished she'd been brave enough to face everything they might have said, every insult they might have thrown at her about not finishing school. Everything they might have been disappointed in—that she'd gotten drunk and wound up getting married in Vegas to someone she didn't know. She wished she'd stood up and taken everything they might have said about all her stupid choices.

If she'd faced them all, then she would still have Keith.

Her bruises had finally healed to the point where a little concealer would cover them. Melanie invited her back to work with open arms.

"I was so scared when you were in that accident! Honestly, when you didn't show up for work the next morning, I thought something must be wrong. You've never been late or not ready for anything!"

"Well, I hope getting cut out of my car by the jaws of life will be my one excuse." She smiled at Melanie, wanting to say how good it felt that Melanie kept her in the job despite the missed time. It meant a lot that she was more worried about Emma Kate than about filling in the position. And that she seemed to think Em was a stellar worker who was always professional. Emma Kate didn't want to say those things. Didn't want to tell her boss who thought well of her that she was known as the family fuck-up. That she'd screwed up her marriage, too. So she smiled and took the compliment. At least this was a job she could keep.

She'd asked Keith via text about the job at the clinic, wondering if this was the end of her work there. He'd written back promptly and told her, "Everyone loved your layout for the front office. So they made the other station match. Thank you."

That was it. Though she'd specifically asked in her initial text if she needed to call Housley and see if there were other days she should come in, Keith hadn't responded about that. It wasn't like Keith to leave a question unanswered and Em could only conclude that he'd seen her concern and simply chosen not to reply about it.

There would be no more work at the clinic. With her work hours cut nearly in half, she buckled down. Emma Kate made dinners for her sister and brother in law several times a week, buying the ingredients herself. She made enough for leftovers and packed them in individual sizes so they could easily be taken for lunches for the three of them.

She was definitely the third wheel in the house, and maybe it was better that she was downstairs and away from the newlyweds. Never intending to stay this long, she'd foolishly believed that Keith would come back and say they needed to be together. Then, when she'd gotten her shit together and gone to apologize, she'd foolishly believed that two simple words would be enough.

She'd hurt him far worse than she'd realized.

So she nursed her broken heart by ignoring it. Staying busy was the best treatment. Em did what she could around the house, from cleaning and straightening to picking up a hammer and helping Finn take out walls when he had a free evening.

The two of them had used her big Sunday dinner to announce their pregnancy. That was nice since everyone had been called together so Em could tell them everything. Now she figured she would just break down in tears and run crying from the room. That would have been a crappy surprise.

Bailey Ann managed to stay out of the hospital for a while, and that made everyone happy. Emma Kate was glad not to be back at the hospital at all. Even more so that it meant her sister and the new baby were healthy and growing appropriately. She continued to be more than a little jealous, even though she knew her sister had waited a long time for this.

She and Bailey Ann painted the baby's room. And Em turned on her camera again. "Hello all! I'm here with my sister, Bailey Ann." Bailey Ann leaned into the shot and waved at the online viewers. "And we're painting her baby's room this beautiful soft shade of purple today. Though she didn't take my advice of searching the already mixed colors paint shelf, we're going to still use a bunch of our painting techniques. And, we're doing stencils!"

She'd talked to the camera and her sister as they worked.

Thinking she would edit most of it out later, she just left the camera rolling.

"Should you even be breathing these paint fumes?" Em had asked her. "It seems like it would be unhealthy given that you're pregnant."

Bailey Ann had laughed at her, "What do you smell? Not the usual paint smell, right? This doesn't have any VOCs. It's safe enough to eat."

"Please don't." Emma Kate had made a face and turned away. "I've seen what you're craving. Please don't add 'organic paint' to the list."

More laughter and smiles came in response and Em wished she could feel that happy, too. "We're painting all the houses with this so I can keep working while I'm pregnant."

"*If* you can keep working," Emma Kate said, "You don't know what will happen with a pregnancy. Remember, you can hire me if you need to. Apparently, I have a lot of free hours now and I'll work for zero dollars per hour in exchange for room and board."

"That's very sweet of you." Bailey Ann had simply reached out and hugged her, paying no attention to the paint getting on either of them. "Hopefully you'll have another job before too long. But don't worry. We aren't trying to get rid of you."

"I was hoping to use Housley in the clinic as a reference to get other jobs reorganizing offices," Emma Kate lamented. She wished she wasn't recording all of this. It wasn't her usual method, but she'd decide later if she had enough good footage to make the right kind of video.

"I suspect you still can use the clinic. You did great work there." Bailey Ann told her. "I can't imagine Dr. Housley would give you anything other than a glowing reference. Regardless of however things ended up with Keith."

Then her sister paused, "What are you doing to fix that?"

She shrugged and turned back to the camera. Waiting a beat for editing space, she said, "My sister is stenciling the walls here. While you can buy stencils, they can be costly. Cheap ones are available, and you should use them if you find one you like. However, Bailey Ann made her own, and it's very inexpensive. Want to tell them what they need?" She turned to her sister and found out that Bailey Ann just might upstage her as an online personality.

That night, she edited and uploaded the video. Her viewership had bloomed into something big. But there were comments asking if she was going to keep working on the tiny house. She didn't answer.

Emma Kate also used her spare time to write on her thesis. Her advisor had approved her initial idea, and she'd even managed to hand in the research for the background section as well as her first draft already.

Her professor's response to it had showed up in her email that morning and Em was more than a little nervous about opening it up, quite convinced it would be completely covered in red lines and edits. She told herself it didn't matter though, that she had until the end of the summer to get the paper done and defended. The defense had to happen on campus and that meant a trip back to UCLA.

However, without having to support a household, pay for anywhere near as much gas, or cover the grocery bills, she had less to pay out and it was easier than she'd expected to save up for the plane ticket. She had friends in Los Angeles, students and recent graduates who had apartments near campus. She was hoping to mooch a couch off of one of them. That would save her a ton in hotel fees, even if it meant sleeping on a couch.

Trying to put her organization skills to work to actually finish something, she'd looked up her last possible defense date to graduate during the summer term. Then she'd back calculated each piece of her work from there. When would she need to have her final draft of her presentation? When would her professors on her committee need to sign off on her paperwork? Could she handle that via FedEx or would she have to make another trip and show up in person and have them sign off on her documents? She currently had emails out to all three of them asking exactly these questions.

Next in her calendar was actually scheduling a room and a time for her thesis defense. The very idea made her nervous, but less so than her concerns about Keith. If she could handle what had happened to her since Vegas, she could handle any rejection they threw at her. If she had to get to LA more than once, she would just figure out how to do it.

When she did open the email later in the day, she was surprised to find that while yes, it was covered in edits and red marks left and right, her professor was actually very pleased with it.

She read through the email a second time. "It's time to pick a date and reserve your room for your defense. You should know that these rooms get very busy toward the end of the summer as do your professors, since everyone pushes it to the last minute. I think given your previous work, and your desire to have a happy defense committee that you should plan this for June. I'm confident you can be ready then. And—if you can do it—your early defense will make room for us to handle other students who push things to the last minute and procrastinate."

Emma Kate felt her mouth hanging open.

He wanted her to defend her thesis at the beginning of the summer. Once the professors all signed off on it, it would be the equivalent of having her degree. She would officially graduate in August, though she wouldn't be able to walk at a graduation ceremony until December. She could basically graduate in June!

She immediately wrote to the department secretary and asked about scheduling her room.

❈ 53 ❈

Emma Kate was proud of what she was getting accomplished, even if she was lonely. She'd worked hard to get here—even if it was without her husband.

Her thesis advisor was now pushing her to work even faster. Because she was living with Bailey Ann and Finn, it was not only possible, it was easy to not take on an extra job yet. That meant she had a part-time job's worth of hours in the week to work on her thesis. She put in every extra minute.

Emma Kate was sending in new sections and updates to Dr. Beeman, her main advisor, every few days. So not only was her thesis moving quickly, it was keeping her mind off of Keith.

When it did wander back to him, her brain trailed in a predictable pattern. How was the office without her? Probably fine, to be fair. How was Keith doing? Probably not eating as well. She wouldn't even entertain the idea that he was dating. He wouldn't. She'd received no papers that dissolved their marriage. He was hanging in limbo like she was. And lastly, how were the kittens? Star and Lucky should be ready to head off to their forever homes any day now—if they weren't already past that age.

Emma Kate had reached out via email asking him how he

wanted to handle that. Because she'd been vetting various emails and requests to adopt one or either of the kittens from her online viewers, she was hoping she could make a video of the kittens heading off. But she needed Keith's input.

After several days when he hadn't responded, she began to wonder if he ever would. If she wasn't depressed about everything in her personal life, the kitten adoption would have been a great motivator. Professionally, student-wise, and sister-wise, she was making great strides forward.

She'd finished the trim in the baby's room herself while her sister was out at work. The stencils were fantastic, and Bailey Ann had turned to Em to figure out the best pattern and what color of paint would show the best.

Em had also assembled the new crib. She'd found it in the box, where Finn had pulled it inside and pushed it into the baby's room for later.

When Bailey Ann and Finn were home, she ate dinner with them, but mostly tried to stay out of their hair. So she worked on her thesis while they watched TV in the rec room. Or she found a project. Finn had come home and found the crib about two hours later. Though he thanked her a too-massive number of times, she'd only smiled. Em knew they were worried about her and she tried to smile genuinely as much as possible.

She'd also spent her own money buying a gliding rocking chair and setting it into the corner of the baby's room with a huge bow on it. Em had left it there. It only took Bailey Ann five minutes upon arriving home to walk into the room and discover it. When she heard the squeal of delight, Emma Kate gave herself a genuine smile, even though there was no one in the room to see it.

Checking a lot of boxes on her to-do list felt good. While she was proud of those accomplishments, it was hard to count her life in the plus column. Everything still felt a little flat.

Melanie's voice reached across the room. "So when you head

out to LA to defend your thesis, what's that like? Is it a full thesis? Did you have to do research and gather data?"

Em smiled at her boss's sudden enthusiasm. She wasn't thrilled to be asking for an extra chunk of time off, especially after she'd just had medical leave and had only been on the job a few months.

"Actually," she replied, "they call it a thesis, but only because it's for a bachelor program. If this was for an advanced degree, it would be considered more of a 'capstone'."

She took a breath, and when Melanie still looked interested, Em continued. "There's a lot of research I've had to do, but it's not data collection. More the information-gathering kind. So I have new ideas, but I'm supporting them with other people's research, rather than performing my own experiments and running any statistical analysis. That's what's made this fast enough to get me through this month."

She shrugged. "It's why I didn't worry as much when I left school."

Melanie tipped her head and brought out another question. "So you're able to do the thesis now, even though you're in Georgia and not L.A.?"

"Technically, no," Emma Kate answered, "I have to be an enrolled student in order to defend. So I'm having to pay for a short summer term of tuition. That allows my professors to advise me and sit in the room while I defend the thesis."

"So, you're paying for a term you aren't really attending, except via email?" Melanie asked, catching on. "That sucks."

"True. But that's the way it's always been."

"Why are you paying it? I mean, you have a job here. And you're not getting classes or anything."

Emma Kate had wondered that herself, but she knew the answer now. "I have to finish. I need my degree. I did too much and got too close to quit now."

"Are you leaving me?"

The question made Em's head snap up. So that's what had brought on this conversation! She shook her head. "I love working for you. I have no intention of leaving this job. I just wish you could give me more hours." She shouldn't have said that last part... *oops*.

"Maybe in the summer. Once we get you with more experience under your belt, we can expand the business. I can take a real vacation."

Em smiled. A real one. That kind of trust felt good. She steered the conversation back to school, now that she had a better idea where she stood. "Well, I knew that going in—that I would have to do this. And the upside is that a half summer term is much cheaper than spring quarter."

"Will you go back for graduation?" Melanie asked and Emma Kate wound up explaining the issues that graduates only walked in December and June.

"But I'll be done. I'll have my degree in hand when the term ends in the middle of August. Technically, I can get what's called a W A D—a 'work all done' form, and that will make me a graduate in barely another three weeks... provided my committee approves my thesis." She shrugged at the last part, nerves still getting the best of her.

"I can't imagine they wouldn't." Melanie smiled. "And just so you know, I give raises for education. You'll get your raise when that W A D form comes in."

"Wow, you don't have to..." Then Emma Kate swallowed that back and changed her answer to "Thank you." The warm feeling in her chest still didn't radiate quite all the way to the edges.

Her world was a little bit dimmer without Keith in it. Pulling out her phone, she checked her email again to see if he had replied about the kittens. Still nothing.

She couldn't blame him. He hadn't been the one to fuck things up. That had been her, and she couldn't fix it. Not yet. First, she was going to get this thesis done.

The next thing on her checklist was getting her husband back.

❈ 54 ❈

Keith set his bowl of Ramen noodles on the table and moved his hand to wave away two kittens who dove for his food. "You've got your own coming. Wait a sec."

His voice was met by tiny mews. They'd gotten louder over the past few weeks, but no less adorable. He was glad his voice wasn't the only sound in the house besides the TV.

Star and Lucky sat back for only a moment. Just long enough for him to put out two little bowls of wet kitten food now mixed with hard kibble. A tiny water dish sat next to each place—another remnant of Emma Kate. Though she would likely have not let them sit *on* the table like he did.

They were too tiny still to sit in the chairs. They wouldn't even be able to peek over the surface, let alone be able to reach their food. He'd taken to eating with them this past week as their schedule moved to fewer, but bigger, feedings each day. So each kitten sat at their own place, a woven place mat defining their spot. It had only been a few days, but they knew where their food showed up.

The place mats had been another beautiful piece of home Emma Kate had left behind. He wondered if she was coming back for all her things. If she would strip the house bare and leave it as gray and lonely as he felt on the inside.

There were four place settings, one on each side of the small, oval table. He used one for himself and his Ramen and one for each kitten. The empty space taunted him, reminding him that he'd made a mistake walking away so firmly. He'd been angry and hurt and he'd lashed out. Hard. Looking back, maybe he should have thought through the ramifications first.

Emma Kate had been emailing him and asking about adopting the kittens out. She was right, it was time. She'd sent him five different applications and asked him to pick two—one for each kitten. She'd even asked if he wanted to match the kitten to the home. She didn't say, "because you clearly know their personalities now better than I do."

Her note—though bordering on professional—put a lot of trust in him. It also put most of the responsibility on her. She volunteered to pick up the kittens, asked what date he wanted that done, and commented that some of the distances would be several hours away to deliver the kittens to their new homes. She would gladly do the driving. She said she hoped to send them each in a separate direction, making two families happy, and noting that she remembered that he told her kittens didn't need to stay together. They might be happier each having their own family giving them individual attention.

He would miss them, he knew, and he wondered what he would do when there were three empty seats at the table. It was more than a little possible that was the reason he hadn't yet emailed her back, though he told himself it was because he was still looking through the applications. When he wasn't lying to himself, he admitted it was because he hadn't yet figured out how to use this conversation to open another one.

He desperately needed to talk to her. He needed her back in his life. But he didn't know how to make that happen. While he thought he could get her back, get her living here in the tiny house with him, it wouldn't be what he needed if things weren't different this time around. If she couldn't be honest with everyone around her about him, then they would just end up in the same place again.

He was torn.

He'd figured it would get easier living without her—the longer she was gone, the less it would hurt. But that was not what was happening. Maybe it was simply because she was Emma Kate, maybe it wasn't because he loved her so much, but because of what she did. She'd come in here and swept her hands like a sexy Mary Poppins and changed everything around her for the better. She'd literally turned the black and while tones of the house to color. And he didn't realize it when he'd walked away at the hospital, but when she left the house—and him—she'd left a hole no one else could fill.

He was halfway through his Ramen, the kittens licking the bottoms of their bowls clean, when the knock came at the door.

Frowning at first, he smiled when he realized it could be Emma Kate. Keith jumped up, the frown disappearing as he threw the door wide.

Though it was a Mayfair, it wasn't Emma Kate. Bailey Ann stood on his doorstep and he could see where Emma Kate had gotten her class. Her sister was wearing a cut blazer with her maternity jeans and even heels. This was definitely a Mayfair thing.

Merely raising one eyebrow, she asked if she could come in without asking a single word. Holding the door back, he waved his hand, welcoming her. "Bailey Ann. It's nice to see you again. Come on in."

The smile that lit up her face reminded him of her little sister and his chest squeezed as he wondered what Emma Kate had told her family about their breakup. He just wondered how that story had gone. Was he the villain? Was Em? Maybe she said it was fate keeping them apart. He had no idea what the woman sitting in front of him thought of him, and he didn't like that.

Bailey Ann Mayfair proceeded to slide out of her jacket and

tossed it over one arm. Still holding onto her things—indicating she didn't intend to stay long—she sat down on the couch, running a hand along the blanket that was stitched into the beautiful slip-cover. She probably recognized her sister's work, but she only admired it a moment before she looked up at him.

"I know things about my sister and you," she said, making him very nervous. "I know how she feels about you. And I know what her regrets are, but they aren't mine to tell. So I can only tell you that I know, and that I'm making my decisions accordingly."

That, Keith thought, he could understand. Though he wanted to know everything Bailey Ann knew, he couldn't ask her. She was telling him she knew, but also that she wouldn't break confidence.

Instead, she looked at him and said, "Emma Kate is defending her thesis next week."

"Oh, wow," he replied, stunned. He wasn't quite sure what to do with that information, beside be impressed. Em had done it. That thesis had been the bane of Emma Kate's existence, something she had put off over and over again. Now it appeared it was almost finished.

"In Los Angeles?" he asked, suddenly calculating how he might get across the country in time to be there.

It seemed, for all of Emma Kate's ability to take something and transform it, to look ahead and see what might be, it wasn't just something that belonged to his wife. It appeared to be a trait that permeated her whole family.

Bailey Ann nodded. "Yes, in L.A. Our sister Harper Rose and I are going to be there for her. So is her cousin Lennon. We have a hotel room booked. Two nights."

"That's fantastic," he breathed the words out, hardly thinking first. He was glad they were going. Emma Kate would enjoy having the support on hand.

Bailey Ann looked him square in the eyes. "Do you want to come?"

He tipped his head asking a question. *How?* But he said, "I would love to. I'll get a ticket."

"You don't need to." Bailey Ann reached into her over-sized purse and pulled out a folded sheet of paper. "I already bought you one. Our flight leaves Tuesday evening. Can you get the time off work?"

"I'll make it happen." Keith reached out and took the ticket from where she held it out to him, hardly believing it was already done.

"Excellent." Bailey Ann smiled widely and launched into logistics. She offered a pick-up time so they could get him to the airport. She seemed to already know that he was dealing with his bike and not a car.

"I'll be ready." He told her this hoping to convey that she could trust him, but she didn't know him well enough for that.

As she slid back into her jacket to head out the door, Keith stopped her, the ticket still clutched in his hand. "This is a pretty big bet on me. You don't even know me."

Bailey Ann turned back and looked at him, her expression almost bland. "You're right. I don't know you well enough to bet this big. But if I can be honest, I'm not betting on you. I can't imagine my baby sister truly loving a man who didn't truly love her back. So, no, I'm not betting on you. This," she tapped the ticket in his hand, "is a bet on my sister."

❧ 55 ❧

Emma Kate stood on the small stage next to the large screen showing her PowerPoint seven feet tall. Turning toward the seats, she looked out over the small crowd that had gathered to see her defend her thesis.

Some of the college professors in attendance were hers, some were just there to see the thesis itself. Some of the students were friends of hers, and some were rising seniors there to witness what the torture would be like.

The room had stadium seating, but only the first ten or so rows were full. Stragglers filled random seats alone or in pairs up to the back of the hall. It was more than enough to give her the jitters. She'd stumbled a little at the start of her talk. The remote hadn't wanted to work until she stood in a certain point on the stage. It did this to her even though she had tested it thoroughly before she started. *Figured.*

She saw her professors—the three that comprised her committee—in the very front row. A table had been pulled up for them and all three were nodding and making furious notes as she went along.

In the back, her two sisters sat alongside Lennon and she looked up at them for comfort every few minutes. They smiled, gave the occasional thumbs up and encouraged her to keep going just by being there. Though she was fine in a social situation, the stage was nerve-wracking and so was the "rest of your life" proclamation that would be handed down at the end of this.

Her professors were basically worthless as far as encouragement went. In fact, she was quite certain from the blank looks on their faces that they were going to fail her as fast and as hard as they could. She reminded herself that it was only the beginning of summer, and she could use the other mini-semester and still make it out in August.

Though he looked glum now, Dr. Beeman had encouraged her all along via email and in their face-to-face talks before she left school back in the winter. It hadn't been that long ago, though she was a completely different person now. So she reminded herself—as she was clearly failing this presentation—she could still graduate at the end of the summer quarter even if she had to do this again.

At last she finished her planned portion of the speech and opened the floor to questions. *Because this wasn't hard enough with a script. Ugh.*

Dr. Lester looked up at her, his eyes cold and hard like obsidian. Let it begin, she thought.

He did. "You've defined the idea of 'old money' more as a state of mind than as an economic condition. Since these are generally social use terms and not commonly defined ones, can you please elaborate?"

"Certainly," Emma Kate smiled. She'd known since she was a small girl that she could offer a smile even when no one else did. So she used that now, and she knew she could answer his question. She took a deep breath to think for a moment, then began talking. "The perception of *old money*, whether by the person or the outside world, is more based on presentation than on an actual bank balance number. There doesn't exist any specific economic level that's achieved to become 'old money.' However, there are certain milestones we can mark in the recent generational history that will match across what we define as 'old money.' For example, a home of a certain square footage, usually owned outright, is one hallmark. Another is that the home has been owned by the family for a certain number of generations as well, usually a minimum of three, anything less than that, and the perception then shifts to 'new money.'

"The major distinguishing factor between what I refer to as 'old money' and 'new money' is the lack of a need to flash the level of success achieved." She thought of her cousin Lennon's fiancé. Gabe and the Zemp family flashed their money, not horribly, but they owned local stores. His father, Bobby Zemp, let everyone know he was a bigwig in town. Gabe's older brother Brodie—when he'd been alive—had driven a fancy sports car and now Gabe did too.

There was something about the change from not having that kind of economic security to having the ability to buy the sports car and the big house that made people want to flash it. Emma Kate talked her way through all of this but never mentioned the Zemp name. "Though I'm using terms not thoroughly defined in the lexicon, they are well defined in common speech. 'Old money' refers in many cases to people who will exhibit behaviors associated with poorer counterparts. For example, they will drive a car into the ground, until it's worthless. But they would never trade the car in. Instead, they'll donate it to a charity, walk to a dealer and buy a new car for cash. The difference in perception is that they don't owe anyone an accounting of their level of worth."

It struck her right then, as she stood on stage, that she would be much better off if she took that advice to heart. She didn't need this degree to validate herself, she just needed the stamp to prove to herself that she could finish it. She didn't owe anyone an accounting of her own level of worth. She felt her shoulders settle, and even though she was near the end of this defense, Em was suddenly much more comfortable. Let them flunk her. She didn't need them.

"The level of money that they have is just assumed to be of an adequate level. What's interesting is that many of these old money families maintain this perception even when they don't have the bank account to support it."

She continued on and answered several other questions.

She was asked how the economics of old money and the social perception of it intersected. She had been ready for this question in particular, and she flashed another smile. She was defending a dual degree, she had to show where her thesis hit both majors.

In the end, her professors were no help. They merely looked up at her, their faces still blank and said, "Thank you." Then they turned to the room and dismissed everyone which left them alone with Emma Kate.

She knew what was coming. This was private questioning. About her thesis, her choice of topic, her coursework, all of it. They asked about her time in school and about her time off. They asked why the dual degree? Why honors? And did she feel she'd earned it? Though, normally, she would have been sweating by the time they dismissed her, she'd settled somewhere along the way. They no longer scared her.

When they at last dismissed her, too, she headed into the hallway to wait out the rest of the time as they made their decision. While she knew the vast majority of people who had come to see her would have left by now, her sisters had likely only gone down the hall to the vending machine and were just beyond the doorway, waiting for her.

But when she came through the door, it wasn't them waiting. It was Keith.

❧ 56 ❧

Emma Kate felt her heart stop. She was in Los Angeles. At school. Why was Keith here?

She wasn't unhappy with that, not by any stretch, but she was stunned. It took a moment for the bubble in her heart to make its way to her brain and let her know that he had come all this way to watch her defend her thesis.

He smiled at her and she almost melted. "You were amazing."

"Thank you," She answered him far too politely for how she felt. "I only hope my committee feels the same way."

"They will," he told her, confidence lacing the words. Then he added, "I've seen enough of these to know that yours went very, very well. You knocked it out of the park, honey."

She swallowed hard at the endearment, hope bubbling inside her. It burst out of her in three little words, "I missed you."

"I missed you, too." Keith whispered it back, the tone soft enough to brush against everything she'd hoped for.

"I'm sorry. I'm so sorry, Keith." She was reaching out to him, touching his shirt, just grateful that he didn't step away. Though she hadn't meant to, she'd wound her fingers into his shirt and was holding on now. "I screwed up and I won't screw up again."

She took a deep breath, waiting as he looked at her. He was

looking at her like he wanted to say something, but she jumped into the space. "I'm waiting to hear what my committee says, but I was coming home to you. I have to get you back."

I shouldn't have said that, the thought streaked through her mind. She shouldn't have told him what her plan was. What if he disagreed?

But he didn't. Instead, Keith smiled at her, and leaned in close. "That's a good plan." Then he paused. "At least I hope it is, because I have the same one."

Hope flared in her chest. "I won't screw up again, Keith. I promise."

"Me either," he said. He'd pulled back and he was looking in her eyes. "I didn't make it easy for you to come back." Pausing, he looked upward as though searching for words. "You aren't a screw up. You've finished everything I've seen you tackle... even this thesis. I think maybe you were like that as a kid or your family said it... but it's become this baggage that you've hauled everywhere with you. You believe it so much that when I was mad it was the nearest, most effective weapon. I shouldn't have said those things. They aren't even true."

He paused again and, when she started to speak, he shook his head to stop her. "The only thing you didn't finish was telling your family about me. You clearly turn everything you touch to gold and you didn't want me to be part of that. That's what hurt the most. I shouldn't have walked away like I did. I should have said what I felt and given you a chance to respond."

Emma Kate was shaking her head no. "I understand what you did. That was on me. You gave me every chance to tell my family and I didn't want to risk their reactions, because they do see me that way. I didn't want to be torn between them and you. I need them. But I need you, too, and you're worth every reaction. You always were. I just didn't know it."

She waited for him to respond and almost smiled as he leaned in closer. But he was kissing her until she melted there in his arms. Maybe because of the kiss, maybe because she finally had her second chance, she finally believed they would work it out.

As she took her first deep breath in more weeks than she cared to count, she was interrupted by the door opening behind her. Her committee was calling her back in.

She'd forgotten to be nervous about her professors taking their time to make a decision about her.

"Emma Kate? Would you like to come in?" Dr. Beeman's face was as flat as ever, but she finally didn't care.

Her fingers were laced with Keith's and she could practically feel him push her away. "Go, you've got this." He whispered the words into her hair, and she knew he was right.

Her three professors stood as she walked into the large room that had now become their private chamber to give her their decision. Just before the doors closed, she heard Keith say, "I'll be waiting right here."

❧ 57 ❧

Keith watched as Emma Kate's eyes lit up again and again during the meal. Her sisters had taken them all out to some garlic-based restaurant they had heard about. The food reeked to high heaven and tasted as amazing as everyone had told them it would. It was definitely a celebration. Emma Kate had been glowing like a Christmas light. Maybe because she passed her thesis defense. Maybe because she was holding his hand under the table and wouldn't let go.

He'd whispered to her that Star and Lucky missed her, but he should have reiterated that he did, too. They'd had a moment to speak briefly after she got out of her thesis committee, but he'd felt uncertain and had wound up sticking to logistics. "Should we pick homes for the kittens? I'll help you drive them."

She'd agreed, then told him her viewership had picked up again, but they all missed the little house. They discussed her job and his. Her sisters' lives. But they'd not really talked again. There was more to do. But it would have to wait until later. For now, he held her hand and hoped she understood.

Though Keith wasn't normally one to eat too much garlic, he was enjoying watching Emma Kate devour it. He'd ordered a meal with only one vampire beside it on the menu. The rating went up to four, but he was hopeful to not smell like garlic tonight. He hadn't said anything yet, but...

As he watched, Lennon pulled out a gift-wrapped box while they all finished up their entrees. The three sisters leaned in and watched carefully as Emma Kate opened it. It seemed they all knew what was in the box, though he had not been privy to that information.

Em pulled her fingers away from where they were laced through his so she could peel ribbon and gift wrap back. The box was flat and square, and Emma Kate seemed to frown as though she recognized it.

Keith couldn't tell if she recognized this exact box—it looked old—or just that it was a jewelry box. She carefully flipped open the lid and found a single strand of golden pearls nestled in a perfect, if ancient, velvet setting.

Bailey Ann nodded as though confirming what everyone already knew—everyone except Keith. "They were Grandma Brown's."

"I thought these were supposed to be yours, Bailey Ann." Em hadn't lifted the necklace out of the box but was reverently running her finger across the pearls.

Now her sister shook her head. "They were left for one of us. I think everyone just assumed they would go to me, since I was the oldest. But there are three of us girls. Harper Rose and I decided that you earned them. We know you got shafted on the family silver, baby sis."

Keith smiled. Even he knew that Em hadn't inherited many of the family heirlooms. In a system that seemed antiquated, she was the proverbial seventh son—the one who got nothing. He watched as she smiled to Harper Rose, and then to Bailey Ann.

It took a moment for him to catch on that she was too choked up to speak. He knew right then that this was the first time Emma Kate felt that she had been seen by her sisters as one of them. Something as simple as a strand of pearls that stayed in the family for years, probably sitting in a jewelry box, unworn, had made a much bigger statement than he would have expected.

Em had tears rolling down her face, and he couldn't help sliding his arm around her waist and squeezing her close for support. "This is beautiful," he told her sisters, though his attention was on his wife.

His wife.

It felt good to be back beside her. He was grateful that he hadn't missed this. It was a big day for her, and he'd had his head so far up his own ass that he wouldn't have known, if not for Bailey Ann. He looked up and gave Bailey Ann a grateful smile as he mouthed "thank you" to her.

She nodded only once and said, "They look perfect on you, Em."

Emma Kate turned and put her head on his shoulder and for the first time that evening, it hit him that he'd failed. He'd come to see her, but he'd not brought a present to celebrate her success.

When they were all leaning back, and moaning with their bellies full, the three women across the table waved their hands at him and Emma Kate. Almost like a trio of witches warding them off.

"We're getting this," Lennon told them in a tone that brooked no argument. "We are splitting it, so you don't have to worry about any of us going bankrupt."

Since Keith had almost gulped at the prices on the menu, he graciously accepted their offer of getting the check. After all, he'd spent all of his money already. Though he'd been following the budget that he and Emma Kate had originally planned out, he was covering an extra set of bills without Em paying her part of the house anymore. On the other hand, he had his own discretionary funds, and without a wife to spend his spare money on, he wasn't using it. Aside from the occasional pizza order, it had been untouched, growing as he added a portion of his paycheck to it, unable to change the pattern the two of them had established. He knew that sticking to the old plan was wishful thinking that she would come back and walk right into her old spot.

Now, he'd spent it all on a hotel for the night. Hotels in Los Angeles were expensive—the nice ones even more so. His plane ticket had a return flight the next day. And, according to one Bailey Ann Mayfair, so did Emma Kate's.

She'd tucked the return ticket into his hand this morning. Then she'd looked him in the eyes and said, "I seated the two of you together on the flight back."

He'd looked at her and again considered what lengths she was willing to go to. "Another big bet on a man you don't know."

But Bailey Ann smiled this time, "Again, I'm not betting on *you*..." She'd paused and looked away, before bringing her gaze back to him, as though she'd made some decision he wasn't part of. "My sister is alternately sweet and bitchy. When she gets going, she's a steamroller. When she's afraid of something, she'll procrastinate to the point of not finishing anything. But she finished this. She's finished all kinds of things because she was motivated by getting back to you. So I got you two seats next to each other. Because I believe in her."

"Thank you," he'd told her. This whole thing was worlds easier with a contingent of Mayfair women as his backup.

So as they left the restaurant, he once again tucked Emma Kate's hand into his. She was looking back and forth between him and her sisters and her cousin. But his backup team had already come to the rescue. He knew that her sisters had told her they had a room for her.

Keith tugged on her hand. Leaning in closer, the smell of her hair almost did him in. Simple things like that were reminders that she'd gone—things he'd had and taken for granted that he missed from the moment he went home without her.

"I have a room for us." He whispered it into the shell of her ear, watching as her eyelashes fluttered at the news.

That was a good response, wasn't it? But he wasn't sure. It was so hard to tell when he'd screwed it up so badly.

He watched, hope shining on his face like a wish, as she turned to her sisters and said, "I'm going to go with Keith, okay?"

"Of course, honey. Congratulations!" Bailey Ann, ever the mother hen, stepped in and hugged her first. He watched as, one by one, she fielded praise and congratulations. Then he was alone with her on a street corner in downtown LA.

"I got us a place up the street. Should I get a car?"

She shook her head. "We can walk. The weather's nice." Then she laughed. "It always is."

"It's no tiny house in Georgia," he commented back, then immediately wondered if maybe he shouldn't have said it. Realizing he couldn't keep monitoring himself—because clearly, he sucked at it—Keith just let it all out. "I want you to move back in with me. I know it's not as nice as your sister's house. I can't offer anything yet. I still have bills, and student loans and—"

She'd stopped. Emma Kate stepped in front of him on the street, stopping his forward momentum and his babbling. "Seeing you there this afternoon was the best thing that could have happened. You don't need to warn me off. If I come back, will you be there?"

"Yes."

"Will you be my husband again? Because all I want is to be with you. I still have no idea how we found each other, but you're all I want."

He nodded. "Give me your phone?"

She clearly had no idea what he wanted, but she handed it over. "What are you doing?"

"Putting myself in as your emergency contact." He didn't look up, though he noticed she'd stilled. Then he saw it. He was already listed. He looked up at her.

"When did you do this?"

Em glanced away. "The day I came home from the hospital."

He'd screwed up, walking away. He'd thought all the mistakes were hers. And some were. But some were his, too. He handed the phone back. "I want you to marry me."

"We're already married." She laughed at him, but he wasn't done.

Picking up her hand, he held it up to her. His, too. "You aren't wearing your rings, and neither am I. I want us to wear them again. I want everyone to know that you're with me. I want—"

She'd reached up to her blouse, under the pearls and tugged at a chain he hadn't noticed before. As she pulled them forward, he saw that she still had all three rings around her neck. "You've been wearing them this whole time?"

She nodded at him as she unclasped the chain and slid the rings into her palm. She pocketed the chain and was reaching for her rings, but Keith got there first. Plucking her engagement ring—a ring for a five-second engagement?—and her wedding band, he stepped back before she could stop him.

Dropping to one knee on the probably dirty street in Los Angeles, he held up the rings to his wife. "Emma Kate Mayfair, will you marry me?"

She nodded, but he wasn't done.

"The real deal this time. No walking away. Not either of us. For better or worse, for richer or poorer, for those days when I'm being a dumbass and I think something is your fault but it's mine, too..." He saw tears rolling down her face and he would have stood and wiped them away, but they were happy tears. "Will you marry me?"

"Yes, yes I will."

Though she tugged at his hands to get him to stand, he patiently stayed in his place. Gently taking her fingers in his, he slid the rings back on. When at last he got to his feet, she didn't let go of his hand.

"You, too," Emma Kate told him in a firm voice, and he didn't know why he was surprised, but he was. He'd forgotten that it wasn't just a proposal on the street corner on a night lit with streetlights and observed by palm trees and passersby.

Em slid his ring back onto his finger and the weight finally felt right.

"Congratulations!" Someone yelled it as they drove by. Several car horns honked, and several celebratory yells came from across the street. But Keith couldn't catalog them. Emma Kate had taken his face in her hands and was kissing him.

It didn't matter where they were.

It didn't matter how he'd found her or that he hadn't remembered her name the first morning he'd woken up beside her.

It only mattered that he had the rest of his life to be with her.

❦ 58 ❦

Ever Halifax walked at the edge of the park, the tiny hand clasped in hers tugging her along faster than she would have walked. Her heels sank into the moist dirt because she wasn't paying attention to where she was going.

She'd been watching a wedding under a beautiful handmade arch of white flowers. It looked expensive. It looked gorgeous. And it looked very out of reach for a woman like her.

In fact, even the dirt over there by the wedding wasn't soft. No one's heels were getting messed up over there, because the sprinklers had been turned off in anticipation. A good party planner solved all problems. She didn't have one. She wasn't having a party so it didn't matter.

Like most things, her problems were the kind of problems that only happened on her side of things. Only her ground was muddy. Only her house had cheap siding that wanted to fall apart. Only she had three kids and just one way to keep food on the table. Only her life had these pitfalls.

Most of her problems were problems only Ever Halifax could have.

The little hand tugged at her. She loved him, but he hadn't been her mistake. He wasn't a mistake at all, but things had left her with more than she'd been able to handle. To say her heels had sunk into the mud of life would be an understatement, but she'd handled it. Maybe it had been her mistake for thinking she could wear heels in the first place.

She certainly seemed to get shut down quickly or harshly—or both—if she tried to "get above her station," as she'd heard said about her more than once. Though at one point she'd hoped she would be having her own wedding in the park.

But she certainly wasn't any Emma Kate Mayfair.

Ever remembered the Mayfair girls from school. They certainly didn't remember her. Who would? But she knew who the gorgeous bride was. She knew that the bridesmaid with the rounded belly was her oldest sister Bailey Ann, proudly expecting her first. And that Harper Rose and their beautiful cousin Lennon were standing in a line in nearly matching dresses.

Everyone knew the Mayfair girls. None of them would have ended up like Ever had.

The small hand that tugged at hers, motioned her forward toward the play sets on the other side of the park. "Ever! Let's go!"

She smiled. "Yes! We are off to play!" She could fake her enthusiasm for the swing sets, but she never had to for the child with her. God knows, she loved all three of the boys.

Even though she could entertain fantasies of being the kind of woman one of the groomsmen would take home, she wouldn't ever be that woman. She was the one who had almost fifteen more years before this little one graduated high school.

As she tried to avoid the muddy patches on the ground, she felt her head turn and look back toward the bride and groom saying their vows now under the Georgia sun. Even the weather cooperated for the Mayfair girls, she thought.

A cheer went up from the crowd and she watched one of the handsome groomsmen—a Mayfair cousin—holler out his congratulations along with the rest of the attendees. She wasn't sure why he'd caught her eye, maybe she'd seen him at work.

If she had, that was just as good a reason as any to turn away. That was not the kind of man she wanted. His kind smile and happy hugs for the groom drew her back in, but Ever forced her gaze away.

She did what she always did and pushed forward, leaving her foolish dreams behind.

AFTERWORD

Dear Reader,

This was both a fun story to write and a tough one! I've never written an "accidental marriage" story before because they are so hard to pull off in a realistic manner. But the problems with quickie weddings are real! Annulments and divorces take way longer (and often so much more money!) than the wedding. Also, Vegas is designed to make you lose your mind and maybe do something a little crazy for once.

When I first imagined Emma Kate, I knew she would have a past she had to shake off. Though small towns have advantages, they have problems, too. Getting pigeonholed and not being allowed to change is definitely one of them. What's worse for Em is that she believes it. I watched along with you as Keith turned his whole life upside down to give them a chance. If you enjoyed their love story and you'd like to leave a review, that would be wonderful. Thank you again for reading. You're why I write.

PREVIEW OF OUR SONG (WILDER - BOOK 1)

The screams tore the air. High pitched and long, they sounded like someone was being stabbed.

Kelsey's head swiveled, like every other head in the store, until she found the source of the wail. Then she relaxed.

It was just a normal little girl, maybe five years old, screaming her head off, but looking quite unharmed. Her head tipped back to make sure that the sounds radiated in every direction. Her straight dark hair slid down her back, looking as if it hadn't made friends with a brush in a few too many days.

"She's upset." Daniel commented in soft tones. He looked up at her from the basket of the shopping cart, his widened eyes and slightly opened bow mouth told what he thought. He watched, but that was all. Daniel had never been one to participate in anything resembling a tantrum, for which Kelsey was supremely grateful.

Her eyes flicked back to the girl, as she let loose another wail. A store employee was rapidly making her way over to help, hands wringing nervously as she gamely pushed her way through the racks.

As the girl took another gulp, Kelsey mentally closed her

ears. She wanted to push her cart and her kids away, but something held her there. She needed little girls' clothes for her own daughter, and she wasn't about to let a screaming kid rule her decisions.

This time the wail got through to Kelsey's shut-off brain. Just as she had picked up the leg of a pair of bright blue jeans, the little voice spoke, "He is *not* my Daddy!"

Well, that made her head snap around again. She barely registered the employee looking between the child and the father, but she saw that the little girl's pants were too short and too tight. Her shirt didn't cover her belly when she tipped her head back to scream. She was unkempt, upset, and glaring daggers.

The father instantly earned Kelsey's sympathy. She wasn't sure why she never believed that the little girl had been kidnapped. But she didn't. And a father didn't deserve to have his kid pull any of this on him—certainly not in public.

She also felt supreme pity for his total lack of parenting skills. Otherwise, he looked strong and capable in fitted jeans and a t-shirt that showed off what he'd worked for. His deep brown eyes and straight nose looked like they belonged on a man who stood his ground. Her heart turned over for him as he stood with feet apart and shoulders straight as he held up a sweet little outfit that was totally dwarfed by the sheer size of him. His dark hair slipped over one eye, only partially obscuring the red that crept across his face and appeared to be setting up permanent residence.

Even though he was facing her down, the child had clearly won.

"Look!" Allie held up a small doll. "Look!" Kelsey blinked for a moment. Only when her eyes landed on a nearby display did she realize that her pigtailed three-year-old had filched it as they passed. With a frown, she looked down and saw the shredded cardboard blister-pack. *Well, that would have to get purchased.*

Now she needed to take the doll away, or get something

comparable for Daniel, who had been an angel. There was no good way around that one. Except, maybe . . .

"I don't want new clothes!" The voice was rude, sharp, and tiny. At least the little girl wasn't shrieking anymore.

"Honey, those clothes are too small." The father stood over her, his voice steady, although Kelsey wasn't sure how he managed that.

"My *mommy* bought me these clothes." The little girl's arms crossed over her chest and she clamped her jaw so tight Kelsey was certain that she'd hear little teeth grinding.

Again his voice was soft, and this time full of defeat. "I know." He absently hung up the outfit on the nearest rack and sighed.

The store employee had disappeared, but Kelsey pushed her way through to them. They probably didn't need her help, but she felt drawn in. Besides, there was that cute doll that she had to pay for and couldn't let her daughter keep. "Allie, give me the dolly."

With a small pout that had Kelsey pressing her lips together, Allie handed over the doll and assumed her own cross-armed position. Kelsey ignored her.

"Would she like this doll?" She was grateful that her voice didn't shake like it wanted to.

The father looked her square in the face, the first time he'd looked *at* someone since his daughter had started wailing in the middle of Target. Kelsey felt something tug inside. His eyes were a combination of grateful and exhausted, the deep brown riddled with shadows and regret. His voice sounded the way he looked. "You are more than welcome to try."

Daniel and Allie looked on with avid curiosity, while she leaned down to the little girl and held up the doll as bait. "Do you think you could help me out?"

There was only a pout and glare as response.

"I'm buying some clothes for Allie and maybe you could try

on some of the same things." Kelsey wiggled the doll, watching its pink nylon hair sway, and she got a great idea. Quickly, she stood and searched the cart, certain that the doll had come with a little plastic hairbrush.

Grabbing it, she began brushing the doll's hair as she walked back to the little girl. Brown eyes were watching her with interest although no other part of the small body had abandoned the furious stance. "This dolly really needs her hair brushed, can you help her?"

Kelsey didn't wait for an answer, just shoved the doll and brush into the little girl's hands and turned past the father, offering a small smile. Grabbing the abandoned outfit from the rack she turned and carefully picked out the same clothes in Allie's size.

"Allie?" She held them up. "Do you like these?"

Allie nodded vigorously and attempted to stand up in the cart. Kelsey held out a hand and shook her head. Allie promptly sat back down, but held her hands out for the clothes.

Kelsey turned back to the little dark-haired girl. "Would you like to try some on, too?"

She didn't say 'yes', but neither did she protest, and Kelsey led the bunch through to the fitting rooms. Only as she walked in did she realize the father wasn't allowed in the ladies' fitting rooms. Kelsey started to explain, but he just shook his head.

"If you can find out if they fit, then you are light years beyond me."

"Okay." Kelsey felt as small as the word, but she plucked Allie then Daniel from the cart and reached out for the little girl's hand. After a moment, there it was in her own. The little face was a little dirty, she noticed from up close, but she didn't say anything. "What's your name, honey?"

The answer came from behind her in a masculine voice lined with a deep sigh, "Andie."

Kelsey felt her back stiffen. *Not another Andy.*

Her hand must have jerked, because the little hand belonging to little Andie grasped a little tighter.

With some resolve, she marched the three of them into the changing room and tried the clothes on the girls. As she had expected, little Andie bore no marks of abuse, just a need for a bath and new underwear. But she tried on the new clothes without much fuss, and Kelsey was pleased to see that the 5T size fit her perfectly.

"Look!" Allie jumped exuberantly in the new outfit, eyeing Andie and smiling that they were dressed alike.

"Let's go show your Daddy." Kelsey stood and walked out, three small children trailing her like ducks. Daniel solemn and sweet, Allie bubbly and charming, and Andie defiant as ever.

Her father stood outside the doors, his head leaned back against a mirrored column, looking like the day had worn him down. He snapped up at the sight of his daughter wearing clothes that fit. He gave an obvious sigh of relief. "They're great."

Kelsey smiled. One screaming fit averted for the day.

"Andie," She choked the name out and then pushed through the rest pleasantly, "I think Allie is going to just wear her new outfit." She reached down and pulled the tags off to ring them up when they left.

Andie motioned for her to do the same, but Kelsey pawned the job off on Daddy. "Can you stay out here with them? I'm going to go grab their old clothes." She didn't really wait for a reply. The pained expression on his face told her he was going to say 'no'. So she simply smiled and didn't let him.

Kelsey gathered small clothes in her arms, and then stepped back out, handing Andie's dad the too-small clothes, and wadding up Allie's. She helped her own kids back in the cart and turned to speak over her shoulder. "She needs new underwear, too."

He panicked. "What size?"

"She was in fours, so sixes should do it. They're right over there." She shrugged and pointed. "The size 5T fit her great, so you can pretty much pick up anything else that size and not worry about trying it on."

Again his shoulders worked through a sigh, and Kelsey felt a pang of pity for both of them. "Thank you." He stuck out his hand, and gave her an odd look before shaking his head as though to clear the thought. "I'm JD. And I can't tell you what a help you've been. How did you do it?"

She shook his hand hoping she looked nonchalant. She wasn't getting into any of that with a perfect stranger. "I'm Kelsey. Good luck."

She wheeled away thinking she needed a new seat cover in the car. She needed to replace one Daniel had ripped accidentally, and do it without upsetting him about the one he had ruined. He was sensitive that way, but no wonder.

She browsed the automotive aisle a few minutes before trying to furtively place the blue Hawaiian slip cover under the cart. But Daniel saw it and his lip began to tremble. At moments like these she prayed that she wasn't seeing vestiges of his father. But the problem was either there or it wasn't; she knew that from experience. No amount of hope or help could change those facts. So she smiled and made the best of it.

"I think we need to re-do the whole car. Maybe these ones with the frogs on them?" She pointed. At twenty bucks a pop they weren't what she was planning on spending. But she could afford it. Just.

Daniel smiled. "They have lizards, too, can we get some of each?"

Allie spotted ladybugs and Kelsey smiled. So the car wouldn't match. Those smiles were worth every penny. The four different covers were all black velvet, so Kelsey figured they wouldn't embarrass her when she went to meetings.

Just before she buried it, she pulled out the shred of cardboard with the barcode for the doll and put it with the tags from

Allie's clothes. This trip had turned far more expensive than she planned.

Pushing the cart to the register, she mentally tallied how much they had spent and tried not to grimace. At least her kids were being well behaved.

What the hell. "Who wants to get pizzas?"

"Me!"

"Me, too!"

Allie jiggled like Jell-O with the prospect, and Kelsey made a mental note to strip off the new clothes before she handed over any pizza.

A few minutes later, Kelsey had tucked the bags and the pizzas into the cart, filled up the drinks, and headed out to the car. Once she had everyone buckled, she pulled out of the parking lot, the passenger seat loaded down with bags. It made her sad the seat didn't have her own Andy in it.

"Mommy! My new shirt is pink."

"Yes, baby, it's pretty." She answered Allie with a pre-packaged smile, grateful to be distracted from memories of Andrew.

"When we get home, can we put the new covers on the car seats?"

"Well, Daniel, I think we need to eat dinner first."

Kelsey went back and forth with Daniel, trying to work out *exactly* when they could put the new covers on. She wasn't sure quite when, but sometime during the conversation she noticed an old grey sedan following them. Andrew's phrasing came to mind: an old Honda P.O.S. he'd always called them. Piece of shit. Kelsey had always argued in favor of any car that stayed on the road, functioning, for that long. But it figured—Andrew had never worried about money. He'd never understood it.

The Honda followed them through the next few turns, ratcheting Kelsey's anxiety up a notch every time it stayed close behind. She had her kids with her. She wouldn't lead someone to her house. She considered driving on to the police station and made the decision just as she drove past her own garage.

They lived in the corner house, so she swung to the right, ready to head around the block, when she noticed that the Honda had pulled into the condos that stood on the corner just behind her house.

With a hiss of breath and a shake of her head, Kelsey cursed her own paranoia. It was only one of her neighbors. If she'd made any effort to get to know them better, she might very well have recognized the car and driver and never thought anything of it. Wasn't that part of the reason she had moved here?

"Okay kids! Out!" She unlocked all the doors and helped Allie down and over to the sidewalk before grabbing the pizza.

"Why are we parked over here?" Daniel looked up with glassy eyes, worry shining bright.

"Oh, I just felt like it."

He nodded, and traipsed off after Allie, only to both be called back. "Daniel, you can close your door, and everybody carries something." The kids grumbled, but they knew the routine, and each picked up a bag and lugged it to the front door.

Kelsey juggled what she was holding and got the front door unlocked. Just as she was marching the kids inside, she heard her name.

She looked up to see JD from Target round the corner, wearing a true grin for the first time. "Kelsey? I thought you looked familiar."

She shooed the kids inside, and set down the groceries before stepping to the front porch and easing the door closed behind her. "You live there?" She pointed to the condos just behind her house.

"Yeah, we just moved in."

He shook his head as if he didn't know what to say, and she realized for the first time that he was younger than she had first taken him for, maybe mid-twenties. He looked nervous there with his hands shoved into the pockets of the jeans she now saw were a bit worn. His sneakers, too, had seen better days. He smiled and nodded, "Well, I'll let you get to your dinner. Thanks again for all your help."

With that, he headed back to the condos and missed the vague, overly-polite smile that passed across her face.

For a moment Kelsey tried to remember the last time she'd had a real smile.

Thank you for reading! I love romances with real love and believable characters, and I hope you found all that in these pages. I want to fall in love right along with the characters, and I do, while I'm writing it.

About Savannah

I started writing when I was eight--I hand wrote an 80-page novella that I believed to be (adult) romantic suspense. I'm proud to say, I've gotten a lot better since then. I've grown up to be a nerd at heart! I love neuroscience and people watching, and if you look, you'll find some of that in each Savannah Kade book. Most days you'll find me in my office, looking out my window at a handful of the neighbor's cows, or watching my dogs or my cat roam the backyard.

Follow me, find me, ask me questions! I would love to hear from you.
www.SavannahKade.com
Savannah@SavannahKade.com